I0576153

REDEMPTION

REDEMPTION

WAR OF THE DAMNED™ BOOK EIGHT

MICHAEL TODD   MICHAEL ANDERLE
LAURIE STARKEY

Redemption (this book) is a work of fiction.
All of the characters, organizations, and events portrayed in this novel
are either products of the author's imagination or are used fictitiously.
Sometimes both.

Copyright © 2018 Michael Todd, Michael Anderle, and Laurie Starkey
Cover by Ryn Katryn Digital Art
Cover copyright © LMBPN Publishing
A Michael Anderle Production

LMBPN Publishing supports the right to free expression and the value of
copyright. The purpose of copyright is to encourage writers and artists
to produce the creative works that enrich our culture.

The distribution of this book without permission is a theft of the
author's intellectual property. If you would like permission to use
material from the book (other than for review purposes), please contact
support@lmbpn.com. Thank you for your support of the author's rights.

LMBPN Publishing
PMB 196, 2540 South Maryland Pkwy
Las Vegas, NV 89109

First US edition, November 2018

REDEMPTION TEAM

Beta Readers

Dorothy Lloyd
Tom Dickerson
Dorene Johnson
Diane Velasquez
Timothy Cox
Sarah Weir

JIT Readers

John Ashmore
Mary Morris
James Caplan
Nicole Emens
Peter Manis
Danika Fedeli
Paul Westman
Angel LaVey
Kelly O'Donnell
Daniel Weigert

If we missed anyone, please let us know!

Weapons Consultant

John Kern
Proprietor
Spurlock's - Henderson NV

Editor
Lynne Stiegler

DEDICATION

*To Family, Friends and
Those Who Love
to Read.
May We All Enjoy Grace
to Live the Life We Are
Called.*

Moloch tapped his foot on the ground as he sat in the chair, realizing he was leaving ash marks from the outer rings as he did so. Lucifer's slaves instantly appeared and began mopping up after him, then rushed out of sight as quickly as they had come. Moloch hadn't spoken to his master in so long he'd almost forgotten what the inner halls of hell looked like. Lucifer's palace wasn't like the rest of hell, nor should it be. He was the king. The leader. The one who ruled it all. Hell was made for suffering, but he did what he could to make himself comfortable. He was, after all, *the* fallen angel, and He had placed him in a shadowy version of heaven that would torment him for the rest of his days as he sat below in the heat and steam.

"He'll be with you in a moment," crooned the divine voice of Lucifer's perfectly sculpted and completely nude demon secretary as she bounced and jiggled around the waiting area.

Moloch kept his eyes off her, though. He knew better than to gawk at one of Lucifer's women. "Thank you."

Instead, he turned his attention to the seemingly endless row of doors peppering the long white marble halls. The hall was opulent; smooth and shimmering, unlike the rough stone from which his own castle had been created. It was hotter here, but there was only one lava stream. It ran through the center of Lucifer's palace, inside a garden Lucifer had created especially for Lilith. She adored Earth's flowers and charms, and he had wanted to keep her happy. Of course, after her disappearance, he let the magic wear off, and all the plants quickly turned to ash.

He did leave the lava waterfall and stream, but the last Moloch had heard, he was tossing demons into it every time he got pissed off. It wasn't really the kind of thing Moloch wanted to think about while waiting to have an audience with an obviously-pissed-off Lucifer. Moloch's eyes darted down the hall as screams rattled through the hallway. A door opened and a demon dressed as a human doctor stepped out, wiped globs of black blood off her claws, and tossed her face mask into a bin. She stared at Moloch for a moment, ran her gaze down his broken body, and sneered before walking in the other direction.

Moloch turned his attention to the eight-foot-tall pictures hanging on the walls in front of him. Adorned with giant golden frames and placards on the bottom, they were some of the most revered humans in history, the most hideous of souls memorialized in places of honor throughout hell. The atrocities they caused on Earth were of monumental proportions, from the genocide of their own people to mass killings all across the world. There were all types of devilish heroes up there with one thing in common: they all committed some heinous deed. Or they all composed a beautiful symphony of evil, depending on who was asked.

"Lucifer is ready to see you now," the nude secretary called from her desk.

Moloch pushed himself up and took a deep breath, preparing himself for an explosive outburst from the king. He swallowed hard as he hopped to the large white doors with twisting black iron handles. He pulled the door open enough to slip through, and it snapped closed behind him, the sound echoing through the vast chamber around him. The room was wide and white, with enormous cast-iron braziers on either side of him. He started down the middle, glancing up only for a moment to see Lucifer lounging on his grand white throne.

On either side of him were his servants. One was a chained human woman, who was averting her eyes from Lucifer's terrible glory. The other was one of Lucifer's longest-running relationships. She had stood by the king of hell through thick and thin, marriage after marriage, and never flinched. Her name was Mania, and she was the Etruscan goddess of hell. She was a great warrior, a fierce lover, and loyal to Lucifer down to the last cursed cell in her body. She was the only one who was allowed to remain in the room while he was conducting business.

Moloch reached the foot of the throne and prostrated himself as best he could. Lucifer stared at him for several moments, his face impassive. He looked at his fingernails and grumbled, "I am displeased."

Moloch laboriously got up. "Your Highness, if I may…"

Lucifer began to tap his finger nail heavily on the stone armrest. The sound echoed across the room and sent shivers down Moloch's back. He winced and tucked his head in. Any movement the king made was a sign he needed to shut the hell up. The tapping continued as Lucifer sat there staring at him. Lucifer had always been capable of changing form, and at that moment he was a bulky, muscular human covered with patches of black scales that wriggled and moved like live serpents.

The tapping was like a dreadful heartbeat in Moloch's head. It wasn't frightening on its own, but it was so different from the norm that it was terrifying. There would usually be screaming, yelling, torture, and possibly death. Everyone knew visiting the king meant being tortured at least for a time, but for most that was an honor. Moloch, however, was already down to one leg, and his arm was hanging by a thread. He was not looking forward to the torture portion of the evening. He had already been through a lot, and the king was acting so very strange. Moloch was sure he had already been through enough that equated to punishment, although he would never tell Lucifer that. He'd beat Moloch and throw him into the lava river just to show him who was boss.

Lucifer got up and walked down the steps of the dais. He stopped by Mania and stroked her cheek, then whispered something into her ear. She looked at him in shock and lowered her head, curtsying. She hurried over and grabbed the human, pulling her out the back door of the throne room. As the goddess left, she threw a nasty look at Moloch. He did his best to ignore her.

When the girls were out of the room, Lucifer turned to

Moloch. His face was calm, but Moloch knew better. He watched Lucifer walk down the steps and wave his hand, conjuring a beverage cart in front of him. He lifted a glass, put three ice cubes in it, and began to pour a generous ration of whiskey. "Tell me everything, and let's start from the beginning. What have all these incursions been about?"

Moloch took a deep breath. "Well, sir, a little while ago I had a visit from T'Chezz. He wanted to find out how to get a seat with the rest of us."

Lucifer nodded and took a sip of the whiskey. "Oh, yes, T'Chezz. Where *is* that demon?"

Moloch shifted nervously. "We aren't sure. He went to one of the incursions, and during the course of things, he had his head removed by...by..."

Lucifer stepped over to him. "Yes? Go on. I haven't cut out your tongue...yet."

Moloch swallowed hard. "By Lilith and her human, sir. We aren't sure if he's in the depths of hell or dead."

Lucifer's eyebrow went up. "Continue."

Moloch looked at the ground. "Anyway, his idea was to show you he was strong enough and evil enough to deserve a seat. He planned to take over Earth as his gift to you. When he died, or whatever happened to him, we, I mean, *I*, decided the plan had already gone too far to stop. So, through a massive number of incursions, we've been making headway into taking over Earth."

Lucifer glanced at his almost-detached arm and missing leg. "And how is that going for you?"

Moloch cleared his throat. "Well, sir, we've had some setbacks."

Moloch watched Lucifer's expression. It seemed

uncaring and unemotional, but there was something more in there. *Oh hell, the fucker is pissed.*

The fallen angel sipped from his glass nonchalantly as he read Moloch's mind. "Perturbed, I would say," Lucifer corrected him.

Moloch nodded. "Lilith has really been at the center of our issues."

Lucifer eyed Moloch. "She does tend to be a thorn in your side, now doesn't she? I remember that all too well. Her passion is her greatest asset and her worst trait."

"Oh, I'm well aware."

"You're aware of her passion?" Lucifer's dark eyes sparkled.

"Yes. I mean, no. Not personally. I've heard the stories. Who *hasn't* heard the stories? That is to say, I am aware of but have not experienced the passion, which is a crucial difference. Sir." Moloch let his eyes drop, ready to be disemboweled.

"Passion." Lucifer drank thoughtfully. "I used to love that about her, but now it makes me want to crush her like a bug." Lucifer's hand tightened on his glass, but his face stayed emotionless.

"We've been trying to kill her, of course, but she always seems to have the upper hand. Her human is not like the other humans, although their union was completely random. We still aren't sure how they've become so close."

Lucifer paced, a thoughtful expression taking over his face. "Who is this human?"

Moloch had known he was going to have to tell Lucifer. "Her name is Katie, but she's no normal human. She's part-angel. Her eyes flash red to blue, she has wings, and she can summon the armor of the angels. Pandora, or Lilith, goes right along with it and has even been seen jumping in and out of Katie's body. It's like they're friends."

Lucifer's lip quivered, but he quickly got it under control. "Friends… What a nasty idea, although I think down here, it might help keep some of you somewhat in line. Have you seen this angel?"

Moloch blinked a couple of times and then just spat it out. "Several times, sire. The humans have devised a way to come to hell. They came here and fought our demons, and ultimately blew me up. That's how I came to be in this position."

Lucifer took a big gulp of his drink. "They came to hell? How is that possible?"

Moloch shrugged. "Pandora—I mean Lilith—brought them here. They showed up with special weapons and suits they designed for the trip. Apparently, they were able to fly drones in to measure the land and the temperatures without us knowing, but I can assure you, we've taken care of all the drones."

Lucifer's eyes went from a dull red to a bright flashing ruby. Immediately, Moloch was terrified. *Fuck, fuckity, fuck. He is bat-shit furious. Oh, fuck, he's going to kill me. I'm done for. He's going to castrate me, lock me away, and then one day chop off my head.*

The dark lord refilled his glass. "This is most unfortunate, isn't it? Lilith is such a whorebag. Has she said anything to you to explain her actions?"

Moloch shook his head nervously. "No, sire. I've suffered her usual stream of slurs that, quite frankly, insult all demonkind. Other than that, nothing. She usually controls the human, but I've seen her exit her human and the two of them fight side by side—although when they separate they don't seem to be quite as powerful. They grow weak much faster."

"Not fast enough, in my book. The world can have Lilith, but it seems you and your band of morons have opened the door to a war unlike any other with humans. One on our soil; one with consequences. When I get my hands on Lilith, I'm going to show her exactly what it means to be married to me and disobey me. That slut has had enough time to play and be free. Now it's time for her to pay for what she's done."

Moloch didn't know what to say. Lucifer looked sharply at him. "And look at you. She's blown your leg off, and your arm is barely attached. She has taken your dignity from you in one fell swoop."

Moloch hung his head. "Yes, Your Majesty, she has. I didn't even see it coming. I just wanted to crush them for stepping on your turf."

Lucifer stuck out his lip. "There, there. Let me see what I can do to fix this."

Moloch felt a bit more hopeful when Lucifer waved his hand. There was a gout of fire and a reek of sulfur, and Moloch's arm snapped back into place. His stump of a leg grew and twisted and became a brand new leg.

Lucifer stepped back and admired his work. "How's that?"

Moloch rolled his shoulders and tilted his neck back and forth. "That feels so much better. Thank you. I am not worthy of all this. Thank you."

Moloch was actually encouraged that Lucifer wasn't, in fact, going to tear him limb from limb.

Lucifer waved the gratitude away as he stepped closer, tilting his head to the side as if in thought. With a flash of red in his eyes, the dark lord threw his drink in Moloch's face and crushed the glass against his chest. Before Moloch could move, Lucifer had grown fifty feet tall, looming over him.

"Oh, shit," Moloch muttered.

As Lucifer's huge hand came toward him, Moloch put up his arms and screamed at the top of his lungs. Lucifer ripped his new arm back off and snapped the other free for good measure. He knocked Moloch's legs out from under him and slapped him in the face with his own hand. Over and over again he picked Moloch up, reassembled him, and ripped him apart again—much like a Mister Demonic Potato Head.

Moloch began to cry and Lucifer paused, holding Moloch's hand in his. He flipped the arm over and back-handed Moloch across the face before reattaching the limb. "Get yourself together, you fool. T'Chezz might have started this entire mess, but I fully blame you for bringing the humans here to hell. We've attacked Earth for centuries, but we've never killed enough humans or destroyed enough property to make them brave enough to come fight us on our own soil."

Moloch kept his eyes tightly shut and his body tense, waiting for the next blow. He sniffled, trying to stifle his tears. "I know, sire. I never thought they would manage to come here. I thought they would keep meeting our advances until they broke. I did not foresee Lilith and her angel meatsack becoming friends and trying to kill me…or invade hell, for that matter."

Lucifer rolled his eyes but spoke in a very even tone. "You didn't think that bitch would be stupid enough to try to take out hell? Yeah, right. I'm shocked she hasn't tried before. Her being gone has merely been a blink of an eye here, but it's been years on Earth. She has learned all those annoying human quirks and foibles, bonded with her meatsack, and even conspired with an angel to do harm. That last bit makes me want to puke, by the way. When she gets back here, I can promise she will not be happy with what I have planned for her. I've had plenty of time to be creative."

Moloch whimpered. "I'm sorry, sire."

Lucifer growled and shrank to Moloch's size. "It's not fair to kick the shit out of you if I'm five times your size, is it?"

Moloch sighed and closed his eyes. "No, sire."

Lucifer roared so loudly it rang through the entirety of hell. Rocks cracked and fell into the lava pits, souls went silent out of fear, and demons paused in their daily routines to look around in wonder. The wrath of Lucifer wasn't often heard, but this time was different.

Lucifer pulled his leg back and kicked Moloch directly in the dick, forcing him to his knees. He punched him hard to the right, then to the left, and then back again. Moloch fell to the ground, groaning and holding his crotch. Lucifer continued to kick the living shit out of him for several minutes.

When he was done, Moloch lay shivering, bruised, and battered, with his eyes shut tightly. Lucifer snapped his fingers, and Mania came running in with a clean towel and some water for him. He kissed her on the cheek before wiping the blood off his hands and the sweat from his forehead. The lord of hell gulped down the water and tossed the glass to Mania, then walked back to his throne.

Moloch carefully stumbled to his feet, groaning as he did. He steadied himself on his good leg. He was definitely worse for wear, but fortunately, his arm and leg were still attached. He waited to be dismissed, his eye swollen and puffy. Lucifer leaned his head back, smiled, and shook his head. "Nothing like a good beating to kick-start your day, right, Moloch?"

Moloch wiped a trickle of blood from the corner of his mouth. "Yes, sire."

Lucifer tapped his claws on his armrest and smirked. "I'm not going to continue because I know everything. I've known from the beginning. To think I wouldn't know what was going on in my own realm is insane. You didn't start this war, and that is the only reason I'm letting you out of here today. Otherwise, you'd have been chained in the torture chamber until I grew tired of you.

"Nonetheless, you continued this ridiculous charade, and you're now responsible for cleaning up the mess. I want Lilith. You're going to bring her to me. As far as the angel goes, kill her and be done with it. One less angel in the world is a good thing."

Moloch nodded but didn't speak. Lucifer took a deep breath through his nose. "Good. You're excused. And Moloch? I'm not giving you forever to complete this task. You need to do it before things get worse. Pain and suffering in hell are caused by me and no one else. I don't want to have to leave my happy throne to take care of this myself. I assure you, if that were to happen, you would learn new definitions of pain. Little demons would tell each other the horrible true story of the Tragedy of Moloch. In the end, your soul would be lost for eternity."

2

So let me get this straight. We had a citywide funeral for a video game character representing Juntto, and now we have Juntto's body in some sort of suspended animation. Is that about right? Katie was tired of all the twists and turns.

Pandora nodded. *Right. By human standards, Juntto is dead, but he isn't really. Leviathans can die like humans, but that wasn't what happened here.*

Katie looked out over the city and zipped up her leather overcoat against a sudden chill. *So it's like a coma?*

Yeah. Or it might be like locked-in syndrome or something. Either way, the big blue bastard is currently checked the fuck out.

And we have to figure out how to bring him back.

Precisely.

Katie sighed. *But it's not just medicine or something simple, of course. It's like a full-on fucking riddle. I hate shit like this. You* know *I hate shit like this.*

Pandora chuckled. *Hey, I didn't do this to him. He did it to himself. I don't know any more than you do at this point. Look at it this way. The character he was portraying actually dies in the storyline, so you gave him an honorable ending.*

I should be happy he's sticking to the video game script? That's idiotic.

Don't be a bitch. I'm trying to be positive here. It might pump up the gamers out there! Maybe we'll get some new fans.

Fans. Fuck me. Katie rolled her eyes, looking down at the people walking along below. Every time she did that, a needle of jealousy stung her. They were living their unassuming lives with no knowledge of how bad things really were. They enjoyed the news reports and used social media to spout off their thoughts on the war, but that was it. They really knew nothing more than the media and the government offered them.

Pandora sniffed. *You know you wouldn't be happy down there with them. You would be damn miserable, actually.*

Katie pulled her knees to her chest. *At least I wouldn't be trying to figure out how to bring a Leviathan back to life. Who, by the way, happens to be chilling in a freezer because he needs to be a certain temperature. We have a Leviathan in a walk-in freezer, Pandora. Do you not find anything about that odd?*

Pandora laughed. *Hey, at least he gets to enjoy some peace and quiet for a little while. We know while he's cryogenic we won't have to worry about him murdering buttloads of people.*

I thought we got over that fear.

He was a bloodthirsty conqueror for a couple of millennia before he took up video games and fucking demons up.

I wasn't aware that a little frostbite and a coma would cause him to revert straight back to Juntto, Total Dick.

This isn't an exact science.

Katie looked bewildered. *We are talking about bringing a*

non-human, non-demon being back to life after he curled up and dusted off. In the meantime, we're throwing funerals, I have an empty casket, and now I've got a hell of a lot more questions than I do answers.

Pandora snickered. *When we get him back, you should tell him he has to do paperwork.*

If we get him back, and that is a big if. There are so many things this could have been, and it's not like we have a Leviathan practitioner available. We're taking care of him as best we can. For all we know, the cold and lack of food could literally be draining what little life he has left in his body.

Katie slapped her hand on the roof and shook her head. She absolutely hated not having any idea how to wake Juntto from the coma. On top of that, she felt terrible for putting Angie through the ringer. Katie hadn't even told her Juntto was still alive until after the service in the city that day. That was when they'd moved him to the freezer section at a local butcher, not trusting the scientist not to carve him up. Katie had paid a shitload of money to exclusively use his freezer until they could get the frost giant moved to a secure facility. But where would they move him? He was huge, and the government was definitely not set up for something like that.

Katie groaned, leaning back on her hands to see the barely visible stars overhead. *What the hell is the answer to this?*

Pandora made a clicking sound, thinking. *We could always go back to his basic instincts.*

I don't think killing a bunch of people in a bar is going to help this.

Pandora giggled. *Not that part. I'm talking about booze and broads. That always got his attention. It has been a while since he's had broads, and he hasn't overindulged in booze since we picked him up.*

Katie shook her head and sat up. *I would never ask anyone to do something I wouldn't do. If the requirement is me screwing Juntto, he just might stay in the freezer for a long damned time. I'm talking icicles growing off him, black appendages, no-longer-has-a-smell long time. They'll be serving meat around his ass.*

Pandora snickered. *That would be quite comical. The locals going in the freezer and high-fiving the frozen guy as they grab a rack of lamb. Can you imagine him waking up in a locker full of frozen meat and vegetables? He wouldn't have a clue what was going on.*

Katie couldn't help but smile and then groan. *There has to be something we're missing. I need help with this.*

Pandora went silent for a moment before realizing what she meant. *Oh. Oh, no. Please don't do this to me. All he's going to do is pile more riddles on top of the ones we have.*

He's been helpful in the past.

Barely. If you want vague bullshit, I've got vague bullshit. A dong in the hand is worth two in the bush. See? It's easy. How do you bang a horny demon? Carefully. Damn, I'm good at this. What's the difference between a left boob and a right boob? The right one is a little bigger. Not sure why since I'm making it up as I go.

Katie rubbed her hands together and closed her eyes. "Gabriel, a little help here would be nice."

Pandora growled. *And she did it anyway—bringing in the backup when it's not even helpful. I mean, do you actually think he will show up this time? He never comes when you call him.*

A voice said from behind them, "Hello, ladies."

Pandora winced. *The one damn time...*

Katie stood up, wiping her hands on her legs. "Gabriel. You came."

Gabriel smiled. "I'm not always indisposed. Besides, you seem to be coming up with some answers that might be a little less than comforting to the Big Guy."

Pandora scoffed. *Please, anything but washing feet and feeding the poor is uncomfortable for him.*

Gabriel kept a smile on his face, not replying to Pandora even though he could hear her. "What can I help you with?"

Fly away and come back with some donuts, angel-boy.

Katie bit her bottom lip. "I'm sure you know what's happened. Now we need to wake Juntto, but we have no idea how to do that. We've racked our brains, but he's kind of a hard one to figure out. I don't know a lot about his kind, and Pandora has told me everything she knows, which isn't much more."

Angel-boy flies to the rescue, and you throw me under the bus. That's cold.

Gabriel crossed his arms on his chest and nodded knowingly. "I see. Well, think about this."

Pandora sighed. *Here it comes. This better be fucking helpful.*

Gabriel rubbed his hand on his chin. "What does that power rabbit need?"

Katie just blinked at him, and Pandora screamed in frustration. *I knew it. I fucking knew it. I told you not to call him down here. All he was going to do was give you some stupid riddle to make the whole thing even more confusing. For all we know, he needs a blanket and a fucking glass of milk. Katie, I need you to give me permission to exit your body.*

Katie found herself agreeing with Pandora. Screw it. *Knock yourself out.*

Pandora mustered her strength and focus and stepped out of Katie's body. Katie stumbled to one side and put her hand on the half-wall beside her to steady herself. She was prepared to see the dark beauty of Pandora's naked demon body, but that wasn't what she saw. Standing there was Pandora in a human form with long, flowing black hair and actual clothes on. She looked like every other human, except that her body was perfect. Her top was a little revealing, but that was to be expected.

Pandora advanced on Gabriel, shaking her finger. "Why do you have to be such an ass? Did God give you some magical command to talk like a fucking Batman villain? Is this payback for my fall from grace? Your help is about as useless as a knitted condom. Seriously, shit just seeps right through the cracks, and we're left with your fucking crap. We're already trying to solve a riddle, and you give us *more* fucking riddles. Are we supposed to use your riddle to un-fuck our original riddle? Now I've said riddle so many times I don't even know what the fuck I'm talking about anymore! You happy? Huh? You get your rocks off doing this?"

Gabriel lifted his eyebrows as Pandora continued her rant. Katie tried not to snicker. Gabriel leaned toward Katie and whispered loud enough for Pandora to hear him, "The *outside* has changed, but it's still the same Lilith on the inside."

Pandora leaned over and tapped him hard on the forehead. He took a deep breath, his animated face going blank. "Not done with you, so stop talking to the one who's admiring my ass."

Katie's head popped to the side from behind Pandora. "Hey! I'm right here, and I can hear you. Besides, I'm just checking out this lack-of-tail thing you've got going on. You always had a nice ass, but without the tail, it's like a perfect peach."

"Aw, sugar, thanks." She narrowed her eyes. "Wait, don't compliment me mid-rant. It's throwing me off my game."

"I'm in awe of it. Really. Why do you not always do this? You might be able to trick the demons."

Pandora looked over her shoulder. "Believe it or not, it's harder to maintain this than it is to just come out in full form. Besides, when I'm fighting demons, they won't be offended by my tail. Some of them have their own. It's kind of a thing in hell. Like 'who has the nicest rack,' but with tails instead."

Katie wrinkled her nose. "I don't like that at all. How do you even judge that? Wait, what does it matter now? I mean, it's not like Gabriel here doesn't know what you are."

Pandora sighed at Katie, who was tilting her head to the side as she looked at Pandora's tail-less ass. "If I looked like a demon, Gabby here wouldn't listen to my point. Angels tend to judge a message by the messenger." She pointed a well-manicured nail at Gabriel. "This has always been hilarious to me, considering your little holy book talks about Jesus not judging anyone. You're the worst of them all."

Gabriel shrugged. "We work for God, not Jesus. And

I'm sure if you read the *good book,* you'd see that God pretty much judges everyone. You of all people should know that."

Pandora narrowed her eyes at him. "Personally I think it's you being lazy. You choose not to look past my outward appearance, even though you know I have little to do with how I look in black scales. That form was given to me when I married Lucifer. Still, you make snap judgments. Maybe it's easier for you. Maybe it's sheer laziness. You want in and out of a situation as fast as possible."

Gabriel shook his head. "It's expediency, not laziness. If you're a demon, do I really think anything you say is going to be the truth? I can't trust you."

Pandora put her hands on her hips. "Until this point, I have gone out of my way to be trustworthy. Think back a little. I should get a gold star, but you just give me shit. You could be respectful and fucking helpful, even if I were standing here in scales."

Gabriel crossed his arms. "You called me, not the other way around. Let's be perfectly clear on that. And look, I am standing here listening to everything you're saying, even though nothing pertinent or even intelligent has come out."

"What-the-fuck-ever," Pandora growled, closing her eyes and taking deep breaths to combat the anger surging through her.

Katie stepped between them and eyed Pandora. "You gonna explode?"

Pandora shook her head and finally opened her eyes, stepping right in front of Gabriel. "What we have here is a Damned war, if you haven't noticed."

Gabriel tilted his head. "How could I not have noticed, with angels and demons working together, gates to hell opening, and Leviathans lying in wait in the freezers of butcher shops?"

Pandora waved her hands. "Okay, then why do I not hear the fancy fucking trumpets in heaven calling the Lord's army down to get their dicks wet?"

"Excuse me?" Gabriel looked mortified.

"I mean get their swords or spears or whatever wet with demon blood. We both know how much the army likes to do some murdering, so stop screwing over my sister here and give us a fucking clue to your riddle."

Gabriel lifted an eyebrow. "Or?"

Pandora gritted her teeth and lowered her voice. "Or I'm going to find a two-by-four and give you a pine colonoscopy complete with splinters."

Gabriel looked at Katie. "She *is* creative, isn't she?"

Katie shrugged.

He looked back at Pandora. "Do you have to be so melodramatic? That was not a trait created by the Maker. Somewhere someone dropped that into human discourse, and it's been a pain in the butt ever since. Probably some stupid joke by Raphael. I swear, he hasn't been serious since that movie used his name and made him into a teenage giant turtle who eats pizza."

Pandora threw her arms in the air. "Do you have to play games when our lives are on the line?" Pandora pointed her fingers at Katie. "You remember her? Your angel? The one you keep teasing with morsels of wisdom that don't mean shit, only to leave her here to combat everything on her own? Do you think she appreciates having to decipher your fucked-up code between demon-killing and trips to hell?"

Katie frowned. "Why are you bringing me into this? You always do that."

Pandora waved her hands at Katie to silence her, but she was still staring Gabriel in the eyes. "She's trying to reform a fucking alien from another planet, then she's trying to save him and perhaps save his soul in the process. All she needs to know is how to help. You can't tell me you don't know. You've *been* to Juntto's planet. You know his people. Hell, if you don't want to be helpful, tell *us* how to get there, and we'll take care of it on our own. Just do *something* to be helpful."

Gabriel stood firm. "It's not the time for that."

Katie interrupted, stepping forward. "Wait, what?"

Gabriel ignored her. "You probably weren't around during this decade, Pandora, but there was a commercial about—"

Katie immediately caught on. "A walking bunny powered by batteries. The Energizer Bunny."

Pandora slowly turned her head toward Katie. "The what?"

"He's a mechanical bunny that runs off of very long-lasting batteries. It's…energy!"

Pandora grimaced. "Shit. You've been infected by his riddles. Maybe if I punch you in the head, I can cure you."

"No, I've got it." Katie grinned. "We need to figure out how to shock him back to the land of the living."

Pandora thought about it for a second. "Like Frankenstein?"

"Without the grave robbing, but yeah."

"I'm not building a weird lair so people can chase us down with pitchforks."

Katie chuckled. "No need. That didn't really work out for Frankenstein anyway."

Pandora nodded, thinking. She turned to Gabriel. "So, we need— Wait, where did he go?"

Katie and Pandora looked around the roof, but Gabriel was gone. Pandora growled and slammed her hand into her fist. "That sonofabitch! He gives us one clue and then poofs into thin air. If you have angel abilities, you need to learn how to poof."

Katie sneered. "I don't poof. Poofing isn't my thing."

"Poof down for some donuts real quick."

"Poofing is not a thing I can do."

Pandora frowned. "You didn't even try."

"I'm trying right now. See?" Katie squinted at her.

"That was a fart."

"No poofing. End of discussion."

Pandora shrugged. "Guess I might as well get back inside."

Katie lifted her chin and stood still as Pandora climbed back inside of her. The tingle that ran through her body made everything hazy for a moment. She blinked her eyes several times, getting herself back together.

Pandora was irritated. *He could have told us what kind of energy we need. It's not like revealing this basic information will harm his good standing as an angel. He's just being typical Gabriel, leading his fucking flock into a dead end and giving them half a ladder. Why not just say, "I don't fucking know, you figure it out."*

He told us enough. Katie smiled and looked at the city

again. *Thank you. I needed this. I needed to feel like I had my feet underneath me again. After everything that's happened, I was starting to feel like I had lost my touch. Without you, I would have been sitting here with two riddles.*

Pandora yawned in Katie's mind. *I got your back, little sis. And let me just point out that without me, you wouldn't have stellar tits, a perfect ass, and a tiny waistline. You would still be playing volleyball and dreaming of your future husband. Let's just say I saved you from a lot of things.*

Katie smiled. *That is true, even if some days I feel like trading back. I would get bored, though.*

Anyone would be bored without me. Now, everything has been revealed that will be, and you have some brain work to do. Unfortunately, I don't think I'll be that helpful, and I'm incredibly tired.

Katie chuckled. She was not used to hearing that from Pandora. *We have a good start. I'll head back to the condo.*

Pandora yawned again, sending pulses of sleepiness through Katie's body. *Good. I'm just going to curl up right here and take a nap. That jumping-out-of-bodies thing is not only creepy as fuck, but it's exhausting.*

With that, Katie spread her wings.

3

Baal ran his finger across a suspiciously shiny wall, and it came away covered in a translucent goop. He grimaced and wiped his finger on a small table covered with papers. The place was dark and smelled of mold. It was also at least twenty degrees colder than other parts of hell, which made it uncomfortable for him. Light flickered from candles set up all over the room, but it was still so dark he could barely see. He hated being there, and he hated having to converse with Beelzebub even more.

The place was far enough away from the center of hell to make the trip unbearable. On top of that, he had to deal with the bullshit of this demon. No matter how powerful he was, it didn't mean he lavished himself in common sense. To Baal, he was just as wild-minded as T'Chezz had been, the only differences being that Beelzebub had confidence and feared no one. Sometimes he even thought the smooth-talking demon lacked the common sense to fear Lucifer.

"If you think I want to be here, you're wrong," Baal

hollered into the dark, knowing the other demon was lurking in the shadows somewhere.

A deep laugh came from the right corner of the room. "Moloch's little errand boy, how cute. I didn't think I would see you again after last time."

Baal wrinkled his nose. "Yes, well, I don't have much choice in the matter. I'm supposed to stay behind the scenes."

Beelzebub stepped out from the shadows, his large, crooked body shifting across the light. His long talons slapped on the stone ground, and a puff of acrid air oozed from his nostrils. "I always thought you and I would make a good team. Me in the front, you in the back."

Baal looked at stacks of human books on one wobbly table. "Yes, well. Even standing in the background, I knew if I teamed up with you, I'd end up with something in the ass. I mean that both figuratively and literally. You are not known to be the most trustworthy of demons."

Beelzebub snickered. "If trustworthy were what was needed in this realm and others we would be shit out of luck, don't you think? No, demons don't know the meaning of that. A trustworthy demon is an oxymoron, my friend."

Baal shivered at the sound of the word "friend." He was anything but friends with Beelzebub. In fact, given the chance, he would gladly take his head as a trophy and shove his soul into Moloch's fireplace. Beelzebub, although he was a hermit of sorts, was highly respected within the confines of hell. He had the master's ear and the rest of the demons by the ballsack. Baal wasn't low man on the totem pole either, but he tended to work his magic in the background. His distaste for Beelzebub came from centuries of listening to him downplay his importance and abilities, only to step into situations when he wasn't needed, take credit for other demons' work, and bask in unearned glory.

He had overstepped throughout history, but until a few centuries ago no one, not even Lucifer, had stood up to him. Of course, Lucifer didn't react out of fear; more brainwashing than anything else. Beelzebub was a smooth talker. He could sell lava to a hell-bound demon. He had played Lucifer, and the worst part was that Lucifer had no idea. He was oblivious to the chaos the demon had brought to the council and the eyes the smooth talker had for his throne. Beelzebub had always had desires far beyond his grasp.

Baal considered the human books. "Your problem is, you don't know when to quit. You don't know what it means to have friends. You had Lucifer's ear for centuries, and now look at you, holed up in this cave, scraping across the floor and writing letters in the dark. I could barely read your letter because the blood you used to write it was old and clotted. I'm here for only one reason, and you're not my concern. You're the last demon I would call a friend."

Beelzebub was smooth, and despite his drop in favor, he was still extraordinarily powerful. The demons feared him more than any other hell-denizen besides Lucifer, and even Baal felt nervous being alone with him in the caves. It wasn't his size or even his demeanor. It was the under-handed ideas he had. It was his willingness to stab you in the back and leave you to take the fall for his mistakes. It was the competitiveness that glowed brighter than the demon-red in his eyes. There was little he could be trusted with, and there was nothing he wouldn't do to make his dreams a reality. Baal was not pleased to be there talking to him, but he had little choice in the matter.

Beelzebub walked closer to him, holding a book in his paws. "So, you got my letter. I really was wondering if I was going to have to kill the messenger. I was expecting it to be either lost or taken directly to Lucifer."

Baal snorted. "Yes, and I'm here to tell you it's a terrible idea. You're absolutely insane. To think that after all this time you would have the audacity to walk in on someone else's plans and suggest the monstrosity you present. I didn't even bring it up to Moloch because I didn't want to stress him out. He's not well."

Beelzebub shrugged. "I thought you'd be happy to ride along. Why be a sidekick to that crippled fool when you could transfer to the winning team?"

Baal ignored the jab. "I'm telling you, it's not a good idea. These aren't angels we're working with. These humans, and especially this Katie, won't respond like you think. You do this, and there will be a reaction. And that will pique His interest."

Beelzebub didn't seem to be moved by the threat. "*Please*. Humans aren't nearly as powerful as you give them credit for, and Lucifer's little ex-wife is nothing but a pest who needs to be exterminated. She will tire of these games and eventually find something else to amuse her. We've all seen her do it a thousand times. Katie isn't nearly as strong of a threat as you think she is, especially without Pandora inside her."

Baal crossed his arms. "I see you've been paying attention."

Beelzebub sat down in an ancient armchair. "Of course, I have. What else do I have to do down here?"

Baal shook his head. "What you're *supposed* to be doing is staying out of the way and not getting involved in this shit. Seriously, you're going to get yourself in deep hell for doing anything to interfere."

"So now you're worried about me? You're worried I'll get in trouble? Be serious. You're worried this will somehow come back on you. You received the letter, and you opened and read it. Your curiosity got the better of you, my dear Baal. Once you read it, you were obliged to come here and say something. If Lucifer found out you knew and didn't attempt to change my mind, he would put you in your own little personal hell. And then what? You wouldn't have your castle or your pets or even your little toy Moloch to play with. I swear, the two of you are like children on a playground. You don't know which way your dicks are swinging, much less how to lead a charge."

Baal narrowed his eyes. "We aren't the ones exiled out here in the boonies. Please forgive me, but I enjoy having the things I've worked centuries for. I sure as hell am not going to let you come into the picture and ruin all of that for me. I've been in this business far too long to have the wool pulled over my eyes."

Beelzebub smiled and looked Baal up and down. "Speaking of working for centuries, I heard that Moloch got a summons to the castle to see Lucifer. First time since all of this drama started."

Baal grumbled. "Pandora and her freaks came to hell and made a huge mess of everything. Moloch got stuck in the middle of the battle trying to stop it and ended up in pieces. He hadn't even regrown his leg yet when Lucifer summoned him. But so what? You don't know what they spoke about or even where the conversation was aimed."

Beelzebub opened his book and set his paws in his lap. "We both know where that conversation was aimed. Which, to me, indicates a probable new seat opening up. Those who respond to the human threat appropriately will have a chance to move up. You do know I was never relieved of my chair."

Baal blinked at him. "It's going to be your funeral, at which I will dance joyfully and drink myself into a stupor. What I'll do on your grave won't pass for flowers. I've given you my advice, and it's obvious you have no intention of taking it. You're not even listening to what I have to say. I'm not sure why you thought to write to me. You had to know I wouldn't be interested in working with you. Was it just a ploy to get back at me for still living my life while you're stuck down here in this cage?"

Beelzebub chuckled. "Perhaps partially."

Baal balled his fists. "Do I need to remind you that you got kicked off the table centuries ago for your last act of stupidity? You're going to fail again, spectacularly. I can't wait to watch. I gave you my advice, so you do with it what you will. Just do me a favor and stop contacting me. I will not have any part in this. Lucifer isn't taking down Moloch, not for this. He'll return in one or two pieces, and we'll go from there. If you want to risk what little life you have left on this stunt, be my guest."

Beelzebub held the book open so Baal could see the picture. It was Beelzebub in his younger years, standing next to some of the highest-ranking officials in hell's history. "I'm the only one left out of all of them. If Lucifer didn't want me to step in at times, he would have killed me like he did the others. That, or buried me deep within the rings of hell. Instead, he put me here with the freedom to come and go as I please. It has been centuries since I was removed, but I assure you, the lord of hell still pleads for my advice."

Baal did his best not to laugh in the crooked demon's face. "I think you might be mistaken. Lucifer needs no one's advice. He's a self-made demon. He does what he wants to do when he wants to do it. Your whispers may be encouraged, but he's only keeping tabs on you. In the old days, I believe he went soft on you to appease the council, mostly those who weren't happy with his temper tantrums when he ripped the other demons apart. He may be the ruler, but he knows some semblance of order and respect are needed, even in hell. You were lucky. That is the point."

Beelzebub slammed his book shut. "Then I guess this conversation is over. You're showing me that you never grew out of being the spoiled little demon you were many years ago. Let me be clear about something: I didn't need your help with my plans. I just figured it might give you the chance to claim a more prestigious seat at the table. After all, you have a squeaky-clean record and are always available. Surely, the master knows this. This could be your moment in the spotlight."

Baal chuckled. "The kind of spotlight I'm looking for doesn't come from doing stupid shit. It comes from careful planning and intense amounts of focus. You think this is something that comes easily? You think screaming from the rooftops will give you a forever seat? No one is guaranteed anything, in this dimension or any other. I thought you learned that lesson long ago when you scrambled for power. You've lost that power now, and you're thirsting for it. I, on the other hand, know how to control my cravings. I bid you a good day, Beelzebub. Please think about what I've said."

Baal started to walk back the way he came but stopped when Beelzebub called out to him. "The spoils go to the bold, Baal. I think all those delicacies you gorge yourself on have made you soft. Perhaps you've realized that hell isn't meant for the weak. You must be strong. Vicious. Simple survival is not an option. You must either thrive or wither. Right now, we are surviving, and that is all. The master makes sure no one gets too big to understand he's in control, no matter what."

Baal turned back to him. "I'm very aware that the master will forever be in control. There's more than one way to skin a cat, Mr. Beelzebub. Survival is only good if you can keep it up for an eternity. From the looks of this place, you may not last the week. You're two steps away from being an angry human cat lady."

Beelzebub laughed and slid his book back onto the shelf. "The days are long here in hell, Baal. They will be even longer with me above you on the council. You might want to rethink your position on my plans. Those kittens, guinea pigs, and gourmet meals are turning your brain to mush, I think."

Baal watched Beelzebub as he yawned and disappeared into the darkness. Baal turned around with tight shoulders and clenched fists. "And I think your stupidity has reached its zenith. I'm going to say I told you so, and I'm going to enjoy it more than anything I've enjoyed in a very long time."

Baal rubbed his hands together and stepped into the darkness, disappearing from the old dripping cave on the outskirts of hell. From the corner in the darkness, two red eyes flashed brightly, and the same maniacal laugh echoed through the space. Beelzebub rubbed his claws over each other and stepped back out into the candlelight. "You will come back, and if you don't, I'll make sure you never have a position again."

4

The condo had been quieter than normal since the
battle in hell. The lack of Juntto's presence had a lot
to do with that silence. Angie wasn't herself. She was
moping around, constantly worried. She barely spoke if
Katie didn't push her for conversation. Everything had
changed, but Katie knew it was only temporary. The lives
of those in Katie's Killers were always changing, but in the
end, they were still the same group who watched endless
hours of superhero movies and devoured box upon box of
donuts.

Katie grabbed her bag out of the closet and set it down
on the bed, looking at all the things she had laid out to
pack. She started by putting her weapons carefully in the
bottom, at least the ones she wasn't going to be wearing.
She was always armed, something she'd learned was a
necessity. She never knew when something would go
south.

Behind Katie, Angie propped herself in the doorway,
crossing her arms on her chest. She was wearing a warm

sweater and leggings with boots. Her hair was pulled back in a ponytail, and her eyes were dark and heavy. "You going somewhere again? I didn't hear any calls about portals or incursions."

Katie put one of her knives in a sheath and set it in the bag before sitting down on the bed. She smiled at Angie, noticing how tired and worn she really looked. "No incursion at the moment. I spoke to Gabriel last night, and he gave me a clue about how to bring Juntto out of his coma."

Angie's eyes lit up and she walked forward. "How?"

Katie hated to get her hopes up. "He said Juntto needs some sort of jolt of energy. He didn't say what kind. Gabriel called him the 'Energizer Bunny.'"

Angie chuckled, looking down at her hands. "He keeps going, that's for sure. Even as an ice cube in the meat locker, he's still making us run around for him."

Katie smiled and put her hand on Angie's. "I know this is hard on you. I know things didn't turn out how you wanted."

Angie shook her head, sniffling. "At least he's alive, and there's a chance we can get him back to where he used to be. This isn't necessarily the final word, you know?"

Katie nodded. "That's right, it's not. He's in some type of weird coma. We aren't sure how he got into it, but we're going to find a way to get him out of it."

Angie let out a sigh. "Where are you going to look for this mystery energy?"

Katie started packing her clothes and toiletries. "Where else? The old countries. I'm sure they had this shit when Juntto was walking around back in the day. Now, we seem to have stopped selling the stuff. Gabriel gave me the hint, and unless he's lost it, the hint has to lead to something."

"What brought him back this last time?" Angie asked.

Katie tilted her head. "I'm not exactly sure, but I'm assuming some sort of dark magic summoned him."

Angie pursed her lips. "Can we try that?"

Katie shook her head. "Unfortunately, we already *did* try that. Pandora tried it right in the beginning, but it didn't work. This stuff I have to buy or find—there's something about it that's separate from both demon and angel. He isn't either of the two, so I guess that makes sense."

Angie furrowed her brow. "And you have absolutely no idea what it might be?"

Katie scoffed. "I wish I did, but in all honesty, I haven't got a clue. It could be anything from a golden dildo to a serum we have to put into him."

Angie giggled for the first time in a while. "Why do I think that between the two, it would be the golden dildo, hands down?"

Katie laughed with her. "I'm sorry this is taking so long."

Angie sighed and shrugged. "Hey, comas make the heart grow fonder. Just wish I'd known I had a fond heart before he went into the coma. I tried to visit and talk to him, but it got weird. He couldn't have stroked out in normal size?"

Katie rolled her eyes. "You know him—he likes to do everything with style and drama. Dude would have done it as an elephant, probably, but he knew we would have left his giant ass right where it was."

Angie chuckled, then her face went blank. "I don't know if he had a choice in the matter. He was struggling to keep you awake and alive, then he just laid down, and that was the end of it. He couldn't keep himself awake."

Katie nodded. "I know. It was very strange. Nonetheless, we're going to try to help him. I need to do it before the next crisis comes along. We could really use his help, and the battles are getting harder as each day passes. Without him being with us in hell, I'm sure we would've had a lot more casualties than we did. He was a huge help. I owe it to him to do what I can to get his ass back here. I told him we were family, and I've said it a hundred times: we don't leave family behind."

Angie was clearly happier now. "Do you want me to pack you anything food-wise before you go? I called and had the plane prepared when I saw you come in and start laying stuff out."

Katie threw a sweatshirt in her bag, figuring she would try to blend in as much as possible while she was in other countries. "See, this is why I love you. Even in your own personal hell, you're thinking about me."

"My job doesn't stop just because bad things happen. In fact, my job is predicated on the idea that bad things are happening. One fell swoop of peace across the world, and I'm standing in line for food stamps."

Katie laughed. "No way. I would never let you go without. Even though it was terrible, that last business in hell got us a bonus from the government. They couldn't count the dead because it was, well, hell, but they did see what was done and felt it would only be fair if we were all compensated. We'll be okay financially for life, unless of course money goes away and I have to start trading with you for things I need."

Angie gave a laugh. "Very funny. Go on and get out of here. The plane's waiting."

Katie put her bag on her back and stepped out onto her balcony. She looked back at Angie, letting so much pass between them unsaid, then spread her wings and jumped. Angie hoped Katie would find the cure for Juntto's coma so they could all go back to the way things were. She hoped that was possible.

Nevada was bright and sunny, the air cooling down with the changing of the seasons. Katie's Killers' home base was calm. Their new perimeter defenses were almost all set up. It seemed like any other day on the base. Everyone was out working on getting everything in shape. The wind was blowing, and the sagebrush and creosote bushes rattled in the breeze.

However, just beyond the surface, something sinister was brewing. The wind began to slow, and everything stood perfectly still. All of the birds and rodents in the area scurried away, and no sound could be heard from any direction. A sudden loud clap rang out, and a gate tore open at the top of an old water tower. The gate swayed slightly, a wave of heat pulsing through the air.

Through the unholy gate came a large, clawed foot. The metal-grated catwalk at the top of the tower creaked under the weight of the thing. Emerging from the gate and seeing the light of day for the first time in centuries was Beelzebub's crooked body. He tapped his talons and stretched his bulky arms. His eyes blinked rapidly, his pupils dilating and constricting, adjusting to the brightness of the sun. He grumbled, putting his hand up to shield himself. "Forgot how miserably bright this planet is."

He walked to the edge of the platform that circled the tower and gripped the railing, bending the metal in his hands. Peering out over the salt flats, he hummed to himself like a child. To his left, the area was clear as far as the eye could see. To his right, the edge of the base was visible in the distance. "Yes, there you are, you silly little humans. Running around like ants doing the bidding of your queen. Little do you know the queen won't be able to save you from what I have in store."

Beelzebub peered at the valley, taking note of everything in his path. He looked at the sky and then back down at the busy soldiers, who were not yet aware he was watching. "How despicable. The answer is right above them. Why does no one else ever think of these things? I guess I shouldn't be shocked, considering who's running this operation. Moloch couldn't find strategy if it were pulling on his coattails."

He took note of the distance from the tower to the base, as well as the placement of guns along the perimeter. "They're quite the prepared little rabbits. No matter. What I have coming for them no gun will be able to deter."

He chuckled for a moment and then listened as sirens began to blare out from speakers placed across the base. Then, a voice came over the speaker. "All hands, prepare for battle stations or whatever it is you do. A portal has been detected on the horizon. Imminent danger. Code Red. Aw hell, just get ready because something's brewing."

The speaker crackled, and the siren continued to blare

as soldiers swarmed the base. Beelzebub's smile widened as he backed away from the edge of the platform. "Don't worry, babies. I'll be back for you."

He disappeared into the gate, which slammed shut behind him. The heat had melted the steel beams of the tower platform, and as soon as Beelzebub left it began to sag. With a grinding sound, the beams crashed down to the ground. After a few minutes, a group of Jeeps and fighters raced across the grounds, coming to a sharp halt in front of the tower. Soldiers piled out of the vehicles and the master sergeant stepped out, noting the heat that lingered in the air.

His scarred brow furrowed as he scanned the area. He saw nothing on the ground, but it was obvious from the collapsing tower that a portal had been produced right where they were. "Stay away from the tower. It looks like it's about to collapse. Just let it fall. It's not being used. Whoever was here is gone now, that's for sure."

The master sergeant walked away from the men and called the base to check in. Korbin answered, "What do we have, Sergeant? Demons?"

The sergeant looked back at the water tower as it groaned, tipped to the side, and slammed to the ground. He grimaced and put his finger in his ear. "Negative, no enemy combatants. The old water tower has been demolished, and there's intense heat coming from this area."

Korbin sighed. "So, whoever was there is gone now?"

The sergeant nodded. "Yes, sir. Whoever was here brought some heat with them, too. Melted the top of the water tower and the steel beams below. Whoever it was must have left as we were driving over."

Korbin rubbed his face. "They probably heard the alarms from the base. Okay, thank you, Sergeant. If you see anything else, let me know. It looks like moving didn't give us much time. When you're done with your search, come back to the base. We need to get ready."

The sergeant agreed. Korbin hung up and slammed his fists on his desk. Stephanie came into his office with a worried look on her face. "No one there?"

Korbin shook his head. "No, and that can only mean one thing."

Stephanie nodded. "Better call Katie. She should know about this. We might need her here, too, especially after the last battle. This base isn't ready to go yet. We still have a lot of preparations to make."

Korbin groaned. "I know, but we're going to have to push and get it done. I want all hands except Timothy out there working. Even those working on the armory. They'll have to take a break. Ammo doesn't do us much good if we can't use it because we're dead and the base has been demolished."

Stephanie gave him a tight-lipped smile and disappeared around the corner. Korbin picked up his phone and dialed Katie's number. It rang and rang, and eventually went to voicemail. He disconnected, knowing that wasn't the end of things. They'd been working on their own for a while. Everyone had been training hard, even the girls in the armory.

He set the phone down and tapped his finger on the desk. Pushing the anger and fear from his chest, he stood up and looked at a picture of the team on his desk. It was from a time long before he'd left the mercs, and Katie was right in the middle. She was smiling almost innocently, and he thought about all the damage his team used to do. "No worries. We got this."

He pushed away from the desk and headed down the hall, stopping in the IT room. Timothy glanced up from typing wildly on the keyboard. "What's up, boss?"

Korbin walked in. "We're all going to have to do whatever we can to get this base operational as quickly as possible. There was a portal but no actual incursion. That can only mean they're going to be back. I know you have to monitor, and I want you to do that, but help with whatever computer stuff you can while you're doing it, okay?"

Timothy grabbed his tablet and swiped his fingers across it, then stood up and walked to Korbin. "Not a problem, I can monitor everything from this tablet. We got this, boss. I don't want you to worry about it. We won't let them take us like they did last time."

Korbin slapped Timothy on the back. "Let's hope not."

Stephanie ran across the base to the armory. Joshua met her halfway, knowing something had happened. "Is it an attack? I didn't get the call to shut down."

Stephanie caught her breath. "Not yet. Whoever came out of that portal went back into it before we got there."

Joshua led her back to the armory. The women inside all looked nervous. "We heard a loud crash. We weren't sure what that was."

Stephanie nodded. "Yeah, the portal must have been atop the water tower. The whole thing came down. It was the old one, though, so we're okay. Korbin wants all hands getting the base ready for attack. We're pressed for time.

He said the armory would have to pause. He needs you, the girls…everyone."

Joshua reached over and slammed his hand on a button on the wall. "No problem. I'll get everyone together and meet you guys outside."

Stephanie smiled sweetly at him as he turned and commanded the room. He had come a hell of a long way since he had joined Katie's team. The meekness was gone, and that warrior he wanted to be was starting to shine through. In some ways, it was sad. He had lost his innocence, to a degree. In other ways, though, it was exactly what needed to happen for he and his team to continue to perform. They were in charge of a crucial aspect of the war, and they were willing to fight to the death.

Korbin stood at the edge of the property looking out over the base. The team was moving double-time, trying to get the base rebuilt and fortified for whatever was coming their way. He had done this multiple times, but it never got easier. The demons were determined to find them at any cost. He was going to have to start thinking about putting a new base underground again—something that couldn't easily be located and was even harder to attack. For now, though, he had to make do with what they had.

His phone buzzed wildly in his pocket and he pulled it out, seeing the general's name on the screen. "General, it's Korbin."

General Brushwood let out a deep breath. "Korbin,

good to hear your voice. We got word there was a possible portal opening near your coordinates. What's going on?"

Korbin looked at the twisted water tower. "Well, there was clearly a portal opened, but nothing was there when the team got to it. The old water tower collapsed from the heat of the thing. We're reviewing satellite images from that time period, but with all the countries all over the world using satellites, it's hard to find our way into the system."

The general scribbled something. "Noted. I'll make sure that from now on, you're given everything you need to be successful. We'll make sure your IT has access to it at all times. I know that used to be a fight, but since we've pulled forces together around the world, there seems to be more availability. As far as what happened, what is your assessment of the situation?"

Korbin rubbed his chin. "Honestly? I think it was a scouting mission. Whoever came through that portal was in and out faster than we could move. They were assessing the area, our defenses, and the lay of the land. Whoever they're reporting to will be given all the details of our location. This probably happened before, but we were unable to track it like we now can."

The general narrowed his eyes. "You think they'll be back, is what you're saying?"

Korbin nodded. "I absolutely do. They don't accidentally make portals in the middle of Nevada. I think they'll attack, and soon. If I were them, that would be my first priority. Otherwise, why scout this location? We're more vulnerable than last time, not just because we aren't fully built out yet but because we're aboveground. The armory is the same situation, and I made sure to put those defenses in first. That's the most important building on this base."

The general agreed. "Thank you for taking time to do that first. I'll send a platoon to help with defense and building, and I hope they get there in time to make a difference. It's anyone's guess as to when they'll reappear and how many they'll be bringing with them. I don't like this at all. We're going to have to find you a better location soon. Someplace highly fortified."

Korbin liked the sound of that. "We should definitely talk about that, but for right now, we're just trying to be prepared for the next incursion."

The general cleared his throat. "Have you talked to Katie about it?"

Korbin sighed. "No. I called her and texted her but haven't gotten a reply. I'm assuming wherever she is, she didn't take her phone with her."

The general was shocked. "I can't believe you haven't gotten word from Katie. She's usually the first one to answer the phones. I'll give her a call and see if that makes a difference."

Korbin was thankful. "We'll let you know if there's any sign of an incursion. Don't forget those men."

5

ngie stood in the doorway of the apartment across the hall holding fresh towels and sheets. She wasn't sure why, but she figured if they did bring Juntto back she didn't want to have to worry about rushing to do that kind of stuff. Sure, she wasn't his slave, but she didn't want him to worry about anything after being an ice cube for so long. She just couldn't bring herself to walk inside. It happened that way every single time. She would approach the door, jingle the keys, and open it wide. Then she would just stand there, staring at the spot where Juntto usually sat.

She didn't know why she did it. She didn't know what it was about the apartment that stopped her in her tracks day after day, but there she was.

She gathered her strength and stepped into the place. It was clean. She had cleaned it the day she thought he died. His scent still lingered there, a mix of man and the really strong deodorant he had pushed her to buy when they were acquiring supplies. She walked to the linen closet right outside the door of the bedroom and set the towels and linens neatly inside.

She could feel the emotion catching in her throat. She tried to avoid it, but it never failed to happen. Angie took a deep breath, wiped a tear on her pants, and shut the door. She put her head down and headed straight out of the apartment, holding her breath. She locked the door and went back to Katie's place. She shut the front door and leaned against it, giving herself a pep talk. "Don't lose it, Angie. He's not dead. That's a good thing. Katie is traveling all over the world to find a cure for whatever happened. Before you know it, he'll be back and driving you crazy again."

Angie let out a long, slow breath. She headed into the kitchen, immediately grabbing the pot from the coffeemaker and filling it with water. She poured the water into the maker and loaded the filter with coffee, closing her eyes and breathing in the scent of the grounds. "This is what I need. A hot cup of Joe, something to really get me going."

She started the coffeemaker and leaned against the counter. Her thoughts went back to Juntto, stuck in that freezer. Just thinking about it made her shiver, and she didn't like to picture it in her mind. On a human level, he was dead, frozen in place at his last breath. But apparently, Leviathans were different, or so she had been told. What that meant, she really had no clue. Either way, she just wanted him back, and she hoped Katie could find the answers they needed.

Angie yawned, watching the coffee start to drip into the pot. A soft vibration caught her attention, and she looked up and around, not knowing where it was coming from. Suddenly, Katie's ringtone went off. It was the Batman theme song, only the last time Pandora had control of Katie she'd dubbed over the Batman part. "Duh nuh, nuh nuh, nuh nuh, nuh nuh, Slut Girl!"

Angie rolled her eyes and went searching for the phone. She looked under the mail, under several stacks of notes Katie had been taking, and under the pile of Juntto's clothes that had been sitting on the table for days. Angie couldn't bring herself to fold them and put them away. She narrowed her eyes at the island, reaching for a drawer at the front of it. She pulled it open to see Katie's phone sitting there.

Angie grabbed it and put it to her ear. "This is Angie."

The general's voice sounded relieved. "Angie, thank God you answered. We've all been worried sick about Katie. She hasn't returned anyone's calls, including Korbin's. Is she with you right now?"

Angie glanced around the room. "Uh. No. She's gone on assignment. Apparently, she left her phone here. I was making coffee, and the Slut Girl theme song started to go off."

The general paused. "The *what* girl theme song?"

Angie shook her head. "Never mind. Don't judge, okay? Every powerful woman needs her own theme song."

The general didn't reply to that, letting out a deep sigh. "I just don't understand it. I need Katie to be on the ball, and she's gone with no way to reach her. Do you know where she went?"

Angie was getting irritable. "I do, but obviously it isn't information I can give out to the public."

The general slammed his hand on the desk. "Goddamn it, of all the times to go on a vacation. We're in a time of war, and I can't find my best man, or rather woman, to get the job done. Meanwhile, her own people are out there having threats made against them, and even they can't get hold of her. I know she's under a lot of pressure, but this is no time for sun and spa. This is time to keep these bastards from doing any more harm."

Angie looked down at her fingernails while she listened to the general rant. Normally, something like that wouldn't bother her. Normally, she would let it slip right out of her mind. This wasn't a normal time, though. This was a time of extreme pressure, and Angie's jaw clenched. She was becoming angrier with each passing second.

The general continued spouting off. "So help me, if she's having some sort of mental or spiritual break, I'll lock her up somewhere. No use in having to worry about her doing something reckless or getting hurt. I can't deal with all this right now. She should be available, that's the bottom line. If she can't be, I will take matters into my own hands."

Angie waited until the general went silent. "You finished? Good. Now you listen to me, and you listen to me *very* carefully, General. I'm not military, I'm not police. I don't in any way, shape, or form work for you so I will not pussyfoot around your bitch-ass attitude. Katie is a one-woman army of PR, and if any of the threats you just made actually happen? Oh, General, I can promise you that I will retaliate accordingly."

The general tried to interrupt. "Angie, listen…"

Angie laughed crazily. "Oh, no, you had your say. Don't you try to silence me, sir. I am a woman, and I will be heard! How dare you insinuate she would take a *spa vacation*? I think if she took any vacation it would be dicks and vodka, and not necessarily in that order. And you know what? Even if she did take that vacation, which she did not, it would be none of your goddamned business, because guess what? She works *with* you, not fucking *for* you. I think you might have forgotten that little bit of information."

The general made sure she was finished. "I'm just upset that I can't get her. I'm always able to get hold of her. I guess, in some way, it scares me when I can't. The last time she was MIA, she was fighting demons in hell and got pretty damn beat up. There isn't much I can do when I can't call her. She could be anywhere—New York, London, or even a completely different damn realm. I trust Pandora to take care of her, but that doesn't mean it doesn't make me nervous. Things can happen, and I want to know what those things are."

Angie modified her tone slightly, sensing that the general might be more invested in Katie as a person than she'd realized. Regardless, Katie was free to do whatever she wanted. "Honestly, if Katie's doing something, then you should take a deep breath and try not to worry. She never does anything without a purpose. If she thought what she was doing was important enough for her to go out undetected, then maybe it really *is* that important. I can't sit here and tell you I understand the way her brain works because I don't, but I *can* tell you I never question her actions. She's got this demon/angel thing on lock. She knows when, where, and what she needs to be doing, and there isn't much that any of us can do to stop her."

The general grumbled. "But what could she be doing that is so important she can't take a phone call? It's not the middle of the night. We know she isn't on a hot date, so she should be able to pick up the phone. Even if she can't tell me what she is doing."

Angie grabbed the coffeepot and poured herself a cup. "Right, and the government isn't known for tracking phones without legal permission. Look, she's focused, and doesn't want to be found at the moment. To be honest with you, I can completely understand that. Sometimes, I'm so focused that I don't want to be found. That happens more times than not these days. It's a wild ride that all of us are going through, and we have to respect her need for privacy even if it inconveniences us."

The general was not a happy man. "I'm sorry, Angie, but I just don't agree with you."

Angie slammed her cup down, splashing coffee every-where. "I'll make this very simple for you, General. You know as well as I do that Katie is not someone who can be ordered around. I hear her tell her own demon to go fuck herself more often than I'd like to admit. She's not going to start taking orders from other people. That's the whole reason she's a merc and not a member of the armed forces. She is your equal, and it would behoove you to remember that. Frankly, I would suggest that anyone who thinks they can bark orders check their idiocy at the door. In this house, we won't stand for it."

The general snapped, "I don't order Katie around. I simply do what we've always done. I make her aware of the job, and she takes care of it. I can't very well fulfill my end of the deal when I'm constantly chasing her down. How can I do my job if I can't get on the phone and tell her a portal opened near Korbin? This is ludicrous."

Angie normally had complete control over her emotions. She'd been in an abusive relationship long enough to know what happened when someone lost control. A blowup like that hurt people both mentally and physically, and she didn't want to be the cause of angst. But Juntto was in a butcher's freezer, and his clothes were sitting on the table. And this entitled man had made her spill her coffee.

Angie took a deep breath and exploded. "I think every single one of you puts too much pressure on this woman. Before she was Damned, she was a regular person. She played volleyball, tutored kids, and went out for beer. She dreamed of a normal future and all that entailed. She was thrust into this life, and now the weight of the world rests on her shoulders. I think you need to take a step back and really think about what you're doing to her. Give the woman a fucking second to do what she needs to do. We're all gone in the blink of an eye, and even when we aren't, even when we're stuck in a freezer asleep, tomorrow's still a fucking mystery. There are no fucking promises in life. There are no sure bets, and sometimes people don't answer their fucking phones. Deal with it."

The general fell silent, picking up on the freezer reference. He wasn't aware that Angie was so invested in Juntto, but her outburst and the whole tone of the conversation now made sense to him. He cleared his throat and spoke softly. "We should both calm down. I know this war is weighing heavily on all of us, including Katie. And you."

Angie wiped fresh tears from her cheeks. The general was right. "I'm sorry, General."

The general understood. "The truth of the matter is you're as tired as the rest of us, and your heart aches. War is hell, that's for damn sure."

Angie chuckled through the tears. "Yes, General. War is definitely hell. No one gets out of it without some sort of blemish on their soul."

He took a deep breath. "Will you just do me a favor? As soon as you have contact with Katie, let her know there's an emergency situation. Have her get in touch with either Korbin or me."

Angie nodded. "Of course. I'll do my best to contact her. I know she would want to know if something was going on with her team. If there's anything I can do in the meantime, just call me."

The general's voice dropped an octave. "The best that we can do right now is pray, Angie. We need to pray that things begin to get better. If they don't, our forces working on defeating the enemy may all fail in a spectacular show of lava, demon balls, and fallen angels. Personally, I don't want to see that occur."

Angie wrinkled her nose. "Especially the demon balls part. I don't think that's something that was in the training manual for this job. Had it been, I might have rethought taking the position."

The general laughed. "You're good at what you do. Don't stop, because you're part of what makes us successful. I have to go to a meeting, but I'll have my phone on me."

Angie nodded. "I'll let you know as soon as I can."

They hung up, and Angie set Katie's phone on the table. The screensaver came on and Angie smiled, seeing a hilarious photo of the two of them on the screen. They'd made superhero masks out of sheets and dressed up one night when they'd had too much wine and watched too much Batman. They'd ended up taking a flight across the city with Angie on Katie's back. The next day, there were photos in the paper of them flying around with black sheet-masks tied on and capes fluttering in the wind. It was both funny and absolutely mortifying at the same time.

Angie needed to follow her own advice and not put so much pressure on Katie, especially when it came to Juntto. She wanted him back more than anything. Having him just down the street but cold and incapacitated made things almost torturous for her. Still, it wasn't Katie's role to be his savior. Hopefully, she would figure it out, but she had to try to be helpful as well.

She grabbed her coffee and the pile of Juntto's clothes and headed to his apartment. She plopped them on top of his laptop and began to fold them. Life had to go on, no matter how badly she wanted it to stand still for her grief. Besides, if Juntto knew how she was acting, he would throw cheese-poof dust over her and swear in six different languages. He would do all that while standing naked in the living room. He would constantly be shifting from one character to another, swinging his dick around. He had gotten bad about that.

Angie's cheeks reddened and she laughed to herself, her giggles increasing in volume. She sat down in the chair and put her head back, laughing hysterically as she thought about him ranting as Arnie or Van Damme or Morpheus. It felt damn good to laugh, and she hoped it would continue, no matter what happened with Katie. Her phone buzzed in her pocket, and she pulled it out to see Timothy's name on the screen. "This is Angie. I'm alone, depressed, and laughing to myself like a crazy woman. Please leave a message."

Timothy hissed. "Girl, do you know how many times a day I do that? If I'm crazy and you're crazy, we'll just go get some of the good pills and sit in a room together. We'll leave all this bullshit to the pros."

Angie smirked. "Right? When this is all over, you and I have *got* to take a vacation. We'll try shopping, drinking, drinking, and drinking."

"Mmmhmm, that's what I'm saying."

Angie tilted her head, smiling. "What's up? I heard you're having problems over there."

Timothy waved it off. "Nothing we can't handle. I called because the general texted me and had the same concerns about you. Figured I would call and see how your lonely broken heart is doing since you're still lusting after the Iceman."

Angie looked down at Juntto's shirt. "Oh, you know—just planning out our future in an igloo with tiny, or not so tiny, frozen children pounding things with swords."

Timothy cooed. "Aw, what a sweet little frosty Viking family you'll have."

"I always wanted scaly children."

"But first, we have to unthaw your boyfriend. He would be an incredibly boring lay right now."

6

"I need six cases of ammo, but I want them to be stacked in the basement for now," Korbin yelled to two of the girls from the armory. "We can't have them out in the open. We don't know what'll happen or how fast it'll occur."

They gave him a thumbs-up and ran back to the armory. Stephanie walked up next to Korbin and put her hands on her hips. "It's insane how different these girls are now compared to when they worked for me. They were a crew of fragile little dolls before, and now they're a brigade of GI Janes running the fucking show. That's what *I'm* talking about."

Korbin put his arm around Stephanie. "There's that feminist spark I've been missing. I was starting to wonder if all the gardening and meal-making had twisted your mind."

Stephanie pointed at him. "Let me just explain to you the root of feminism. None of this new-age man-hater bullshit; it means that as a woman I can do anything I damn well please without judgment or control, penis or no penis."

"No penis. I've checked you out."

"Shut up. If I want to be a gardener and housewife, I'm empowered to do so. If I want to run out into a sea of demons and rip their 'nads from their bodies before slicing them in two, I'm empowered to do that, too."

Korbin put up his hand and gave her a high-five. "Yaaass, queen."

Stephanie laughed. "You sound like Timothy."

Korbin shrugged. "Hey, sometimes you just got to embrace the other side of things."

Stephanie smoothed the wrinkles in his shirt. "Before we know it, you're going to be shopping with us. Turn into a real diva."

Korbin gave her a side-glance. "I doubt that. I guess it all depends on whether we survive whatever the hell is coming for us. I feel it, Steph. I feel a surge of demons like I've never felt before. Something dark is brewing out there, and we're undoubtedly the targets."

Stephanie looked at the sky, which was starting to grow dark with cloud cover. "How's the build-out coming along?"

Korbin looked around. "It seems to be going okay. Everyone's busting their asses. Even if they hit us tonight, we'll be better fortified than we were yesterday. Every extra minute we get to prepare is something else crossed off our checklist."

Stephanie kissed him on the cheek. "Then let's not waste it. I'll get back to work. You make sure you're stopping to eat, okay? It won't help much if you're weak when this thing comes to a head. Without Katie around, we're going to need all the strength we can get."

Korbin nodded and watched Stephanie walk back toward the main building. His phone vibrated in his pocket, and he pulled it out. "This is Korbin."

The general's voice was tired. "Hey, Korbin. How are things coming along over there? I know you guys are monitoring portals, but please know we are keeping an eye on things, too. The platoon I sent should be there soon, and they have some serious weaponry."

Korbin squinted at the sun, which was beginning to take a dive toward the horizon. "We're better than we were but not as good as we'll be in another few hours. Just taking things one step at a time, you know? We knew this was a possibility from the beginning. Luckily we've been training for it."

The general sighed. "Good, I'm glad to hear it. I spoke to Katie's assistant, Angie. She said Katie was off doing something important and that she had left her phone at the condo. Apparently, whatever it is will be keeping her out of contact with us for the foreseeable future. I'm not too thrilled about that, but as Angie pointed out, I'm not her boss. I have to learn she's my equal and is free to come and go as she pleases."

Korbin smiled. "It took me a bit to realize that myself. I guess that was why she brought Stephanie and me back, General. She can't be everywhere."

The general wasn't happy, but he knew Korbin was right. "I will learn to let it all go. Just gotta give me time to do it. I care about her too, you know. It's not all business. She's become like a daughter to me over the years. I want to make sure she, and Pandora, for that matter, stay safe. I can't do that when I can't get hold of her and have no idea where she is."

Korbin shrugged. "I'm sure that if you wait long enough, you'll spot her on television somewhere. Those reporters don't give her any leeway."

"Man, they're relentless, although I don't blame them for taking pictures when she's flying around drunk in a floral cape in the middle of the night. Not one of her prouder moments, I suppose."

Korbin laughed, turning back toward the building. Before he could reply, his face fell, and he stared at the sky above the main building. The air was shimmering and wavy, just as it had been before when he'd watched a portal open. His gaze shifted to Stephanie and then to the front door as it flew open. "General, I'll call you back. I think it's happening."

He turned off the phone as Calvin bolted out of the door, waving his hands in the air. "Portal! Right over us! Take cover!"

Stephanie started running for the building as the sky cracked open and a great tremor shook the ground. She stumbled and fell as a blast of heat hit her hard, taking her breath away. The portal split wide open above her, and all she could see was eternal darkness.

Korbin took off, yelling to Stephanie, "Get out of there!"

Stephanie shook off the trance and got up, running to the hatch and locking it behind her.

Korbin turned to Calvin. "Lock down the armory and get into position."

The alarm was already blaring as Timothy rushed for the main building. He needed to be at his desk to properly oversee their defenses; namely, to turn on all the weapons that were controlled remotely. The soldiers took their positions behind their weapons. With a great mechanical whirring, the retractable cage slammed down over the armory. Joshua and a large number of his team were standing in front of the building with various armaments.

There was a sound like thunder, and demons began falling from the portal above them. Stephanie ran out of the building with her guns drawn and stood next to Korbin. "Here we go. Fuck these bastards."

Calvin cocked his weapon. "Come to Papa. It's been a while since I had some fun."

The demons scaled down the main building, a grotesque horde that came running across the base toward the group. Korbin threw down his arm. "Now! And don't fucking shoot us!"

Calvin, Korbin, and Stephanie yelled a battle cry as they took off toward the demons. They fired their weapons into them before slamming into them head-on. Stephanie took careful aim and fired shot after shot, hitting demons right and left and filling the air with demon dust. When her magazines were empty, she holstered her guns and grabbed her knives. She crouched and suddenly sprang forward, deadly blades flashing around her as she cut the throats of four snarling demons. She pulled her knives back and another demon swiped at her, slashing her across the shoulders. She hissed, and her eyes flashed bright red. With lightning speed, she stabbed the demon in the throat. She pulled the knife out and watched the demon fall, spitting on its body as it turned to dust.

Korbin blasted the crowd of demons with a shotgun, pumping the weapon after every shot. The spray of pellets struck several demons at once, taking them down in hissing, writhing heaps. A fat beast ran for him as he reloaded his gun and Korbin kicked the demon in the stomach. It stumbled backward but recovered, then bared its teeth and roared. Korbin narrowed his eyes. "Okay, fucker, you want to do this the hard way?"

He let his shotgun fall to the ground, and from sheaths on his back, he pulled twin swords. Korbin slashed them, raising one in front of his face and dropping the other low. "Well, come on, then. Show me how low those balls really swing."

The demon growled and lunged at him, managing to get a talon deep into his shoulder. Korbin winced and his swords flashed, cutting off the demon's hand. The beast wailed and stepped back, leaving his claw stuck in Korbin's shoulder. Korbin yanked the demon's hand out of his flesh and threw it to the ground. He raised his swords to finish the job when a shot rang out. The demon's head exploded. Joshua blew the smoke from his large-barreled pistol. Korbin nodded to the young man, and they fought on.

They fought hard, slashing through demons at every turn. Every fighter was gashed and struck and bloodied in the process. Several of the soldiers were taken down, and more were being carted off by Joshua's girls with extremely serious injuries. The demons just kept falling from the sky above them.

Calvin ran up next to Korbin, creating a circle of dead demons around him. "Sunny with a chance of fucking demons? This is fucking insane. We need to get that portal shut."

Korbin looked at their defenses, but the weapons had either been taken out or mangled by the demons. "We need more weapons. We need something to blow right into that portal to close it, but we can't take the chance of opening the armory."

The portal was shimmering and wavering from the heat it was producing. Calvin holstered his weapon. "What if I took a shit-ton of grenades and launched myself up there? That would blast the hole shut."

Korbin shook his head vigorously, then his eyes went wide and he raised his weapons and shot three demons approaching them. Calvin didn't flinch, just courageously held his head high. "Not a chance, buddy. We aren't losing anyone else today. There has to be *something* we can do; something that can launch explosives up there. Not everything could have been damaged that quickly."

Just then, the sound of tires crackling over gravel echoed behind them. The extra troops sent in by the general were arriving, looking hard as hell and ready to go. The troop carriers came to a sliding stop, and armed men flooded into the base. They laid down covering fire, shredding waves of demons as they came.

A middle-aged man with a scar down his cheek jumped from the troop carrier and put on his lid. "Korbin?"

Korbin put out his hand. "That's me."

The man shook it and yelled over the firefight, "First Sergeant Elroy, platoon leader of this fine group of men. How can we help?"

Korbin looked at the portal. "You got anything that can blast that hole back to hell?"

Elroy chuckled, the scar twisting his face. "Damn straight, we do."

Elroy waved at a Humvee, and three men grabbed a rocket launcher from the back and ran over. They unloaded the launcher and the missiles. "This should do the trick. Stand back. It might be a big blast."

Korbin pushed Stephanie back, and they covered their ears as Elroy loaded and launched several RPGs at the portal. The first one hit and exploded, but the second two flew right through. As the portal began to shudder, the smaller demons went scurrying to the building, trying to get back to hell. They were too late. With a loud snap, the portal shut. The demons on the ground were stuck on Earth.

Sergeant Elroy handed the launcher to one of his guys and waved his hand in the air. "All right, boys, let's clean house. No demon spared. Send these fuckers whence they came."

Gunfire echoed through the valley. Korbin winced as he limped across the battlefield. There was a messy gash on the back of his thigh he hadn't noticed until then. He wasn't alone. They were all beat to hell. Many of the defenders were seriously injured, and many had given their very lives. It had been a success, though. They'd defended their ground.

"*Puoi sentirti libero di guardare attraverso i libri ma non ho conoscenza di ciò di cui parli.*" The woman behind the desk spoke quickly, and Katie didn't speak Italian.

Pandora did, though, and translated. *She said she doesn't know anything about it, but you're more than welcome to dig through.*

Katie nodded. *Can you tell her we already searched the floor? Ask her if there are archives in the basement?*

Pandora took over Katie's voice. "*Abbiamo già controllato il piano principale. C'è un archivio nel seminterrato?*"

She pointed to a staircase at the back. "*Giù le scale e a destra. Ha degli archivi scritti sulla porta.*"

Pandora nodded Katie's head and gave the woman a smile. *Down the stairs to the right. It will say it on the door.*

And ask where she got those shoes. What? I can afford it.

Katie walked across the museum and down the steps. She was already exhausted from their search. They'd been at it for hours, combing through museums and scouring for sources that might lead them to understand what Juntto needed. So far, nothing had come up. They reached the door to the archives, opened it, and blinked at the mess on the other side.

With a groan, Katie leaned against the doorway. *This is insane. I thought museums were organized. It looks like a small tornado had its way with the room. It's going to take forever to go through all of this shit.*

Pandora sniffed. *It's not categorized, either.*

Katie walked through the room, looking at different stacks of paper and flipping open boxes. *None of this stuff has any connection to demons or the Leviathans. They're refer-ences to historical wars in Italy, not wars of the Damned.*

There was no use going through it all. If there had been an ancient text about the demons, it would have been cataloged. She left the archives and shut the door behind her. Frustrated, she trudged back up the steps. She waved at the woman as they walked out onto the busy sidewalks.

She was tired and annoyed, and felt slightly hopeless. *I just don't get it. I have no clues to follow. It's not like I'm going to walk along and accidentally trip over a giant battery that's labeled "Life for Juntto."*

Pandora chuckled. *No, but it would be funny if you did. I mean, let's think about it. What might be the source of energy Juntto needs but is not getting? Even with everything I know about his people, nothing pops into my mind. There are many differences, of course, but nothing that would help us. They don't walk around with plutonium milkshakes or inject uranium vita-mins or even stand out in the sun without sunscreen to keep them going.*

Katie walked along the medieval streets and wracked her brain. *What if it's not something ingestible? What if it's like a spell or a magic word that transfers whatever energy source he needs to him? I know that sounds hokey, but I'm part angel, you're a demon, and we're talking about an alien here. Nothing sounds too crazy these days.*

Pandora clicked her tongue again, thinking.

Katie shivered. *Do you have to do that? Can you think without clicking your tongue? When did you start doing that, anyway?*

Pandora scoffed. *Okay, snappy bitch. Calm the fuck down. I can't tap my fingers, obviously, and I can't rub my chin. It helps me work through my thought process. If I need energy, I eat a dozen donuts. To be honest, I have no idea how it works for Juntto. He was all outward emotion. I mean, he constantly was bragging about how he was the greatest Leviathan in the universe. He was angry ninety-nine percent of the time. He would stub his toe and have a fucking meltdown and massacre entire cities.*

Katie nodded. *He was a fighter too. He was almost happy to be causing pain to people. There was something about the adrenaline he glommed right onto, but none of those things really carried over when he joined us. They weren't keeping him alive, or he would have collapsed long before the battle. Or at least, I'm assuming he would have. Maybe he stores that or something. I mean, I'm not familiar with the anatomy of a frost giant Leviathan.*

Pandora wasn't sure either. *Who knows what he has in that body? He's probably full of angst and teenage hormones. I mean, the guy never ate or drank anything out of necessity. He ate a lot, don't get me wrong, but he did it because he loves food. He could go long periods of time without a meal and be fine. He was always so angry you would never be able to tell if he was hangry instead.*

Katie shook her head. *Drinking, too. He would down tequila, drink beer, or even swig soda, but I never saw him take a single sip of water. Even after being in hell, he didn't seem thirsty. Nothing seemed necessary for him. Not showering, not grooming, not food, not water...nothing. He could eat an entire pizza in one sitting, but it didn't seem to change anything for him energy-wise. And the frozen thing, that's like a capsule for him. No human or anything like a human could withstand that. Cryogenic freezing isn't really a thing.*

I heard Walt Disney's head is frozen somewhere.

Who told you that?

Nobody, but his headless body's in hell, so I assumed his head was still here. Great fun at parties.

Still, it's not something you want to do if you want to remain among the living.

Pandora sniffed. *Speaking of food...*

I was not.

You totally were...sometime today. I remember. You should go into the patisserie and get us something. I'm starving. We can brainstorm what's next. It's obvious we're going to need help from someone more educated on the matter than we are.

Katie walked toward the bakery, not paying any attention to the people staring at her in awe. Even in Italy, they knew who she was. She was a sensation across the world. She had gotten used to it, though, especially living in New York where there were people around her all the time. She went into the restaurant and allowed Pandora to place the order in Italian. They took the food outside and had a seat in the sun.

Katie took a bite of her *zeppole* and sipped her espresso. *So what's our next move? I mean, we obviously need help on this one.*

Pandora was silent.

Katie lifted an eyebrow. *Hello? Did you get lost in the pastry?*

Pandora sighed heavily. *I can't believe I'm about to say this. Seriously, I'm beginning to think I'm losing my mind. If you think I'm crazy, I want you to put me down easy, okay? I've been your friend these last couple of years. Put me out of my misery.*

Katie rolled her eyes. *Dude, spit it out. What the hell are you talking about?*

Pandora groaned. *Okay. We need help figuring out this battery situation. My thought was that the people who would know are those who've been heavily invested in these sorts of issues for the longest time, right?*

Right.

Pandora paused but decided to go with it. *I think we should go to the Vatican.*

Oh, boy.

Wait. We should go to the Vatican and ask their research people. They have a secret library where they have stuff hidden.

How do you know that?

If there's one place on Earth that has a secret library, where do you think that is?

Okay. Point taken.

They will for sure have information on Juntto's people even if they don't have the answer we're looking for.

Katie cringed. *Can we just roll up to the Vatican like that?*

I don't see why not. You are Katie, and I promise you they're curious about us. Maybe we'll even high-five Popie MacPopePope while we're there. I will refrain from telling him that God doesn't think he's any better or worse than Joe Lasagna who goes to church on Easter and Christmas.

Katie sipped her espresso with a smirk. *Yeah, I would probably stay away from calling anyone Joe Lasagna or telling the Pope how inconsequential he is, especially if we're looking for his help. I've heard the Catholic church doesn't look too kindly on those who question their importance and authority.*

Pandora started laughing. *Nope, not in the least. They enjoy burning people at the stake, murdering them in wars, and*

*condemning them to a life of house arrest for having—gasp!—
ideas. For now, we'll play nice.*

Katie shook her head. *Is that something you're capable of?*

*I'll do my fucking best to keep my goddamn language clean
and my words on point. I won't mention dicks or balls while
we're there, scout's honor.*

Katie waited until the evening hours to take her trip to the Vatican. She was trying to keep a low profile, so sprouting wings and soaring over the city in heavenly armor at noon probably wasn't the best course of action. Once the sun was low in the sky, she stepped off her hotel balcony and spread her wings. She soared higher and higher until she was right below the clouds. She hoped that at that height she would be mistaken for a large bird.

Pandora scoffed at the thought. *Maybe if it was the Jurassic period and you were a fucking pterosaur.*

Katie's jaw dropped. *Uh, excuse me? Did you just name a random flying dinosaur from the Jurassic period? Please tell me how you knew that.*

I would have you know that I've been through an Ivy League education. I have traveled the world. I've studied with wise men and monks.

Katie snorted. *I fell asleep while watching Jurassic Park on television and you stayed up.*

Pandora paused. *Yeah, okay, I did. But education is educa-*

tion. I learned something new, and if you hadn't remembered watching tv, you would have thought I was a genius.

Do you think this is a bit much? The wings and the armor?

Hey, dress to impress, I always say.

Katie smiled as she descended into St. Peter's Square in front of the Vatican. Immediately a slew of guards rushed forward with their guns pointed at her. She put both hands in the air. "Easy, boys. I'm here on business. If you don't know who I am, name's Katie. I'm half-angel, half-Damned."

Pandora cleared her throat. *Let me. They speak Italian, my dear.*

Katie let Pandora take over her voice. "*Ragazzi facili, sono qui per affari. Se non sai chi sono, chiama Katie. Sono mezzo-angela, mezzo-dannata.*"

The guards looked nervously at each other until one stepped forward and waved his hand at her weapons. "*Devi rimuovere le tue armi prima che ti permettiamo in chiesa.*"

Katie rolled her eyes. *Let me guess. They want me to take off my weapons.*

Yep.

Katie shook her head. *Translate the following, please. I have angelic attributes. My wings, my weapons, and even this armor are all heavenly gifts. Do any of you young men have the ability to take away these weapons? If not, you can move to one side and let me through. I don't go anywhere without my weapons, even in the Vatican.*

Pandora chuckled and relayed the message. "*Ho attributi angelici, le mie ali, le mie armi e persino questa armatura. Qualcuno di voi giovani ha la capacità di portare via queste armi? Altrimenti, puoi semplicemente spostarti di lato e lasciarmi passare. Io non vado da nessuna parte senza le mie armi, nemmeno il Vaticano."*

A man dressed in black stepped forward. "Katie, it's good to see you. I'm sorry, but we must insist you remove all your weapons."

Katie tilted her head to the side. The man was good-looking and had a killer Italian accent. "I appreciate your need to keep everyone safe, but as I've told every world leader I've met in my travels, I do not remove my weapons for anyone. It's not a matter of fear, but preparation. I might have to defend you. You'd be surprised how often demons drop in wherever I am."

The man crossed his arms, an amused look spreading across his face. "Then I believe we are at an impasse."

Katie looked past the man in black to a figure approaching them. "I don't know if that's true."

The man in black saw who was coming and stepped to one side, lowering his head. The armed men parted, and the Pope walked across the cobblestones. Katie found she was nervous, though she wasn't sure why. To her, he was like any other man. A shorter and older man, but still just a man. She thought it had something to do with Pandora, but she wasn't about to call her out on it. The Pope was dressed from head to toe in robes so white they almost glowed. He looked as regal as ever. He put out his hand, and Katie leaned down to kiss his ring.

Pandora made a gagging sound. *Do I call him Mr. Pope?*

Pope isn't his first name. I think the proper title is "Holy Father."

Nope.

Katie smiled at the old man in the robes. *Maybe His Holiness?*

Seriously?

I have no idea.

Pandora and Katie stood in the evening breeze, chatting with the Pope, who thankfully spoke English. "Thank you for seeing me, uh, sir. I know I kind of flew in without notice."

The Pope smiled. "It does not surprise me to see you here. With the world in turmoil and the Enemy and his demons attacking, I assumed I would meet you before this."

Katie smiled and cleared her throat. "We have some things we would like to ask you. We, as in my demon and I."

His Holiness nodded. "I'm aware that your demon is Lilith. I'm no stranger to the first wife of Adam."

Katie's mouth dropped open slightly. "I'm sorry? I thought Eve was the first wife of Adam."

The Pope put his hands together. "There's little we know about the Garden of Eden, but it is widely thought that Lilith was the first wife of Adam. She was created by God, perfect."

What have I been telling you? I'm perfect.

"To be more accurate, I suppose, she was *almost* perfect. She was unruly and headstrong. She wished to dominate her husband. When this did not occur, she ran away. God sent three angels after her. The stories after that are strange and conflicted, but we Catholics believe she became one of God's angels. Lilith was a fierce warrior for God until her fall from grace."

Katie was blown away as she listened to everything the Pope said. "I was not aware of her importance."

The Pope offered his hand, and after a moment Katie accepted. Together they strolled toward the huge columns of St. Peter's Basilica. "She was the queen of the demons long before Lucifer took her to wife. We Catholics know she fought beside our trusted warriors in the Holy Wars." The Pope looked up at Katie. "And some say she will sneak into a crib and steal children not protected by God."

Pandora scoffed. *That is total bullshit. I don't even like kids. And no, before you ask, I did not eat them.*

Katie was shocked to hear that Pandora had been involved in so many historic moments. She never would have believed it, although the dominance thing made perfect sense. *You wanted to dominate the first man created by God?*

Pandora huffed. *He always wanted to be on top. It was so boring. Missionary this, missionary that. I was like, come on, bro, let's liven this party up. Plus, Adam wasn't an especially giving lover. Not a cunning linguist, if you get my drift.*

The Pope paused at the bottom of the steps. "Although she is demonic, I appreciate the good she has done for our people and many others across the world."

Katie appreciated the Pope's restraint. He could have started spouting off a laundry list of Pandora's sins. They would have been standing there for the next century.

The Pope looked at the basilica and sighed. "What is it that I can do for you?"

Katie had almost forgotten why they were there. "Oh. We're in need of historical research. The kind that's not readily available to the public. We have a Leviathan who is seriously injured. I believe he is in a coma, and we're looking for a cure. The angel Gabriel pointed us in the right direction, but we need help figuring out exactly what we're looking for."

The Pope arched a gray eyebrow. "Gabriel speaks to you?"

Katie nodded and patted her armor. "Kind of comes with the new job."

The Pope chuckled and put out his arm. Katie took it. "Please, come in. We'll get you whatever you need."

Katie followed the Pope up the stairs and into the main portion of the basilica. The domed ceiling loomed high overhead in marble and gold, and grand statues decorated every corner of the sanctuary. It was more beautiful than she could have imagined. The Pope had a small army of people following him around, and he began barking orders in Italian. Katie had no idea what he was saying.

Pandora listened carefully. *He's ordering a couple of people to grab one Father Okenhoff, someone who works in the secret museum beneath the church.*

The Pope beckoned to Katie and she followed him down the halls of the Vatican, around several corners, and through a door that shut quietly behind them. He put his hands out. One of the younger priests stepped forward and spoke in English. "The Pope is inviting you to the vaults. There's all the history you would ever need to know in here. There are scrolls from the dawn of the written word. Some books were thought lost to the world, but we have the last remaining copies. I'm to order the others to search the entire library to find any hint of the information you need."

Katie felt incredibly special. She knew the church was very secretive, especially when it came to their historical texts and relics. She thanked the Pope profusely.

Another priest scurried up and whispered into the Pope's ear. The Pope nodded and spoke to the young priest in Italian. He translated for Katie. "He says that unfortunately, his historical relic expert is not in the church at this time, but everyone else will be more than willing to help you."

Katie nodded kindly at the Pope. She never imagined they would welcome her with such open arms. She hoped that together they would find the answer to her problems.

The staff working with Katie spoke English, though some were more skilled than others. She had an entire team at her disposal to go through the books and scrolls, writing down pertinent information, and bringing their findings back to a large table in the center of the library. Katie went through each, hoping to find something of value.

One of the priests pointed to a picture of a vase or water pitcher. "What about this? It was said to have some sort of healing powers. Drinking from it would make the person well again."

Katie glanced at the picture and shook her head. "No, I don't think so. What I'm looking for is a relic that contains some sort of power. Some sort of energy. The way it was explained to me, I need to find a type of battery. You have to remember that this being is not human. He's not from this planet. They have different physiology, so they need different things to survive."

The Pope walked in, taking a seat at the table with them. Katie smiled at him and continued going through the mounds of papers. One of the priests stopped and looked up, obviously thinking. "What if it isn't an object that we can see?"

Katie looked at him strangely. "What do you mean?"

The priest put down the papers. "What if it's simply the energy of emotions? It may sound strange, but emotions are fluid in every living being. Whatever happened to him, he might need a specific emotion to wake up."

The Pope asked, "What was different about the last battle, the one where Juntto fell ill?"

Katie thought about it for a moment. "We were in hell. We were fighting, and many were dying. Juntto saved several people. He sustained injuries, but nothing that bad."

Pandora sighed. *It's absolutely true that Juntto shouldn't have died from what happened down there. He was hurt, but he heals even faster than the Damned do. There was no physical cause for what happened.*

The Pope nodded. "And what about his emotional state? Was it different? More intense? Complicated in some way?"

Katie shook her head. She looked down at the table, trying to replay the whole thing in her head. There had been so many people there, and it had been so stressful. She had a hard time remembering exactly what Juntto went through. She had been in her own sea of emotions during that battle, but most of hers was anger, which wasn't uncommon in the heat of battle. Not Juntto, though.

If she recalled correctly, it was the calmest she'd ever seen him.

Katie looked at the Pope. "He was feeling empathy. Compassion. Things I couldn't remember seeing in him before that day."

The Pope nodded. The priest shook his head. "Fascinating. I wonder if the new emotions caused him to shut down? Especially if those weren't emotions typical to his kind. That can be off-putting, even traumatic for some. Those emotions were not known to him, correct? Even as children, the beings on his planet don't know those emotions. If I read the situation correctly, his people are almost totally devoid of human emotions. He learned anger and fear from humans but not empathy or compassion. Until, because of you, he did. It might have been a big enough shock to his system to cause him to shut down. He may still be processing those new emotions."

Katie handed the papers back to the priests. "You know, I think this might be the best answer to the situation we've found. I'm not sure what to do to help his body pull through it, but at least that gives me a starting point. Thank you so much."

The Pope got up with Katie and walked her to the door. "Katie, do you think you could stay for a few minutes and answer some questions?"

Katie nodded. "Of course. After everything you've done for me today, I owe you. I should warn you, I'm not positive I can tell you anything you don't already know."

The Pope smiled and put his hand on her arm. "Actually, we wanted to ask Lilith a few questions about the past."

Pandora laughed and asked the Pope a direct question. "How are you going to know if I'm lying?"

The Pope smiled. "I guess we'll have to get your answers and then find out."

Pandora sank into the background, and Katie poked her. *Do you want to do this? I mean, of course, you don't, but will you? It would be a very nice gesture after all the help they gave us. But if you aren't comfortable, I'll tell him no.*

Pandora let out a deep sigh. *How do I get myself into these situations? Yes, of course, I will. We may need these guys again one day, and the last thing I want to do is piss them off. They aren't known for having the best temperaments. Besides, I already know what they're going to want to know. People are so obsessed with history it just blows my mind. In the end, barely any of it made a difference to today's society. Although I have to admit, they live like it's still the eighteenth century at the Vatican.*

As long as you're comfortable.

I already know the kinds of questions he'll ask. What's God like in person? What do angels smell like? Do demons have buttholes? I can even do a little show-and-tell for that one.

Pandora, sweetheart, please don't show the Pope your asshole.

Katie smiled at the Pope and followed him out of the room. Once Pandora took over, she hoped the demon would mind her manners. Katie really didn't want to cause an international incident. She could only fight one war at a time.

8

The questions weren't hard for Pandora, and they were incredibly interesting to Katie. She listened in the background, letting Pandora take over. Pandora wasn't comfortable showing her true face to the Pope. To his credit, the pontiff understood and didn't judge her for it. Three high-ranking churchmen sat next to him and watched intently as she spoke. It was obvious they'd never had the chance to speak to someone like Pandora in person.

When they were done, the Pope thanked her profusely and walked her out. Waiting on the steps outside were all the priests who had helped her search for information. They wished her well, and a couple of them gave her their cards in case she needed more information.

Katie stuck all the cards in her pockets, but Pandora scoffed. *Right, like I'm going to call up some strange priest halfway across the world so I can ask him a question. I would call Damian first. He seems to have a bit more common sense.*

Katie looked around Vatican City. *I feel bad for being so*

close to Damian and not being able to visit him, but I need to get home. I've been having this gut feeling that something's going to happen soon. Hopefully we can figure out the secret to Juntto's coma before it does.

Pandora chuckled. *Most people have emotional issues, and they go see a doctor. Juntto had to get all dramatic on us and curl up into a frozen coma. I swear he's more of a diva than Timothy.*

Katie spread her wings wide. *Don't let Timothy hear you say that. He'll take it as a challenge. We'll never hear the end of it.*

Katie waved at everyone, and even the Pope waved back. Several of the priests snapped pictures as Katie rose off the ground. She ascended slowly, giving them a good view of her wings. None of them had ever seen an angel in real life, and several of the priests had tears running down their cheeks.

Pandora chuckled. *Look at you, showing off for the Church.*

Katie flapped her wings, soaring into the sky. *Hey, maybe they'll put a statue of me in St. Peter's Square or some-thing. They'll make me look all demure with these beautiful feathered wings. People will put roses at my stone feet.*

Pandora laughed louder. *I wonder if they'll give you tennis shoes in the sculpture and make your tits as big as they really are. I bet they scale down those boobs and that ass. It's a little too risqué for the Catholics. Lusting after a statue might get you taken down.*

Katie soared across the city toward her hotel. "You know what? The Pope was like, super-intelligent. Who would have known the Pope would be so knowledgeable about old Mesopotamian history?"

Baal's large claws tapped on the cold stone floor as he walked through an old building in the Greek hills. He went from room to room, holding a lantern over the bookshelves and boxes of old books, hoping to find the tomes he needed. He reached into an elaborately-carved wooden chest and grabbed a book, but the ancient thing turned to sludge in his hand. "This is just nasty."

He dropped the blob back into the chest and ran his hand across the wall, wiping it off. There was nothing useful in that room, just as there had been nothing useful in the four before, but he knew the tome was here. If he just focused, he would locate it. He still had three more sections of the massive compound to go through, so he wasn't panicking quite yet.

He exited that building and moved on to the next. There were fewer documents, scrolls, and books in that one. Against the wall was beautiful and ornate furniture that had degraded along with the building. No one had taken care of the items left behind. No one had cleaned the couches or organized the sculptures. That would have been up to the church, but he doubted they even knew of its existence. If they had, they would have plundered it long ago.

The next room was stuffed with old rugs and tapestries, but the third building he explored was full of ornate boxes of tomes and scrolls. He rubbed his hands together and began going through each box. He stacked the papers carefully, trying to keep them off the soggy floor. Not only was there a plethora of very important historical accounts of human history there, but there were things valuable to the demons as well. Moving the documents would be Baal's biggest problem. They would all combust in hell, and there was no one on Earth he could trust to guard them, so they remained in the Greek hills. They would be there until they either decomposed or someone else discovered them.

He stayed in the third building the longest, carefully pouring over the ancient texts. In one of the middle boxes, he found an old scroll with the broken seal of Lucifer. The paper was singed on the edges, which was a good sign. If it was what Baal was looking for, the scroll was from one of the very few times Lucifer had actually walked the Earth. He carefully unrolled it and read the contents. When he was finished, he rolled it back up and clutched it to his chest.

Baal had never been one to explore history, but recently he had become an avid student. He had a feeling that the contents of that specific scroll were going to become vital to his survival. Beelzebub had been right about one thing. The whole world operated on the premise that they had to be better if they were going to survive.

Baal was no different. He opened a gate and disappeared.

Baal stepped out of the gate into Moloch's mansion and walked to the fireplace, holding the scroll in front of him. He had put protections on it so it wouldn't combust when he got home.

He stared down at the tiny souls writhing in the fire. He

was wondering what to do next when the door opened behind him, and Moloch walked in with a slight limp. Baal slipped the scroll behind a large statue on the mantel.

He smiled at Moloch. "You're still alive! That's fantastic!"

Moloch barely glanced at him. Instead, he growled and limped over to the whiskey. He poured himself a glass and downed it quickly. "He beat the living hell out of me. He uses his power, his mastery of fear and pain, to manipulate even his inner circle. I didn't think he was going to let me go. I thought for sure I would be strung up in his dungeon for the next millennium undergoing beating after beating. Did you know he slapped me with my own damned hand? Talk about humiliating!"

Baal couldn't figure out why he was bitching. "You have your leg and your arm back, though."

Moloch grumbled. "The leg is a bit short, so I have a permanent fucking limp. Just what I need—a goddamned limp. He kept pulling my limbs off, beating me with them, and then putting them back on."

Baal stifled a laugh. "He beat you with your own limbs?"

Moloch shrugged and walked to the chair, plopping down heavily. "He probably forgot I came to see him with the arm barely attached."

Baal walked over and sat down across from him. "What did he say? Was he too angry for words?"

Moloch lifted his eyebrows. "Oh, no. The master was definitely *not* too angry for words. He let me have it."

"But he spared your life, so it couldn't have been that bad," Baal replied.

Moloch nodded, staring at the fireplace. "He did spare

my life…for now. He noted that I wasn't the one who started the wars, so he is giving me a chance to fix it. He believes I was responsible for fucking it all to hell. He wants Pandora, and he wants that meatsack of hers. The meatsack will die a slow, painful death. He has plans for Pandora."

Baal nodded. "I can see that. It makes sense to me."

Moloch shook his head. "Oh sure, it makes sense to me, too. The biggest problem with it is that I have to be the one to do it. I have to make sure I kill Katie and bring Pandora back, or the next time he summons me the torture will be even worse. I'm going to end up thrown out of the inner rings. I'll be exiled, living like a hermit in the outer ring. I wouldn't survive it, I tell you."

Baal immediately thought about Beelzebub. "You won't be expelled. We'll get those two and take them down. If you kill Pandora instead of bringing her back, at least she's out of the way. Besides, if you kill her, she'll end up back in hell. Lucifer can still have his way with her. We'll just have to retrieve her from the depths. I know a guy who'll do that for a nominal fee—just a dozen or so souls."

Moloch looked stressed. "Sounds easy, but we both know that together, those two are a force to be reckoned with. By the end of it, they may harm me more than Lucifer ever could. I'm not quite sure how I'm supposed to kill her when I haven't even been able to pin her down."

Baal cleared his throat. "We know where the base is now. Maybe we can wait until she's there."

Moloch looked up, surprised. "We know where the base is?"

Baal nodded. "Apparently Beelzebub got in on the

action and sent an incursion over there. He didn't kill anyone important, but it definitely dampened their spirits."

Moloch cringed. "I hate that guy. I suppose I should ease up on him, though. I could be his new neighbor out in the middle of nowhere if I'm not successful. I wonder if he would rent to me?"

Baal clapped his hands. "Stop that talk. You have your body back. You have all your limbs, short or not, and you have another chance to save your ass. You shouldn't be looking at this in such a negative light. Get yourself together. This is no time for a damned pity party."

"You know what, you're right. I have to keep pushing through. Eventually, we'll come up with a plan. I won't let this get me down. Thank you, Baal. You're truly a good friend. You're always so motivating." Moloch got up and headed for his room. "I'm going to rest for a while. He kicked me so hard my balls are still in my stomach. I'm hoping a nap will pop them back out. It might even help my leg grow a few inches. Otherwise, I might be that demon limping along in one platform shoe."

Baal nodded. "Hey, you might just start a new fashion down here. It's been a century or two since we've had one."

Moloch snorted as he went into his room. Baal sat there for a moment staring at the mantel. He waited until he could hear Moloch snoring and then stood up, retrieving the scroll. He looked at it for a moment and then opened a gate. He had something up his sleeve.

"I want Team A to go right and Team B to go left. We'll take the main hall and meet in the center. Make sure you check every single room. We've been assigned by the general himself. Do not fuck this up, gentlemen," the old sergeant advised his men.

They were a team of American soldiers in Greece, searching their way through a dilapidated ancient castle. The old sergeant followed Team A inside and searched the grounds with them. He stayed close, keeping his weapon at the ready in case any demons or creatures were hiding in the dark corners. They moved slowly through each room, searching through old bookshelves and boxes.

The castle grounds held several different buildings, and they were responsible for going through the entire compound until they found the source of the portal. They had detected it only hours before and been ordered to explore it thoroughly. When they reached the first building, the sergeant put his fist in the air, stopping his men. He walked slowly to the wall and stared at a streak of still-wet goop dripping from the stone.

He pulled out his gloves, removed a chunk of the slime from the wall, and put it in an evidence bag. "It looks like a demon came through here. They probably were not happy with that book turning to mush in their hands."

The sergeant flashed his light on the ground, picking up a large footprint that led into the next building. The soldiers tracked this, checking out the different scrolls and writings in each room. The second room was nothing but furniture and tapestries, and they didn't see any signs of anything being disturbed.

All along the way, ornate boxes had been thrown open and papers were strewn all over the place. The sergeant picked one up and raised his eyebrows. "This is very old. Very, very old. I would say this is an extremely important find."

One of the soldiers walked up to him. "It looks like it was just one demon, and he was frantically trying to find something. There are objects from so many time periods here, I don't know what it could be."

The sergeant walked to a dusty old box and ran his finger over the imprint of a scroll that had been lifted from its tomb of encrusted dust and cobwebs. Whatever was there had been taken by the demon, but he had no idea what it might have been. No one went to that old castle. It was privately owned, and not a normal tourist destination. The castle had had dark beginnings and was said to have been home to death cults and dark magicians. They had also apparently used it to stockpile important historical documents.

The sergeant shook his head. "I don't know what that bastard was looking for, but he might very well have found it."

The soldier rifled through a couple of documents in the same area, but there seemed to be no rhyme or reason to their placement. "What would you like us to do, sir?"

The sergeant rubbed his chin. "We can't just leave all this here."

The soldier whistled to the others. "Listen up, men. We are going to start bagging and tagging all of this."

The sergeant turned. "No, no. Wait. We're going to need a group of specialists in here to do that. Some of this has been around since before the Greeks spoke Greek. We need well-trained personnel in here, or we'll end up buggering the whole find. I'll save your asses—and my own —and call this one in."

One of the other soldiers walked into the room. "Sergeant, can you come look at this?"

The sergeant handed the other soldier his phone. "Get the general on the phone. Tell him what we found, and have him send some specialists out here to start collecting things. Tell him we'll maintain protection on the building until they arrive."

The sergeant followed the other soldier across the castle yard to the first building. He pointed at the floor and shone his light on black burn marks. "Between the markings on the floor and the increase in temperature, I believe this was where the portal opened."

The sergeant stared at the black streaks. "Good job. I guess there's nothing we can really do about that, but at least we pinpointed it."

The soldier moved his flashlight. "To solidify your theory of one demon, there's only one set of footprints going in and out of this spot. I'm assuming it was one demon looking for something in particular. I have to think this was the entrance point, and most likely, you'll find similar burn marks on the floor in the third building."

The sergeant turned without a word and rushed back into the third building and to where the scroll was missing. Sure enough, on the floor were several singe marks. He put his hand against the shelf against the wall, feeling how hot the wood was to the touch. "You're right. It looks like he took the scroll and opened a portal right here. It couldn't have been that long ago because everything's still very warm. Damn it, we need those specialists here right away.

In the meantime, you guys write down the temperature of every building in the castle. I want to make sure we have that information."

Everyone went to work, carefully carrying out their orders. No one wanted to be the idiot who destroyed a key piece of evidence. The sergeant stared at the outline of the missing scroll. There was something to that. He just didn't know what it was.

9

Katie flapped her wings hard and put her feet forward, landing on her balcony. She tucked her wings behind her and took a moment to wave at her fans below. They yelled and cheered for her. She remained on the balcony, letting them take a couple of pictures.

Pandora was loving it. *That's right, vogue for your adoring fans, my dear. Strike a pose. There's nothing to it.*

Katie lifted an eyebrow. *Since when did you become a Madonna fan?*

Pandora scoffed. *Please, who do you think gave her the cone tit idea? I didn't like her much, so I thought maybe it would bring her some ridicule.*

Katie laughed. *Little did you know.*

Pandora pouted. *How was I supposed to know women would love the idea of using their tits to flag traffic? I thought it was ridiculous. Humans are ridiculous, though. There's nothing I can do to fix that.*

Still smiling, Katie opened her bedroom door. *Hey, just*

think of it this way. You helped influence some of the worst pop culture fashion in history. You should be famous.

Pandora laughed. *Oh, darling, I am famous.*

Katie took off her belt and laid her guns in a drawer in the dresser. It was early, and she wasn't sure if anyone else was awake yet. Katie was in a good mood after finding more information about Juntto, and getting some much-needed sleep on the plane ride back hadn't hurt, either. Even Pandora was in a good mood, which was rare and made Katie laugh to herself.

As she went to pull off her shirt, there was a knock on her bedroom door. She cursed and yanked it back down. Katie found Angie standing at the door in her robe and slippers. Katie smiled and grabbed Angie's hands, pulling her into the room. "I have good news."

Angie just looked at her. Katie cleared her throat, not really noticing her shocked expression. "We couldn't find anything at first. We searched through museum archives, church archives, everything. Then Pandora had the brilliant idea to go to the Vatican. The Pope welcomed us with open arms. We searched their secret archives for hours, and then one of the priests had a thought. He said it just might be the energy of emotion that was keeping Juntto under. He was feeling emotions he'd never felt before, and that basically shut his system down. Now all we have to do is figure out what emotion he needs."

Angie swallowed, her facial expression not changing. "Katie."

Katie pulled her hair back in a ponytail. "I know it's not definitive, but it's more than we had."

Angie clasped her hands in front of her. "Katie, you left your phone here."

"Yeah, I just wanted to be able to focus."

Angie's face looked sad and worried. Katie stopped what she was doing and walked her to the bed. "What's going on?"

Angie took a deep breath. "Everyone was trying to get hold of you yesterday morning. The general, Korbin—they all needed to find you. Apparently, a demon came and scouted the base, then left."

Katie stood up angrily. "What? Then I have to get there. There could be an incursion at any minute."

Angie reached out and grabbed Katie's wrist. "Call Korbin. There already *was* an incursion. Some of the troops were killed, and some were seriously injured. Korbin, Stephanie, Joshua, and Calvin sustained pretty hard-core injuries too."

Katie's face fell, and she tapped her pockets looking for her phone. Angie reached into her robe and handed it to her. "Just try to stay calm."

Katie nodded as Angie left the room to give her some privacy. She dialed Korbin's number and waited until he picked up. "Korbin! Is everyone okay? Are *you* okay?"

Korbin cleared his throat. "Good morning to you, too, Katie. I'm okay. We have scratches, gashes, and bruises but Stephanie, Calvin, Joshua, and I will all live. There were a couple of troop casualties, and one of Joshua's girls was injured. Some of the soldiers were flown out because of their injuries. The base wasn't damaged that badly, but we'll need to repair the defenses quickly."

Katie shook her head. She felt guilty for not being

there. "I'm so sorry, Korbin."

Korbin chuckled. "Don't ever apologize. You can't be everywhere at once. But Katie? This was a surprise attack. Not because we didn't know it was coming, but because they literally opened a portal above us and dropped demons like rain. Somebody out there is changing the rules, which is not very polite of them."

Korbin walked out of the room and quietly shut the door behind him, letting Stephanie get some sleep. Her shoulders were killing her, and her lip was swollen. Her demon was working on healing her, but she needed to sleep. Korbin put the phone back to his ear as he limped down the corridor to the kitchen.

Katie was obviously feeling guilty, but Korbin didn't want her to feel that way. "Look, Katie, you had something to take care of. That's okay. We all have things going on, and you put us here because you can't be everywhere at once."

Katie sighed. "I know, I just... You're my team, my family. I should have had my phone on me."

Korbin flipped on the kitchen lights and grabbed the coffee pot. "Let me guess—you weren't in this country. I'm telling you, even if you'd answered when we identified the first portal, you wouldn't have made it back here in time. The incursion lasted maybe forty minutes and then it was over. We had some help from the general. They shot several RPGs into the portal to close it. After that they swept the field, killing everything else on the ground. I have to say, I've never seen anything like it. It was like the sky ripped open and all you could see was black."

Katie was pissed. "Someone thinks they can fuck with us. Someone thinks they can change the rules."

Korbin poured the water into the back of the coffeemaker and replaced the glass pot. "You have to understand something, though. We've been fighting demons for centuries. There have never been, and will never be, rules of engagement in this war. They do what they can to strike us down. They will kill you running away, and they will kill you from overhead; they will do whatever it takes."

Katie leaned against her dresser. "Then we'll do the same. Period. We'll play dirty too. I'm going to get some breakfast and repack a bag, then I'll be on a plane out there."

Korbin shook his head, filling the filter with ground coffee. "No, you stay put. You have a lot going on in New York right now. I've got this under control here. If we detect any more signs of an incursion, I'll call you right away. Just make sure you have your phone on you."

Katie sighed. "If you need anything, and I mean *anything*, please don't hesitate to call me immediately."

Korbin chuckled. "I promise. Go eat some breakfast before Pandora takes you down."

They both laughed and hung up. Korbin crossed his arms and waited for the coffee to brew. He was thinking about the battle the day before. It had been brutal, but they had been lucky. If Katie flew all the way to Nevada, she wouldn't really get anything accomplished. The worst of it was over.

Calvin leaned against the kitchen counter, surprising Korbin. "Good morning. You know, Katie never did listen to me."

Korbin smiled and winked. "You aren't me."

Calvin chuckled and handed Korbin a coffee mug. "Figured we would start getting anti-aircraft weapons in place, so this shit doesn't happen again."

Korbin poured them both a cup. "Sounds perfect. Just aim and shoot right into the portal as it opens. Not sure if it'll work completely, but we'll definitely have a better chance of stopping the bastards before things get out of hand."

Calvin took a sip of his coffee. "That was crazy yesterday. Made me miss living in the tunnels like a sewer rat. Being underground definitely has its advantages."

Korbin nodded. "It does, and that's why I ordered the men to start digging deeper. My goal is to eventually move the whole base into the ground below this building. That way we're protected by the building and by the earth. There'll be an entire system below. It'll take time, but we need to do something, especially with hell raining down from above."

Calvin tipped his mug. "Literally."

All I'm saying is, maybe you could throw me a bone. Literally.

Timothy rolled his eyes, tired of his demon's constant bitching. It had gotten even worse lately. He just wouldn't shut up about getting some. *I told you, I'm not interested in girls in the slightest. You could put me in a room with a gaggle of naked coeds and my dick would stay as calm as a spring breeze. Not gonna do it.*

His demon growled. *So you're just going to stay chaste for the rest of time?*

Timothy picked up his tablet and left the IT room. *We could do things my way. Go over to the Iron Horse Lounge to see what we can see.*

Not happening.

Then we can both enjoy chastity for all eternity.

Timothy's demon angrily yelled, *You are impossible!*

Calm down, now. You're going to give me a stroke or something. Timothy made his way outside to where Korbin and Calvin were working. Stephanie was sitting in a chair. She tried to stand when she saw Timothy, but Korbin growled at her.

"You're weak. Rest."

Stephanie smiled at Timothy. "Morning, boo-boo."

Timothy put his hands in the air. "Morning, my beautiful babies. Aw, momma, you look like you've been run over."

Stephanie chuckled. "I *feel* like I've been run over."

Timothy bent down next to her and kissed her cheek. "Well, I watched you on the screen while you were fighting, and let me just tell you, you were slayin' it. Just absolutely fucking slayin'. Badass queen is what you are."

"Thank you, my darling. What are you doing this morning?"

Timothy pulled a lawn chair next to her and fanned himself with his tablet. "Girl, let me just tell you, this demon shit is for the birds. My demon will not shut the fuck up about getting laid. I told him it's not going to happen. He would have to add a dick to the menu for me to go to that restaurant, and still, it would be weird. Titties flying around, her bringing more drama than me. We might end up having a catfight mid-fuck."

Stephanie giggled. "That would be interesting to see."

Calvin chuckled and looked at Timothy as he moved one of the guns to point higher in the air. "Or you could just give in and let him have his way. Not all the time, just every, oh, I don't know—two years or so. It'll be his reward for being a good demon."

Timothy wrinkled his nose. "Mmm, no. I don't think so. It's like children. You give them one treat for being good and going potty in the yard, and then all of a sudden they're jumping on you every five minutes."

"Timothy," Calvin ventured. "What kind of kids you been training?"

Korbin tilted his head. "Do you mean children or dogs?"

Timothy waved his hands. "Same thing. Wet noses, fleas, and they shed."

Everyone laughed as Timothy looked down at his fingernails. He grabbed Stephanie's hand and looked at hers as well. "We need some loving time. Look at these fingers. Manicures are on the house tonight, girl."

Stephanie looked at her fingers, the chipped nail polish slightly singed at the edges. "That's what you get when you're hit with a heat wave and then forced to stab demons in the throat with daggers. It's a shame. They should make warrior-proof nail polish."

Timothy smacked his lips. "That they should. It would be fabulous, that's for sure. It would have to be like steel polish or something, though."

Calvin looked at them. "They should make gloves that have the special steel fingertips. That way you could claw your way through like Catwoman."

Timothy's eyes lit up. "Oh my God, I'm fainting. I could totally wear the whole getup. The lycra suit, the wig, and those special claws. I would even wear the little furry ears. Holy hell, this bitch would be fabulous."

Stephanie elbowed him. "You could wear those spike-heeled Prada boots we saw."

Timothy shook his head, continuing to fan himself. "Girl, I am in *love*. Where is Joshua? I need that man to put down the grenade launchers and get his ass in gear. Momma needs a brand-new pair of claws."

He stood up and strutted toward the armory building, Stephanie whistling after him. Everyone smiled as he curtsied and threw open the armory door, yelling Joshua's name at the top of his lungs. "Joshua! We have fashion to make."

Beelzebub shook off his scales as he appeared in one of the gorges in hell. It was off the beaten path, so no one would pay any attention to him being there. No demons were out that way, and the only other being was the specialist Beelzebub had summoned. He kicked one of the stones into the river of flowing lava and put his hands on his hips. A large lavafall cascaded over the edge of the cliff above. The goop dripped down the fall and plummeted into the small pool below, making gargling and bubbling sounds.

"This is an interesting place. Don't know how I haven't

found it before," Beelzebub muttered to himself, looking at the lava pool.

The specialist demon walked over with an air of nervousness surrounding him. "This has been here for centuries. It was created when Lucifer banished Hindleroth to the depths of hell. He slammed his body into the rock and created the gorge. The lava just flowed right over. Beautiful sight, really."

Beelzebub lifted an eyebrow and walked closer to the falls. "Yes, well, it will be even more beautiful if my plan works the way I hope it will. How much lava is flowing per minute here?"

The demon pushed up his invisible glasses. "It would really depend on the viscosity of the lava, where it was flowing, if there was an eruptive force behind it, and so on. In hell, things move differently than on Earth, of course. Lava flows at about half the rate of water."

Beelzebub sighed. "How about for this?"

The demon looked at the lava pool. "I would guess between two and five cubic meters per second, nearly twenty million gallons of lava every few minutes. Then again, the temperatures in hell are very high. I would wager that if this lavafall were in, say, Hawaii, it would flow much slower because the air is cooler. It would thicken the lava considerably. We would still see around five million gallons of lava every few minutes."

Beelzebub put his hand on his chin thoughtfully and walked to the edge of the gorge. "Hmm. That is not bad at all. I will have to select an appropriately-sized town. If the city is too large, the lava won't do nearly enough damage."

The demon looked at him nervously. Beelzebub waved

his hand. "You may go. But remember, not a word about this to anyone. Do you understand?"

The demon nodded fearfully and raced off through the gorge. He jumped onto a wall and scampered out of sight. When he was gone, Beelzebub waved his hand again, and a world map of Earth sprang into view. He studied it closely.

"This will be a beautiful test for those meatsacks. I will test their agility and courage, then pour this lava straight down on one of their precious little cities. They won't even see it coming. They'll be too busy fighting the initial demons I send in," he mused.

He waved the map away and paced up and down the edge of the lava pool. The hot molten liquid churned and bubbled below. He had seen what lava did to humans. He'd been there when Vesuvius erupted on Pompeii. That had been an exciting sight, but it had been random. The opening gate had sparked the volcano and created an event that would live in infamy both in hell and on Earth. Vesuvius had been a fantastic accident. The next major eruption would be purposeful.

Beelzebub continued his trek through the gorge, talking to himself as he went. "Baal talks about these humans being so tough and so strong. He lets them get the best of him and Moloch, but I do not believe it for a second. The humans I know are weak and fragile. They only fight for their own skins, not for others. Those two have seriously overestimated them. I'm going to prove that. There's no better way to extinguish the light of a rally than to burn them all straight into the ground. Fires will rage, my dear Baal, and when the lava hardens to stone, we will see who is left standing."

10

Katie giggled as she flew through the air, this time with an actual cape latched around her neck. It wasn't a sheet. She had purchased it online. This time she wasn't absolutely wasted, either. She and Pandora had needed to fight some crime, take down some demons, and generally blow off some fucking steam. Between the general and the attack on her base, she was starting to lose her mind.

Pandora laughed as they dove between buildings, the cape flapping between her widespread wings. *What you need is to kick some ass. Feel that rush again. Feel like you're doing something good and it's all worth it.*

Katie soared to the right. *You're right. I* do *need a reminder.*

And what better way to do that than as Slut Girl?

Katie and Pandora both started singing her ringtone. *Duh nuh, nuh nuh, nuh nuh, nuh nuh, Slut Girl!*

They laughed as they swooped toward Brooklyn. Katie

reveled in the wind on her face and enjoyed the flight. *This is such a perfect fall night. I love it.*

Pandora sniffed. *Uh-oh, I smell trouble. To the east, about three city blocks.*

Katie put on her game face and swooped right. She soared down a row of apartment complexes, keeping her eyes peeled. As she reached the fourth block she slowed, hovering above an alley. Below were three guys, all with red eyes. They had cornered a young black woman, who had her pepper spray out in one shaking hand. Katie could hear the desperation in her voice. "Stand back. I have pepper spray. I'll use it. I will."

The three guys looked at each other and laughed. She released the spray into their eyes, and they all coughed wildly. Victorious, the woman tried to make a run for it. One of the demons grabbed her, faking a hacking cough. They all began to laugh. The pepper spray had had no effect on them. He twisted her arm until she dropped the canister, the clang of it hitting the ground echoing down the alley. He snarled, "We just want to play."

Katie growled and descended into the alley. She tucked her wings as she landed behind the demons. The girl looked up and gasped at Katie's bright blue eyes. The guys sniffed the air and slowly turned. The lead demon dropped the girl's arm. Katie looked at the woman and pointed down the alley. "Go. Keep going until you get home."

She grabbed her things and went, yelling her thank-yous as she ran down the alley. Katie turned back to the three guys and snarled. The one in the middle, the only one without fear surging through him, chuckled. "What the fuck are you supposed to be, Whore Girl?"

Katie smiled and rammed her hand into the guy's chest, grabbing his demon. "Actually, it's 'Slut Girl.'"

She yanked the hissing demon out of the man and tossed it into the air. The other two watched, horrified, as it wheezed and snarled before bursting and disappearing. They turned to make a quick getaway but Katie lunged for them, grabbing them both by the backs of their necks. "Where do you think you're going? I promise I'll be gentle."

She released their necks and shoved her claws through their backs, pulling out their demons. The two guys fell unconscious on top of their friend as Katie held up the snarling beasts, which exploded and were gone. She dusted her hands off and nodded. "That should do it. You boys stay out of trouble, now."

Pandora laughed. *That was fucking brilliant. I loved it. Let's find another mess.*

Katie smiled and took off straight out of the alley. An old newspaper flapped around the alley's walls in her wake. They flew over the city again, this time heading for the Bronx. As they passed over Times Square, Pandora sniffed again. *I smell it. Two blocks down on the right. A jewelry store. This is a good one.*

You gonna get the number of blocks right this time?

Pandora scoffed. *I'm a demon, not a bloodhound. Just go.*

Katie laughed as she soared ahead, stopping two blocks down across the street from a jewelry store. She hovered in the air and watched the action through a window.

The man's face was covered with a black ski mask. He had a sack in one hand and a gun in the other. "Just put the money in the bag, and there won't be no problems."

The lady behind the counter shook with fear as she

opened the register. She filled the sack with money, then emptied the glass cases of jewelry. She shoved the sack back at him. Slowly, Katie descended in front of the window. The woman's eyes grew wide, but the robber didn't notice.

He chuckled and took a bow, still pointing his gun at the woman. "It's been a pleasure, sugar tits."

He reached to grab the door handle, but Katie was already holding it open. Her cape flapped in the wind behind her as she grabbed the sack of goodies from him. "Give me that, sugar tits."

The thief yelped and pulled the trigger, shooting Katie in the arm. She gritted her teeth as she looked down at the bullet hole. The robber watched in horror as her finger grew a claw and she dug the bullet out. She held it in front of her face and turned it from side to side so she could examine it. "Just a regular old bullet."

She threw the bullet down and grabbed the guy by the neck. *He's not Damned.*

Pandora giggled. *Nope, just a regular old dumb-ass robber.*

Katie found it odd. *How did you sense that? Usually, only I can sense that kind of thing.*

Pandora cleared her throat. *Might be leftover from my days as an angel. Who knows?*

Katie shrugged and lifted the guy into the air, then slammed his face on the ground. "You don't call women 'sugar tits' unless they ask you to, asswipe." She pulled out a pair of handcuffs she'd borrowed from the station and cuffed the guy, then growled in his ear, "And you don't shoot before figuring out just what the fuck you're dealing with, dickwad."

Katie stood up and beamed at the woman behind the counter. "Call the cops. Tell em' Katie did it, and he shot first."

The woman behind the counter nodded and quickly picked up the phone. Before she could dial the number, Katie was gone.

She flew over the city, proud of her good deeds. *Kicking ass...*

Pandora chimed in, *And not giving a fuck about the names.*

Katie put her arms out in front of her like Superman. *Damn fucking straight. Now, I know there are some leftover donuts at the apartment. Let's go chow— Wait, do you hear that?*

Pandora listened intently and instantly became enraged. *Sure as hell fucking do. Oh, fuck yeah, this is going to be a good one.*

Katie turned right and went low, listening as the muffled screaming and whimpering grew louder in her ears. She dropped to the ground near a window looking into the basement of a brownstone. Katie crept closer and wiped dirt off the glass. Peering through the grime, she could see a leaky old basement. There were some ten-gallon buckets, mold on the walls, and an old workbench with what looked like shiny new tools laying on it.

Katie frowned. She knew she'd heard a voice coming from inside.

She looked into the corner, where a slowly swinging light flickered on and off. She put her hand over her mouth to muffle her gasp. Against the wall were a half dozen metal dog cages. Inside each of the cages crouched a barely clothed, battered, and broken woman. A figure walked from the corner. He was a tall, muscular man in a dirty wife-beater and a pair of brown work pants. He snapped his leather belt on the floor and screamed at the girls, "I told you not to make a sound, bitches. I told you when it was time for you to go get fucked and make me some money, I would take you out of there. Now, since you can't follow directions, it's punishment time."

Katie growled. *Oh hell, no. He will* not.

She grabbed her phone and sent Detective Shultz a text with the address.

Bring all the boys. This one's going to be good.

Katie summoned her angel powers, and golden armor encased her body. She grabbed the bars on the window and planted her feet, groaning as she pulled. She snarled and the bars came free, ripping the entire window out and a ton of brick along with it. She tossed the window into the street and jumped into the hole she had just made.

The guy backed against the wall. "What the fuck?"

Katie glanced at the cages, then narrowed her eyes at the man. "Tsk, tsk, tsk. That's no way to treat a lady. I think it's time *you* got fucked."

She ran forward and slammed her fist into the side of his face. He winced and fell back into the wall, but bounced back red-faced and furious. He cracked his belt at her. "Come on, bitch. You'll make a good addition to my collection."

Katie smiled without humor. She snatched his belt, and before he realized what had happened, she spun him around and jumped on his back. She wrapped the belt around his neck and whispered into his ear, "I would kill you right here, but I think you need a little quality time with Bubba in Cell Block Five."

Pandora snorted. *Don't drop the soap. Or do. Whatever floats your boat.*

The guy growled and grabbed Katie's arms, flinging her over his head into the worktable. She grunted and rolled off the table to find him charging toward her with a knife in his hand. She grabbed a pair of pliers, waiting until he got close enough. As soon as he did, she caught his knife with one hand and jammed the pliers at his crotch with the other. The man yelped as the pliers' jaws clamped down on his nuts. His eyes went wide and he wheezed, falling to his knees. "Silly sex offender, your balls are too gross for me to touch with my bare hands. Now, come on. I think you know where you belong."

Katie led him to the cages by his balls. She opened the empty one on the end, threw him inside, and locked it, then smashed the locks off the other cages. "You're safe now. That dog is going where he belongs."

The girls came tumbling out, but they stayed in a tight group. They hugged each other until the cops arrived.

She flew out through the hole she'd created, knocking Schultz's hat off as she flew by. He laughed and waved at her as she rose. It was a short flight back to her condo. When she arrived, she landed in front and walked past the doorman. He tipped his hat to her. "Nice cape."

Katie curtsied. "Why, thank you."

She took the elevator to her floor, feeling renewed and refreshed. Pandora had been right. She *had* needed to remember why she was fighting so hard. As she walked toward her door, she slowed down. Rose petals marked a path to her door. She looked up and down the hall, but no one was there. She walked inside slowly. A smile grew as she followed the petals to the bathroom, where there was soft music playing, candles lit, and a bottle of bubble bath on the lip of the tub.

There was also a note on the sink.

Katie picked it up.

Get comfortable. I just ran out to get us some fresh food. Won't be too long.

Xoxo, Brock

Pandora whistled. *Oooo, girl, you got him on a chain. He's over here breaking and entering just to get some of that poon. Yep, perfect way to end a really good night.*

Katie's cheeks went red, and she picked up one of the long-stem roses and lifted it to her nose. *Well, might as well go with the flow. That's what I never say.*

Pandora giggled. *Hell, yeah. Now get you some of that bath and do some cleaning. We can have a real nice surprise for hunky monkey when he gets back.*

Katie wrinkled her nose. *Don't ever call him that again.*

Katie turned the music up a bit and stripped. She swished her hand under the running water until it was nice and hot, then stoppered the tub. She grabbed the bubbles off the sink and opened the cap, taking a big whiff. *Mmm, lavender and vanilla. He's starting to catch on.*

Pandora scoffed. *If he was catching on, he would be here to get in the tub with you.*

Katie shrugged and sat on the edge of the tub, waiting for it to fill. When it was about three-quarters full, she dipped her body into the steaming water. She looked down at her breasts floating in the soap. *If I didn't know you were in there, I would think they were fake.*

Real as can be. These flotation devices can be a drowning hazard, though, so be careful.

Katie smiled and sank lower in the tub, enjoying the candlelight, the scents, and the relaxation. It had been a long time since she'd done anything like that, and she had to admit, she appreciated Brock for thinking of it. It was a surprise that he was there in the first place. *I wonder where Angie is?*

Pandora purred. *Probably making herself scarce. I have to admit, this is like heaven.*

Oh, really?

Pandora groaned. *Stop reading into everything. I can't even explain heaven to you. Not like I'll ever see it again, anyway. Can we just relax and not think about all that? We gotta get prepared for a hot night in that bed of yours. Boy has it coming.*

Katie chuckled. *Sure, I think I can manage that. When he gets back, though, we better be ready for him.*

Katie grabbed her luffa and lathered herself, then grabbed the razor and went to town, making sure everything was perfectly trimmed and smooth. Pandora winced as she shaved her nether regions. *Jesus, girl. You need to keep up with this shit. You got Chewbacca down there. We really don't want that thing sounding off during sex.*

Pandora made the Chewbacca sound, and Katie choked, laughing hard. *I've been a little busy, okay? Besides, this way it'll be nice and smooth.*

Pandora sighed. *Remember the days when we could order beautiful bras and lounge around?*

Katie raised an eyebrow. *No, not at all. The bra thing, yeah, but it's your fault we don't fit in them anymore.*

She laughed evilly. *Yes. My plan is working. Biggest titties ever!*

The doorman opened the door for Brock and tilted his head. "Evening, sir. That smells delicious."

Brock smiled as he strolled in. "Thanks. Gotta feed the hungry warriors."

The doorman grinned. "Enjoy your time."

Brock climbed into the elevator and pressed the button, tapping on the takeout containers as he whistled a tune. He was proud that he'd been able to set everything up for Katie. He only wished he'd been able to get there sooner and have dinner waiting for her. He knew he could seduce her into spending time with him with a delicious meal. Hopefully, the rest would fall into place. She hadn't exactly been playing hard to get, but keeping her attention with bombs going off in hell, Leviathans dropping, and demons attacking her team was more than a little difficult.

When the elevator doors opened, he headed to the apartment. The rose petals had been kicked around a bit, which meant Katie was back. A surge of nerves shot into his stomach, and he took a moment to compose himself. Hell, it was just Katie…and Pandora, but she kept quiet during their time together. Katie could be incredibly intense, though. He hoped he could face her with courage and sexuality.

He opened the door and headed to the kitchen, where

he set the food down on the counter and looked around for a moment. The music was louder, and the smell of lavender and vanilla permeated the house. He smiled. "Katie, I'm back! And before you jump out and take me down, Angie allowed this. I did not sneak in. There was no illegal breaking and entering."

That's a shame, a voice whispered in his mind. He swiveled his head back and forth, not knowing what the hell that was or if he'd heard it correctly. He shrugged and walked back to the kitchen, removing the takeout boxes from the bags.

He grabbed a couple of plates and some silverware and began to set the table. "I got us Italian. Angie said it was your favorite. Sorry I didn't cook. I'm not that handy in the kitchen."

You're handy in other areas. Brock stopped and looked around. He tapped his finger on his temple. Was he really hearing a voice in his head or was he imagining things? He stood still for a minute to see if it said anything else.

As soon as he reached for the food, the voice said, *Leave it for now and come to my bed immediately!*

He froze. "Yes, ma'am?"

Brock carefully walked down the hall to Katie's room. He opened the door and went into the dark room. The only light came from the flickering candles.

A shadow moved on the bed, and his jaw dropped to the floor. It had definitely been Katie's voice.

The wind blew wildly through the Carpathian Mountains. A bright yellow sun was just peeking through the sparse clouds. Lynxes, wolves, and bears stalked across the mixture of rock and foliage the mountains offered. Suddenly, the small animals all became alert, sticking their heads up and shifting their ears from side to side. One by one, they began to run for hiding places. They sensed impending doom heading their way.

Before a small, frightened marmot could flee, the first of a hundred gates tore open right where it stood. The fluffy woodland creature burst apart in an explosion of blood and fur. Another gate opened higher up the mountain, then another, and another. Finally, the Romanian mountainside was covered in shimmering gates, all pumping the heat of hell onto the mountains. Steam pumped out as the blast-furnace heat hit the cold air. On the ground, several patches of early ice quickly melted and began to boil.

A clawed foot stomped out of the first gate, then the

demon's head poked out and looked at his surroundings. He snarled at the bright light and jumped out into the woods. Several more rushed after him. More growling fiends clawed their way out of the other gates. Before anyone even knew they were there, thousands of demons were flooding down the mountain. They tore trees from their roots, sent bridges crumbling down to the valleys below, and pretty much destroyed everything in their path. Nothing was safe.

They approached an overlook on the edge of the mountain, bunching up as they came to a stop. They all growled and hissed as they took in the small town of Sighișoara below. It was a vibrant Romanian town, boasting scenic views and a population of about twenty-five thousand. From their perch, the demons could see the droves of unsuspecting people milling around, going about their days as normal. None of them had the faintest idea that death was waiting high in the mountains.

One of the larger demons let out a loud bellow that echoed across the mountains. The other demons growled and followed suit, tilting their heads back like wolves and howling. The trees shook, and rocks crumbled and broke away from the sides of the mountains. A young boy playing on the outskirts of the town looked up from his toy trucks and stared at the ledge high above the town, then stood up and narrowed his eyes. Even in the daylight, he saw the hundreds of red balls of light staring down at him.

He dropped his truck and turned to the town, screaming, *"Demoni! Ei vin pentru noi!"*

"Demons! They are coming for us!"

The remnants of dinner and the remnants of round four were mixed together in a mess that sprawled across the kitchen. Empty food containers were strewn across the kitchen counter, and plates had been stacked in the sink. A half-empty bottle of wine sat on the counter above a pile of discarded clothes. The apartment was silent as the sun peeked through the windows.

Down the hall rose petals were wilting on the floor, curling and twisting where they lay. The candles in the bathroom had been extinguished, and those in Katie's room had melted down to nubs. The smell of freshly extinguished candles mixed with the scents of Italian food, lavender, vanilla, and a wild night of sex and booze. It was definitely not the norm for the apartment, but at that moment no one cared.

Katie lay across her bed sideways. Her dark hair was strewn in a wild halo around her. Her naked body was wrapped in a sheet, the comforter in a clump on the floor. A small puddle of drool emerged from her lips where her face was pressed into the mattress. She had passed out, under the spell of a relaxing night. She gradually woke, and she smacked her lips together to remove the stale taste of wine. She turned her head to shield her face from the beams of light coming in through the curtains.

Her hands flexed and released the sheet. She squeezed her eyes closed, attempting to keep at bay the dizziness that threatened to overtake her. She could tell Pandora was not even close to awake. Her body still trying to metabolize the wine she'd drunk straight from the bottle the night before. She hadn't felt that way since college, after going to her one and only party at the local frat house. That night had been full of alcohol but definitely not sex. She had left the party early, staggering back to her dorm and passing out on the floor.

Waking up on a comfortable bed was a lot better than waking up on the carpet with her roommate standing over her with a glass of water and some aspirin. That night had not been her best. At the moment, she was proud of what she'd achieved in her little New York City condo. She'd let it all out and had no regrets. She had let Pandora's and her own sensual nature completely take over.

When she heard the shuffling, she opened her eyes and blinked hard. Brock stood near the bed, smiling at her. He was pulling the last of his gear out of his black duffel and finishing suiting up. Katie groaned quietly and wiped the drool from her chin, then turned on her back and took a moment to ground herself.

Brock chuckled. "Feeling okay?"

Katie's voice was raspy. "Like a ten-ton demon dropped his ass on my head."

Brock laughed as he put his guns in his holsters. "You'll be fine. Just guzzle some coffee and grab a shower. You'll be better than ever. My demon already went to work on the hell that was bubbling inside me when I woke up."

Katie slapped her arms on the bed beside her. "Mine seems to be taking a vacation right now."

Katie turned over on her side and propped herself on her elbow. "That's not really what I would expect you to wear for a stroll through New York on a beautiful fall day."

Brock smiled and sat on the bed next to her. He pushed

the hair from her face. She stared at him with her bright blue eyes, and his eyes met hers. He leaned forward and gently kissed her lips. The oxygen rushed from her lungs but she pushed back against it, trying not to go all googly-eyed over Brock.

He broke off the kiss. "My team has been called to an operation in Romania. They said it's pretty dire. Lots of demons, lots of portals. I checked your phone, but it never rang. Must not be Katie-worthy."

Katie groaned and plopped her head back down on the bed. "Good. I could use about nine days of recovery after last night."

Brock grinned. "I'll take that as a compliment. But yeah, I gotta leave. The team is already at the base, and they're waiting for me. There's a car downstairs."

Katie held the sheet to her chest and sat up, flipping her wild hair to one side. She leaned forward and kissed Brock deeply, taking in his fresh, clean scent. "Be careful. I know I don't need to tell you that, but I felt like I should say it. These incursions are getting crazier."

Brock ran his finger down her cheek. "I know. I heard about your base. They said demons were dropping out of the sky. They're ramping up their assault tactics, I see, but no worries. You know us. We'll go in and knock some heads."

Katie gave him a sweet, sleepy smile. "You know how to get hold of me if you guys need help. I can jet over there in no time. Never been to Romania."

Brock stood up and slung his bag over his shoulder. "Sorry to leave you with the mess."

Katie waved her hand. "Meh, gives me something to do

to wake my ass up. Don't want to scare the hell out of Angie when she comes back."

Brock smiled again and walked toward the door. He paused and looked back at her, flashing one of his toothy grins. "Last night was—"

Katie giggled. "Yeah, I know. Go, before I have a dozen military guys busting down my door to drag you out."

Brock tapped his hand on the doorframe. "Going. I'll call you when we get back stateside."

Katie stared at the doorway until she heard the front door close. Suddenly, the house seemed a little less lively. She sat there for a moment to gather her thoughts, then jumped out of bed. Nope. Too soon. She grabbed the dresser to stabilize herself, then put her hand to her head and groaned. "Ugh, take it a bit slower, Katie."

She opened her dresser drawer and pulled out a pair of panties and some jogging shorts and threw them on. As she walked toward her closet, she paused. Brock's t-shirt was laid neatly over the chair. She smiled and grabbed it, throwing it over her head. It smelled like him, or at least how he'd smelled when he'd walked into the condo the night before.

Katie took stock of the disaster that was her room. She knew the kitchen was even worse. She immediately started picking up all the clothes and throwing them in the hamper. She pulled the sheets off the bed and tossed them in too. She grabbed a fresh set of sheets from the closet and spritzed them with fabric spray. She still hadn't heard a word from Pandora, which was not in the least like her.

Katie spread the sheets on the mattress and made the bed, putting all the decorative pillows back in place like

Angie always did it. She put her hands on her hips and chuckled. *I'm so domestic. It's kind of gross.*

Pandora growled and mumbled almost incoherently. *Shh. Sleeping, bitch. Don't fuck with my sleep.*

Katie narrowed her eyes and shook her head. *Oh hell, no, hooker. This is fucking payback for all the times I just wanted to sleep in, and you couldn't fucking shut up about donuts. You're going to wake the fuck up. Turnabout is fair play.*

Katie started to pick up the candles from around the room, singing loudly and trying everything to annoy the hell out of Pandora.

"*This is the song that never ends,*

it goes on and on, my friends!

Some people started singing it, not knowing what it was,

and they'll continue singing it forever just because!

This is the song that never ends..."

Pandora huffed. *You know I have the power to give you fucking saddlebags and acne, right? How would you like that next time you decided to get wild with Brock? You take off your clothes, and you have back acne.*

Katie smirked. "Good morning, bitch! It's about time you woke your happy ass up and joined the goddamned world."

Pandora groaned. *I am so tempted to fucking make your hangover worse. One swipe of my hands and your ass will be puking in the nearest trash can.*

Katie wasn't going to let that dampen her mood. "Oh, come now, Lilith. That's not very nice of you. What would Adam think?"

Pandora laughed loudly. *That motherfucker would tell me to get into the advertised position—missionary—so he could insert his manly seed. Bro would be talking about me populating the Earth and shit. Please, son. I am not going to put this body through that. And millennia before the epidural was invented? You have got to be kidding me.*

Katie wrinkled her nose as she continued to clean up her room. "Man, the entire Earth? Talk about a hot dog down a fucking hallway. Those babies would fall right out of you after a while."

Pandora cleared her throat. *No, bitch. I've been telling you. It's all about the Kegel exercises. I've been doing them for you throughout the day since you don't seem to care.*

Katie paused for a moment. "I'm not sure how I feel about you messing with my vagina when no one is looking. Or when everyone's looking, for that matter. Is nothing sacred?"

Hell, no. You're my bitch now, although I guess if you want to be loosey-goosey, be my guest. Ask Brock first, see what he has to say about it.

Katie chuckled. "I have a hard time believing that my once-in-a-blue-moon bone sessions would get me anywhere near loosey-goosey status. I think someone is projecting."

Pandora gasped. *How dare you! My cat is nice and tight. Never any complaints.*

"I don't know, centuries of throwing that thing around like it was public property might have caused serious damage. You might need a little tune-up, if you know what I mean. That thing still under warranty?"

Pandora was getting irritated. *I will have you know that even after sleeping with big dick Lucifer I'm still ready to go, thank you very much. We demons have elasticity.*

"There's a difference between being tight and having a shriveled-up mummy-cooch, you ancient pain in my tits."

Little did Katie know, while she was having her morning conversation with Pandora, Angie had come home. She had taken one look at the disaster that was the condo and gone straight to Katie's room, just to make sure it was a wild night and not a hostage situation. When she walked around the corner, she stopped in the doorway. Katie was talking out loud to, she assumed, Pandora. There wasn't anyone else in the place. She stood there for a while just listening, her eyes wide.

After a few minutes she stifled a giggle, and Katie spun. "Angie, you're home!"

"I am. And I have to say the half of that conversation I could hear was, shall we say, *enlightening.*"

Katie laughed. "Yeah, you know, fucking with Pandora. She's having a fit."

Angie shook her head. "You two are seriously going to drive each other nuts before the war is over."

Katie tossed a sock in the hamper. "Oh, we are long past crazy, my dear."

Angie set a hot cup of coffee down in front of Katie after helping her clean up the kitchen. She stared at the sink. In it were a potato masher, a pair of tongs, and two wet aprons. She scratched her head. "So, you said you didn't cook last night?"

Katie glanced at the sink. "Yeah, just let this one go. It's hard to explain. I'll take care of that."

"Good, because I was considering just lighting a match and letting the place burn down."

Katie laughed and took a gulp of her coffee. With Pandora finally up, her hangover was going away quickly. Katie was pretty sure Pandora was leaving just a bit of the hangover intact to punish her for getting her up that morning.

Her phone buzzed loudly on the countertop. It was the general.

"Morning, General. What's the good word today?" she answered.

General Brushwood grumbled into the phone. "You sound awfully cheerful for being up this early in the morning."

Katie shrugged. "You stole my company this morning. Brock said you had an assignment you were sending his team on?"

The general cleared his throat uncomfortably. "I'm not going to ask about you and Brock. As far as the assignment…yeah, pretty nasty incursion."

Katie hated to hear that. "Do you need me for it?"

"I don't think so. It's a shit show, but the demons seem to be slowing down. I think by the time you could get there, everything would be over."

Katie shook her head. "It's crazy to think how much our response has improved. Two years ago your teams would be all but demolished by now. Good work, General."

"I owe a lot of it to you," he replied.

Katie didn't care where the teams had learned it, as long as they had. "What can I do for you today?"

"I was calling to see how your trip went."

Katie suddenly remembered Juntto. "Oh, yeah! I got valuable information. I have a few really good ideas on how to wake that fool up from his coma. The goal of the treatment will be to get emotional energy into him."

The general wasn't sure what she meant. "Okay, and how do you do that?"

Katie sipped her coffee. "I have a few thoughts on that. Actually, when I'm done with my coffee, I'm going to head to the base and try them. They finally got Juntto moved out of the meat locker. I appreciate that."

The general took a deep breath. "Yeah, we couldn't really have a Leviathan hanging out at the local butcher, could we?"

Katie giggled, looking at Angie. "I'll give you a call if anything works. I think I'll take Angie with me."

The general remembered his and Angie's conversation. "I think that would be good, especially if it works. We could all use a little good news these days."

The choppers hovered over the small Romanian town. Brock's team dropped the ropes to the ground. Brock stood to one side and nodded to his teammates as they rappelled down. There were demons everywhere and screams echoed off the mountains.

Brock reached the end of his rope and unclipped himself. He gave a thumbs-up to the chopper above and it sped toward the safe zone, leaving the guys standing in the center of town. Turner had his M4 carbine ready. Eddie and Sean were facing down opposite sides of the street, surveying the area. Brock put his hand on Turner's shoulder and took in the scene. There were bodies everywhere. The stone fountain in the center of town was decorated with gore, and parts of arms and legs were hanging over the edge. The water ran red with blood.

Buildings were crumbling under the demons' attack. Several humans had emerged from the ruins with glowing red eyes. Not only were the demons attacking and murdering whoever they could, they were also summoning demons to take over bodies. It was a grim scene.

Brock motioned for the guys to get close. "Okay, here's the deal. We're late to the scene. I think the best tactic is working a grid. We go house to house accounting for the living and helping the Damned. We aren't priests. We can't take the demons out of them. If we find infected like us, we get them to a safe space. After that, the military will handle them. We kill any demon who comes near us, no questions. These fuckers are on a mission, and it seems like chaos is the word of the day."

Turner pulled the trigger of his gun, spraying bullets across a group of demons approaching. He took down five of them, but two survivors turned and ran. Turner lowered his weapon and watched a little girl emerge from the dust and fog. She was clutching a bloodied teddy bear in her arms and walking toward him with red eyes. "Uh, Brock?"

Brock turned to the girl and pulled up his weapon. "Hey there, sweetie. I can see you need some help. What's your name?"

The girl stopped, and her head bent drastically to one side. A deep voice tore from her throat. "Today is the reckoning. You will all die."

Turner whimpered. "Holy fuck!"

The little girl launched herself at them. Brock raised his weapon and pulled the trigger, and her body flew back and crumpled to the ground. It quickly dissolved into ash and dust. Turner turned toward Brock with wide eyes. "That was the scariest fucking thing I've ever seen."

Eddie held his rifle loosely in his tattooed hands,

staring at the mound of dust. "That was scarier than the time I banged Sean's sister."

"Fuck yourself." Sean shook his head. "Nasty fucker."

"Seriously. She looks just like you. She has the same whiskers on her chin. I got real conflicted at the end." He raised his eyes thoughtfully. "I finished, though."

Turner murmured, "What kind of fucking mission is this?"

Brock sighed and looked around. "I don't know, but something tells me it's going to be a whole new ball game."

***

Moloch had been locked in his room for two days, and Baal hadn't heard a peep from him. He decided to go back to his own castle. He didn't want to be there when the other demon finally emerged. Besides, he had information to look into.

Baal's castle was quite a bit smaller than Moloch's, but it was perfect for him. He'd acquired several demons from the pool of souls in hell, and he forced them to play classical music on instruments he had snuck in from Earth as he lounged in his living area. He had put a shield around them so they wouldn't burst into flames, but they didn't sound quite right. Still, the music relaxed him and helped him think more clearly.

As the strum of the cello and the throb of the bass echoed through the house, Baal sat in front of his fireplace, his feet on an ottoman. He slowly unraveled the old scroll, waving his hand over the document to reinforce the protection spell he'd hastily put on it. The edges were a little singed, but other than that, it was still in one piece.

He began reviewing the scroll, running his eyes over the symbols on the paper. He grabbed a kitten from the bowl, ignoring the tiny mews as he popped it into his mouth and chewed. As he swallowed, he remembered what Beelzebub had said and grimaced. He pushed the bowl away. "Damn Beelzebub, fucking with my appetite."

He grabbed his glass of wine and took a sip, some of it trickling down his chin. Wiping his face on his arm, he continued reading. He scanned the first two sections and paused when he heard a loud banging on the door. With a sigh, he remembered he didn't have the service staff that Moloch had. That was no one's fault but his own. He liked his solitude when he went home, but it seemed he had become accustomed to Moloch's way of living.

He rolled up the scroll and set it in a stone box on the table next to him. He waved his hand over the stone, and the lid clicked closed. Slowly, he dragged himself across the room. He opened the front door and lifted an eyebrow at the twisted mess in front of him. It was a wobbly human figure dressed in an expensive Armani suit. The skin of the human drooped on one side of his face. A well-manicured hand reached up and pulled his hair back, which pulled the skin tighter around his body.

Baal chuckled at the elitist, who was carrying a smoldering leather suitcase, his suit perfectly pressed. He gestured for the droopy human to enter. "Staying as a lawyer this time, Belphegor? I have to say, the look suits you, although the skin might be a bit big."

Belphegor snorted. "It will shrink just like a sweater in the dryer."

Baal closed the door behind him and led Belphegor into the living area. "Can I get you a drink?"

Belphegor sat down in one of the chairs. "No. I'm here on official business."

Baal refilled his glass, the wine boiling as it hit the sides of the cup. "And when did you ever come here when you weren't on official business?"

Belphegor lifted his eyebrows, thinking about it. "I suppose never."

Sitting comfortably back in his chair, Baal crossed one leg over the other. He raised his glass to Belphegor and took a sip. "So, what official business can I help you with today?"

Belphegor cleared his throat and fiddled with the top of his tie. "I've been informed I need to review what's going on with the humans. Our Lord Prince is a bit perturbed, to say the least. I was given the order as he tortured one of his servants. Did you know he likes to beat people with their own limbs?"

Baal choked into his glass, thinking of Moloch. "Yes, apparently that's his new thing. Whatever floats his boat. I suppose after millennia of torturing souls, he had to start getting creative to scratch the itch."

Belphegor shrugged. "Now, about this human business?"

Baal waved his arm. "You need to talk to Moloch. The gist of it is that Moloch started all this shit by encouraging T'Chezz. He had a plan for getting rid of Lilith, thinking it would please Lucifer. It seems he underestimated her and the skinbag that she wears. She ended up changing sides to help the humans and the angels. During what the humans call 'Incursion Day' she chopped T'Chezz's head off, and we have no idea what happened to him after that. We're assuming, with her history and her human's, that he is dead."

Belphegor glanced up from his notes. "Her human's history?"

Baal sighed, drinking his wine. "Yes, something about her being part-angel. She's the one who has been leading the charge in hell. Doesn't even have to wear one of those nifty protection suits the humans made to walk around down here."

Belphegor put his pen down. "They made suits to come to hell and fight?"

Baal rolled his eyes. "Where have you been, man? This is old news. It would take me books and books of notes to explain everything to you. My suggestion is, get the Cliffs-Notes if you value your sleep. You could seriously sit here for years hearing every detail of what has happened. But I digress. You should talk to Moloch. He has the first-person account of everything. I was just in the background making sure he didn't get hell blown up or anything."

Belphegor harrumphed. "Well, you didn't do a very good job managing that. Part of hell *did* get blown up."

Baal slammed his glass down and sat up. "Don't you put that on me. You know Moloch. When he gets something on his mind, he just goes with it. He's higher-ranking than me, though not by much. You know I can't order him around. Going to Lucifer with it would have been bad. There was a good chance I would have been the first to be beaten with my own damned arms."

Belphegor put up his hands. "Calm down. I didn't mean to offend you. This just seems like a big fucking mess. So where is Lilith now?"

Baal relaxed back in the chair and shrugged. "Somewhere on Earth, I suppose, although she has been known to make random appearances in hell. She's out there trying to rid the world of demons. Sometimes, I wonder if she hasn't realized that the souls are pretty much limitless. We could continue to flood the Earth with demons every day for a century and still have enough to cook, clean, and play music."

Belphegor tilted his head. "I think you're forgetting that most of the demons this human and Lilith kill actually end up dying completely. Gone forever. I'm not even sure if *they* realize that yet."

Baal grimaced. "Well, if they don't know it now, it won't be long until they figure it out. That human is smart. With Moloch now completely focused on killing her I would like to say the incursions will slow, but that may not be the case."

Belphegor was confused. "Why not?"

Baal sighed. "Because Beelzebub is planning something. He's determined to take over this fight and regain his seat at the table. He has done it repeatedly throughout time."

Belphegor growled. "I hate that fucking guy."

Baal nodded. "I know, right? He has no manners, and can't help coming up with foolish plans."

Belphegor shook his head. "He fucked up World War II by having his Japanese puppets attack the United States. I had kept the US neutral until that point. We were really getting somewhere, too. Hitler was reigning supreme, and his forces were capturing the majority of the world. Best of all, the US was not a threat. Every day I kept them neutral was one day closer to conquering them, too. But no, asshat had to come in and bomb Pearl Harbor. They decimated their Navy and killed a bunch of their men, and after that, it was pretty much over. The US rolled through the world making heroes and martyrs out of every soldier they sent to either front. Beelzebub wasn't even supposed to leave his damp, disgusting cave, much less stick his nose into a war. When Hitler's demon got back to hell, Lucifer was so distracted by him he didn't even punish Beelzebub. The idiot should have been locked up and the key thrown away."

Baal could tell Belphegor was getting all worked up, which was exactly what he wanted. He didn't want the spotlight anywhere near him. Having the suit sitting there asking questions let Baal know that Lucifer was aware he'd been involved in the most recent attacks on humans. That was a dangerous place to be, especially when the dark lord was extraordinarily angry about the whole thing.

Baal sipped his wine, watching Belphegor angrily scribble notes. "You know what you should do? You should find Beelzebub and give him a true warning, right from Lucifer. I tried to talk him out of it, but you know him. He thinks his power will allow him to get away with anything. He's been in exile for so long that no one pays attention to where he's going. From my understanding, the most recent attack on Lilith's human base was orchestrated by none other than the Bee himself. Of course, this is all speculation."

Belphegor shook his head. "This is absolutely ridiculous. Lucifer will lose his mind if he knows Beelzebub is working on his own plans behind everyone's back. Does Moloch know about this?"

Baal scoffed. "No. And he shouldn't, not yet. He has enough on his hands after being blown up, beaten up, and now tasked with killing someone who almost seems unkillable."

Belphegor closed his book. "No one is unkillable, not even us. You just have to go about it the right way, that's all. I'll probably have more questions for you, but I think right now it's important that I get to the caves and find Beelzebub. I don't need another headache on my hands."

Baal stood up. "That's a good idea. Feel free to call or come by any time you need something. If I'm not here, you'll probably find me at Moloch's. Of course, you probably already knew that."

Belphegor looked him up and down. "Hmm. Yes. Anyway, thank you for the update. I will be in touch."

Baal walked him to the door and flashed a fake smile as Belphegor walked out, his suit steaming in the boiling heat. Baal closed and locked his door, then leaned against it and rolled his eyes. "It's raining annoyances."

He clapped his hands, summoning his demons to resume playing music. They jumped to it, immediately started Concerto Number Five, Baal's favorite. He sat down in his chair and waved his hand to the song, the music soothing his stricken nerves. He unlocked the stone box and pulled the scroll back out to study its contents. He breathed deeply and swayed his head from side to side as he read.

The kittens mewed across the table from him, but he ignored them. "Maybe I should back off the kittens for a while. Damn you, Beelzebub."

"Get inside! Hurry!" Brock yelled, waving to his team and the few survivors they'd picked up along the way.

They had been caught in a relentless firefight with several dozen demons who had swarmed them, and now found themselves backed into an old church. They stood staring at the open door of the church as a demon squealed loudly, making a run for the opening. It hit the doorway and flew back as if it had encountered an invisible wall. Turner blinked and put down his gun. "What the hell?"

A voice came from behind them. "This church was blessed by the Pope. Some say even Jesus walked here when it was a temple, although the church has been rebuilt many times since then. It was built on very holy ground." The team turned. A priest was with several nuns in the nave, all of them huddled together in fear.

Brock rubbed his chin thoughtfully. "I forgot that the demons who aren't in infected struggle to penetrate holy places. This is good. Turner, you watch the door and shoot anything that gets close."

The priest came forward with a blanket and wrapped it around one of the survivors. "We can help these people, but we aren't sure how long we can survive. We don't know how long this attack will last."

Brock looked at him for a second. "You speak English. I just realized it."

The priest nodded. "And Romanian. I'm from the States. I came here a few months ago to protect this church. The sisters and I have kept it open in these dire times to help those in the town who needed assistance."

Brock was glad to hear a familiar accent. "This woman kept yelling something to me, but I couldn't understand her. Would you translate?"

The priest put his hands on the woman's shoulders. "*Ce încercai să-i spui acestui bărbat?*"

The woman swallowed hard and tried to calm herself. "*Fetița mea. A dispărut la început. Purta o rochie albastră, cu părul sălbatic, și purta un ursuleț de pluș. Au văzut-o?*"

The priest patted her back and looked at Brock. "She says her little girl is missing. Blue dress, wild brown curls, carrying a teddy bear."

Brock's heart dropped. He glanced at Turner, who closed his eyes and shook his head. Eddie and Sean went quiet. They had all seen that girl. Brock looked at the priest again but didn't say a word. He didn't know what to say. The priest already knew, so he held up a hand to silence Brock. As the priest relayed the information to the woman, Brock turned away, trying to escape her cries of agony.

He lifted his assault rifle as two demons attempted to push through the door. He walked toward them, pulling the trigger until neither of them was left standing. He was tired of death, and tired of killing. That little girl had done nothing wrong, but she had been sentenced to death by hell.

Turner walked forward and put his hand on Brock's shoulder. "Hold it in, man. When we get out of here, we can have a good long drink."

Brock nodded. "Right now, let's just kill these sonsofbitches."

13

Katie landed at the secret base, set Angie on the ground, and folded her wings. Soldiers were going about their normal routines everywhere. Several stopped and waved at Katie, and she smiled and returned the gesture. Angie, on the other hand, looked a bit nervous.

"We'll go directly into the left hangar. They converted it into a freezer for Juntto. Gave us more space so we could lay him out comfortably."

Katie started walking toward the hangar but stopped, realizing that Angie hadn't moved. The woman stood there with her arms wrapped around her body, just staring into the hangar bay. Steam oozed out of the building. Katie walked back over and touched Angie's shoulder. "You okay?"

Angie swallowed. "I have never seen him up close."

Katie wrinkled her forehead. "But I thought..."

Angie chuckled. "It's stupid, really. I went to the butcher shop and just stood outside the freezer door. I wanted to visit him. I wanted to be close to him, but I was too afraid. I didn't know what he would look like or feel like. I didn't know if he would even be recognizable in his true form. I didn't want to lose that image of him in my mind. You know, the one that makes me smile when I think about it?"

Katie bit her lip and nodded. "I get it. But this time, it's okay. I'll be right there with you the whole way. I think you might be able to help me think of a way to get him the energy he needs to wake up."

Angie nodded but didn't move. She still wasn't convinced. Katie pursed her lips and turned her head toward her assistant. "After I rescued you, I asked you to make a lot of sacrifices for the cause. I know it's been hard on you at times. I'm afraid I am going to have to ask you to do it again for this. Everything relies on us figuring out what this answer is. Bringing him back is not only the right thing to do because he's family, but he's vital to our fight. Juntto is part of the puzzle, just like you are. We don't leave family behind."

Angie took a deep breath and shook her head to clear it. She reached out and took Katie's hand. "Okay, let's do this. Who knew the man of my dreams would be a popsicle?"

Katie giggled. "Might be the best way to keep a man. Just unthaw him when you're feeling frisky."

Angie couldn't hold back a laugh. "That sounds like something Pandora would say."

Katie giggled. "I know. I'm starting to think we're melding together. No one else seems to mind, though. I have to admit, she's a badass."

Angie reached out and opened the door to the hangar. "Like *you're* not?"

Katie pointed at her as she walked past. "You have a point."

They walked into the preparation room where racks of gloves, coats, and caps lined the walls. Katie pulled two sets down and handed one to Angie. "You'll need this. It is as cold as a witch's titty in that bitch."

Angie pulled on the thick coat and the fur-lined leather gloves. She tucked her hair back and pulled the stocking cap down over her ears. Katie reached for the second door and looked back at Angie. "You ready?"

Angie nodded nervously and Katie pulled open the door. A rush of cold air slammed into them, and Angie's teeth immediately began to chatter. She carefully walked into the room and stared at Juntto. He was huge in his frost giant form, and his scaled body was blue and muscular. Hair covered his face, and his eyes were closed. A silver streak still wound its way through his hair. As cold as it was, his chest still rose and fell. His nose expelled shallow steaming breaths that floated toward the top of the hangar.

Angie ran her hand along the large table beneath him. "I didn't expect him to look…"

Katie smirked. "So normal? Yeah. I mean, he's huge, but he is still Juntto."

Angie laughed. "I seriously pictured him covered in ice, with icicles hanging from his nose and eyebrows. Maybe even a frosty beard."

Behind them, the door opened, and one of the scientists walked in. "Hello. I'm Doctor Ozu. I've met Katie, but not you."

Angie put out her hand and shook his. "I'm Angie."

The doctor nodded in recognition. "Ah, yes. Another

brave warrior and close confidant of Juntto. So nice to meet you."

Katie clapped her hands. "So, what we need to do is figure out what kind of energy Juntto might need."

Pandora shivered. *The fucking energy of heat. This is like the opposite of hell. This is a goddamned man-made tundra.*

Dr. Ozu stroked his chin. "When you called me with this theory, I started to go through all the techniques used in psychology to create a rush of emotion in someone. These techniques are usually centered around creating the emotion a subject needs versus the one they are currently having issues with. I thought perhaps electroshock therapy might help. The problem is, we don't know what to tell him to help bring forth that emotion."

Katie winced. "Yeah, I don't know if it's such a good idea to shock the giant frozen alien. We might not live to see the results. I would say stay away from physical intervention until we have exhausted all other ideas."

Angie looked at Juntto's frozen face. He looked so peaceful and quiet. It was quite the opposite of what he normally was. As that thought wormed through Angie's mind, her eyes got wide. She realized something right then and there.

Angie bit her lip. "Opposites."

Katie raised an eyebrow. "Attract?"

Pandora shushed Katie. *Hold on. Ask her what she means.*

Katie stared at Angie. "What do you mean by that?"

Angie walked around the table, gathering her thoughts. "I mean that right now, he's the complete opposite of what he normally is. He used to be loud, happy, angry, and funny, and now he's silent. There's not a single whisper of a sound coming from him. His face is blank, and his eyes are closed. He always had some sort of expression; a glimmer in his eye that let you know he was alive—really alive. And he never really slept."

Pandora clicked her tongue. *I think this chick is onto something. He has been through a massive change in recent weeks. Think about how he was when he tried to kill me, and how different he had become when he fell into the coma.*

Katie started to pace. "You're right. It *is* the opposite. During the fights, the rogue murders, and everything else, he was angry. Just like everyone else in battle, he was constantly feeding on negative emotion. When he was fighting, he had his game face on. He took all the rage he had bottled up and laid it out in the form of violence."

The doctor started taking notes. "But he had been fighting for centuries. What was different about this latest battle?"

Katie tried to replay the fight in her head. "He was bashing heads. That was just what he did. He was launching himself into crowds of demons to try to get them away from the front-line soldiers."

The doctor pointed at Katie. "Empathy. What else?"

Katie imagined herself in the battle. She pictured herself protecting him. Pandora made a snapping sound. *Dude, that's it. That is the emotion that is different. Tell them.*

Katie looked at Angie and at the doctor. "During the fight, he saved several people, then was overpowered by demons. I went back for him. I saved him and got him out of that shitstorm. From then on, things really started to change. I mean, he had already mellowed out, but that was because Pandora had threatened him. After I saved him, he started to really fight on our side. It wasn't about the killing anymore. It was about protecting the Earth from the demons."

Angie's face was full of emotion as she looked down at Juntto. "He was becoming human. He was feeling all the things humans feel, more than just anger and annoyance. He felt solidarity. Compassion. Maybe even love. Then he just shut down."

Pandora snorted. *I've heard of men denying their emotional side, but this dude gives a whole new meaning to shutting down emotionally.*

Katie tried to hide a smirk. The doctor tapped his pen on his board. "But how do you correct the shutdown? You obviously want him to experience all these things. You just have to figure out how to make that change."

Katie was about to say something when the speakers crackled and alarms began to blare. "Well, this can't be good."

14

Thunder rolled outside, and large sheets of ice that had collected on top of the hangar's insulation began to crack. Angie jumped, scared to death of what was going on. Katie planted her feet, rocking back and forth as the ground shook. Whatever was happening, it was big.

Pandora sniffed. *Uh-oh. You better get prepared, lady.*

Katie jumped into action, grabbing Angie by the arm. "You're going to be okay. You and the doctor can stay here with Juntto. Do you have your gun?"

Angie lifted her jacket, displaying two holstered pistols on her hips. Katie patted her on the arm and smiled. "Good. Just in case. Anything demon comes through that door, you start shooting. Got it?"

Angie braced herself. "Yeah."

Katie turned to the doctor. "This is important. We have to keep Juntto out of the hands of the demons. If things are dire, you look to Angie. There's a failsafe built into this room. If they take over and she gives you the word, blow this bitch. The safety of the world depends on your actions. Are you able to do that?"

The doctor was more than calm. "Absolutely. I spent nine years as a Marine. Can do."

Katie smiled. "Good. For now, stay put. Hopefully, I can handle this quickly."

Katie ran toward the door, taking off her jacket as she went. She flung the first door open and tossed her jacket to the ground.

Pandora pouted. *Shit. I loved that jacket.*

We can buy another one.

Katie pulled Tom and Harry from their holsters. She paused at the outer door and took a deep breath, slowly letting it out through her nose. *You ready for this?*

Pandora laughed. *Please, I was* born *for this. Some pagan circles praise me as the goddess of battle and war. Let's do this.*

Katie stepped outside with her guns up. The hot wind from the portal blew into her face, and she had to put up one arm to protect herself. She narrowed her eyes at the swirling black hole in the middle of the gate.

Oh, balls.

A giant paw reached out to grab the edge of the portal. *Uh-oh.*

Pandora gasped. *This motherfucker decides to show up now?*

A large clawed foot stomped out onto the ground, shaking the planes and choppers around it. Slowly, Moloch pulled his large body out of the gate. Steam poured off his scales as the cold air hit him. He twisted his neck right and left, looking down at the line of troops below him. They all looked nervous, but they kept pointing their weapons at him.

One of the soldiers in the middle of the line yelled an order and began firing, and the rest followed suit. The bullets bounced off his thick scales as he stepped on a helicopter, crushing it like it was made of tinfoil. With one swoop of his arm, the great demon plowed through the line of soldiers, injuring several and killing more. Katie kicked the door shut behind her, determined to hide Juntto from Moloch. There was no way she was going to let him have the Leviathan. She suspected Moloch had other plans, though. She thought he had come for her.

Pandora growled loudly. *That sonofabitch thinks he can come to my base, fuck with my hot soldiers, and prance away scot-free? Oh,* hell, *no, bitch!*

"Fuck it." Katie shoved Tom and Harry back into their holsters and gulped a breath as she summoned her armor. A bright light enveloped her as heavenly armor encased her body. The sun shone off it and caught Moloch's attention. He narrowed his eyes, letting out a mighty roar. The air hit Katie in the face, and she waved her hand. "Fuck, you could have eaten a Tic Tac before coming to Earth. Jesus."

Moloch was beyond angry. His body grew stronger and mightier with every spasm of rage that pulsed through him. He charged Katie, trailing streaks of energy in his wake. He waved his fists as he ran, easily smashing the nearby planes and choppers. Shards of metal flew into the lines of soldiers, and they took cover where they could.

Katie shook her head and took a deep breath. *Well, here goes nothing.*

Balls. Here goes fucking something!

She took off across the landing pad and launched herself into the air. Her wings caught a gust of wind as she pulled her guns and blasted Moloch in the neck and chest, the shots sparking off his heavy hide. The bullets lodged in his scales, which just pissed him off. She flew closer and fired into his face, but he swung a huge claw at her. He made contact with a loud crunch, and Katie's wings went limp. She plummeted to earth and slammed into the asphalt of the base's airfield.

She jumped to her feet and shook her head, her eyes turning from blue to red. There was a Katie-sized imprint where her body had hit the ground. She growled and leaped from the hole, flying up past his slashing claws. She landed on his shoulder and punched him as hard as she could. Blood flew from his mouth, but he was quick. He swatted at her, but Katie jumped before his hand could reach her.

She landed in front of him and holstered her guns. "Hold still, motherfucker."

Moloch leaned down and put his gigantic face in front of Katie. "Only if you will, whore."

Pandora was not having that. *Oh fuck, no. Do* not *disrespect us like that. Let me at him.*

Katie pulled her holy sword, and its glory nearly blinded the demon. *Calm down. The fight has just begun.*

Moloch reached back to pound Katie with his fist, but she dodged. She tucked her wings and rolled across the ground, slicing his shin with her sword. His hide was like armor, but her sword was not of the human world. It bit through scale and flesh and came out dripping with black blood. Moloch screamed and grabbed his leg, hopping up and down. "Twat! I just got this shit put back on."

Katie made a tsking sound with her tongue. "Maybe you should have stayed down then, asshole."

Moloch snarled and snatched Katie around the waist with lightning speed. He had her arms pinned to her side, and he lifted her into the air. "I would love to be home, but I have to worry about your dumb ass. Why don't you be a good girl, give up Pandora, and fucking *die?*"

This fucker's gotta go.

I got it, Pandora.

Katie leaned her head back to snarl at the giant demon. "I don't give up like that, you half-bright hell-turd. I blew you the fuck up once, and I'll do it again. They'll be picking up bits of Moloch 'nads in every circle of hell. Lucifer won't even be able to figure out which bit is your nose and which is your knob-end." As she cursed at him, her hand slipped down and pulled Tom slowly from its holster. "Jesus, you are one dumb dingleberry, even for a demon."

Katie yanked her gun out and pulled the trigger, shooting Moloch in the eye. He dropped her and grabbed his head, groaning and moaning. Katie's wings spread and she descended to the ground, hoping the bullet had gone into his brain.

Pandora chuckled. *Knob-end? Are you fucking British now?*

It just came to me, and it felt right.

I guess it has its appeal.

Moloch roared, and Katie held her sword at the ready. She watched in horror as he yanked his eyeball from the socket and shook it. There was a light metallic clink when the bullet hit the ground. Her jaw dropped as he popped his eye back into its socket and shook his head, then gnashed his teeth. "Okay, you're a tough one. Got it."

The demon narrowed his eyes and grabbed one of the mangled choppers from the airfield, heaving it at Katie. She ducked as the chopper flew over her, slamming into the hangar bay. The building rocked, sheets of ice falling from its roof. Katie took a deep breath and sheathed her sword. She sprang into the air and drew both of her special-metal daggers. She heaved one and then the other with all her might. The metal glowed as they turned end over end, finally burying themselves in each of Moloch's arms.

Moloch barked a laugh and yanked the knives out. Great gouts of foul blood sprayed Katie, and she shook the stuff off her hands. *That's fucking disgusting.*

Pandora winced. *God, it smells like dead rats and patchouli. What the fuck has he been eating, hippies?*

Katie took off at a run, vaulting over a large mound of twisted metal that had been a helicopter. Moloch tried to follow her, but she was much smaller and faster. She darted to the side and doubled back behind him. She backed up as far as she could possibly go, eyeing the mound of scrap metal, then took a deep breath. *A little boost when I jump, okay?*

Pandora was all about it. *Just gotta make sure I do it at the right time. Don't want to launch you into his ass.*

Katie chuckled and dug her feet in, then raced across the tarmac. The soldiers cheered her on as she hit the pile of metal and launched herself into the air. She pulled out her sword as she flew and slashed it across Moloch's back.

The scales broke and fell to the ground. Her heavenly blade dug into Moloch's black flesh. Black blood flowed out through the wound and Moloch arched his shoulders, throwing his head back and howling with rage. Katie grabbed a ridge of broken scales and held onto the demon's back, ready to strike again.

Moloch's eyes flashed bright red, and he roared loudly. "Fuck, that *hurt*! You bitch!"

He reached around but felt only warm blood pouring down his back. He tried to look back to see where Katie was, but she was out of sight. He began to throw his body back and forth, raging wildly. The burning pain of the sword was ten times worse than any torture Lucifer had ever devised. He grabbed a jagged chopper blade and swung it around his body like it was a giant deadly back-scratcher. Katie ducked her head once, but on its return, she had no choice but to jump.

Katie hit the ground and slid across the grass, digging a deep furrow in the dirt and collecting a pile of dirt and sod behind her. Moloch continued to lash out furiously. He grabbed soldiers and threw them as hard as he could at the buildings. One soldier careened into the hanger where Juntto was being kept. He slammed against the building, went limp, and fell to the ground. Katie groaned, reaching back to investigate a lump on the back of her head. "This motherfucker is tough."

Pandora scoffed. *Please. Give me your speech, and I'll add some extra oomph to your next hit.*

Katie pulled herself out of the dirt. *And how exactly would you like me to hit him?*

Headfirst. Like a fucking freight train.

Katie sighed and got into position. "I should have bought a helmet for this shit."

She took off across the ground, putting her head down as she got close to Moloch. Pandora poured a burst of power into Katie just as she slammed into the demon, throwing him into a building behind him. The bricks and cinder blocks crashed into each other with such force that a wave of energy rippled outward, knocking several soldiers off their feet. Katie grabbed Moloch's leg and pulled herself on top of the giant demon.

Pandora, using Katie's voice, yelled at Moloch, "Hey, asshole! I told you a long time ago that you can't just roll into places uninvited, nuts swinging. You will be put down."

"Your husband has been asking for you, dear." Moloch groaned and pushed a chunk of the brick wall off his chest. "I have orders to bring your disgusting ass back to him."

Pandora put Katie's hand to her chin, pretending to mull that over. "Hmm. Nope. I think I'll pass on that one. In the meantime, you can go back with your balls in your throat."

Before Moloch could react, Katie reared back and kicked him as hard as she could in the crotch. Pandora giggled. "Fuck, I've always wanted to do that to you."

<hr>

Angie stared down at Juntto's heavily bearded face, seeing the same man she had seen before he left her. He didn't look cold at all. He looked natural. His blue scales were not tough and rigid but smooth to the touch. Of course, she could feel the frigid temperatures, but it was like his body enjoyed it. She couldn't even imagine what he was going through. She wondered where his thoughts were. Was he dreaming? Could he hear her? They were the same questions most would have for a coma patient, but this particular patient was blue, gigantic, and thriving off the subzero temperatures.

Angie looked at the scientist, who was watching the monitors near Juntto's body. She wanted to ask him a question, but she was afraid of the answer. She gathered her courage. "How do you know he's in there? How do you know it's not a situation where his body is preserved because he's alien, but he is gone?"

The doctor offered her a kind smile. "He has brain activity. Come here and let me show you."

Angie looked up at the sound of gunfire. The doctor waved her over, and she followed him to a bank of computers. He pulled up a screen with jagged lines moving up and down across it. "These are his brain waves. We can detect them much better now for some unknown reason. When he came in, these waves were smaller because there was much less activity. However, as time has passed, they've become larger and sharper."

Angie watched them move. "Does that mean he's coming around?"

The doctor sighed. "I don't know. Humans can have normal brain waves and still be comatose, but Leviathans? This is all new to us. We have nothing to compare his data to. All we know is that the baseline of his vitals has not changed, and his brain activity continues to fluctuate. I—"

Just then, a loud roar sounded and the building shook.

Angie grabbed the table and waited it out. As the shaking began to fade, something huge slammed into the side of the building. The shape of a humanoid body indented into the side of the hanger. The lines carrying the cooling agent to the building snapped and hissed. Clouds of frost floated through the air, and the lights flickered wildly above them.

Angie gasped and ran to Juntto's side. She climbed onto the table and threw her arms across his wide chest. She was frightened and felt weak, but she knew Juntto would comfort her. She laid her head next to his and closed her eyes tightly, talking to him out of fear. "Oh, Juntto, I wish you were here. There is a huge demon is outside right now. I don't know if he wants you or Katie or both of you, but he's on a rampage. His anger is so great that I can feel it."

The building shook again as a wave of energy rippled over it. Angie whimpered and pressed her head against the frost giant's neck, whispering, "Please come back to me, Juntto. We need you."

Across the room, Dr. Ozu typed wildly on his computer. He wasn't going to sit there and let this happen without some sort of protection. He went to the door and opened it, calling one of the soldiers. The man rushed over. "Yes, sir, what can I do for you?"

The doctor grimaced at another loud bang. "I'm not hearing much gunfire now. Why is that?"

The soldier let out a deep breath. "The bullets don't seem to be doing much good. The demon is huge, and his scales are incredibly thick. There aren't any heavy weapons out because we weren't expecting an attack. The armory is on the other side of the base, but the men are preoccupied, if not dead already."

The doctor thought about it for a second. "What about the building next door? We had extra weaponry in there."

The soldier led him to the other door and cracked it for him. He gazed out at the crumbled remains of the building and the large demon stomping back and forth in front of it. A winged figure was blasting the demon with two guns, but it didn't seem like that was doing much good.

"The building has been remodeled, sir.

"Oh. Well, shit."

They went back inside. The doctor shook his head. "We need something big; something that can pierce that monster's hide. Soldier, I need you to take two men into that rubble and get as much ammo as you can. Rockets, artillery—all the big stuff, if possible. On your way back, grab any kind of twisted metal from those choppers. If you have tools, get those too. I need this done as quickly as possible. We have got to help Katie. She's fighting this demon on her own, and it doesn't look good for her."

The soldier saluted Dr. Ozu and whistled to two other men. The doctor went back inside the room, glancing at the numbers for Juntto and then moving to his desk. He put his computer on the floor and shoved a stack of paperwork off, grabbed a pencil and a piece of paper, and pulled his chair up. They badly needed weapons. If he was going to be part of this war, he was going to use his know-how to help however he could.

He started to sketch different weapons, labeling the various parts and listing what he would require to build them. He needed something powerful but easily put together. He sketched for several minutes, looking nervously at the door and waiting for the guys to return.

Bodies and debris continued to hit the building, rattling the entire place. After fifteen minutes or so, the outer door flew open, and two of the three guys came rushing in with their arms full.

The doctor ran to them. "Where's the other guy?"

The soldier wiped his forehead, catching his breath. "That last body you heard? That was him."

The doctor grimaced, then nodded. "Okay, what did you get?"

They started going through the gear. There were several large ammo shells and a bunch of mid-sized ones. There were also long shards of metal, and they had been able to grab a couple of damaged weapons. The doctor held the guns up, narrowing his eyes. "Definitely won't be able to use these, but we can use the parts or modify the other stuff. Good job, guys. Thank you. I need one of you to go monitor those screens and make sure Juntto doesn't redline." He gestured to the other soldier. "I'm going to need you here. Let's get Katie the help she deserves."

15

Brock pointed his rifle at the charging demon and pulled the trigger. The bullet flew through the air and struck the demon in the forehead. A little bit of blood splashed from the front of his head, but the back of his head exploded black gore. The bullet had gone straight through and hit the demon behind him in the chest. Brock looked at both of them, shocked, as they fell over and turned to dust.

He laughed and looked at Turner. "Did you see that?"

Turner slashed his daggers through the air. "Sorry, hero. Too busy saving my own ass."

Brock snickered. "Jealous much?"

He raced toward the screams coming from inside one of the houses. He kicked open the front door to find a woman and her dog trapped in a corner, both of them slashed and bleeding. The demon attacking her growled at Brock, then leaped over the dining room table and lunged at him. He held up his rifle and pulled the trigger, but the magazine was empty. *"Motherfuck."*

The demon landed on him and they rolled across the floor, slamming into the television. Brock grabbed the demon's wrists, keeping the claws from slicing him. The demon snapped its sharp, jagged teeth at Brock, who slammed his knee into the demon's balls. The demon whined and fell to the side, choking on his own spit.

Brock stood up, breathing heavily as he reloaded. "Sorry, dude, I know that wasn't fair play. Seriously, your fucking teeth are a dentist's nightmare."

He pointed the freshly loaded rifle at the demon and pulled the trigger, putting it out of its misery.

Outside in the street, Turner flipped backward, avoiding the sharp ends of a demon's claws. As he landed, he threw one of his daggers and it hit the demon between the eyes. The demon wobbled, then burst into dust. Turner ran, then dropped to his knees and slid through the dust. He snatched his dagger before it could hit the ground, then jumped back to his feet, crossed his arms, and sliced in a wide arc, taking the head off another charging beast.

The gooey black blood splashed his face and he groaned, wiping it with his arm. "Fucking disgusting. I'm so tired of that. Why the fuck does demon blood smell like fucking fried chicken?"

Brock laughed as he ran up next to him. "Who knows? Maybe we've been missing out all along. Crazy demon shish kebobs."

Turner nodded and imitated a sophisticated voice. "Why, yes. I'll have the demon flambé with a side of zombies' fingers, please. Make it crispy."

Brock faked a gag and slammed his foot into an oncoming demon. The two guys pressed their backs against each other and faced the snarling demon hordes. Turner pulled out his pistols and screamed as he fired. They cleared a wide area around them before running out of bullets. As they reloaded, more demons charged from the shuddering portals.

Turner took a deep breath. "This shit is monkey-nuts crazy, dude."

Brock smirked. "Yeah, but when is our life not?"

"Good point."

Brock stopped and tilted his head to the side as something new wriggled from the portal. "Uh, dude? Looks like they're letting all the freaks out of hell."

Turner spun his guns toward the nearest portal. An impossibly tall long-necked demon lumbered toward them. His skinny arms dragged on the ground, and a gray tuft of hair blew around the top of his head as he walked. His bottom jaw stuck out, and his eyes were huge and round. "When the fuck did they start with demon trolls?"

Brock furrowed his brow. "He looks like he's made of spaghetti."

Turner shook his head. "Guess it's meatballs for dinner, then."

"Holy *fuck*, this is going to hurt," Katie yelled as she flew toward the hangar bay.

Three soldiers jumped to catch her, not realizing how fast she was going. Katie slammed into the group, and the four of them crashed onto the ground. Katie groaned and rose on shaking legs. "You guys okay?"

The three soldiers shook it off, rubbing their heads. Katie nodded and looked back at Moloch. "Good catch, that's for damn sure. I could have taken down that entire building, which would not have been great for Juntto." She grimaced and straightened her armor. "I need something a little more substantial to protect me."

Just then, a loud crack sounded, and light flashed overhead. Katie narrowed her eyes as a golden shield fell from the sky. She leaped into the air and caught it. "That's definitely what I call super-fast service."

Pandora scoffed. *Some of us have to do it the old-fashioned way with brawn and strength.*

Katie grinned as she took off across the field, heading straight for Moloch. He pulled his fist back and swung at her. Katie gritted her teeth and held the shield up in front of her. "Let's see what this baby can do."

Moloch's fist met the shield with a huge clang and stopped dead. Katie put her foot back and her head forward, pushing hard against his fist. Sparks flew from the surface of the shield as it scraped his knuckles. Moloch looked at her with wide eyes. "Fucking angels."

Katie grinned maniacally. "That's right, asswipe. Fucking angels coming in hot every damn time."

Pandora giggled in excitement. *Holy fuck, that's awesome. You're just like Wonder Woman. No, even better than that. You're Wonder Whore. Fighting crime and deep dickin' on the side.*

Katie couldn't help but laugh. *Wonder Whore is losing steam here, honey.*

Oh, shit. Sorry.

Pandora used her strength to push back, and Moloch

withdrew his fist. Katie stumbled forward but caught herself before falling into a baking pile of metal. She straightened and rolled her shoulders, impressed by the shield.

Moloch let out a deep nefarious laugh. "You stupid bitches. Do you really think a tiny shield and a pointy little golden sword can stop me? I have Lucifer at my back."

Pandora took over Katie's voice and yelled, "Are you fucking kidding? This bitch has the Almighty at *her* back. And if I'm not mistaken, he's the one who threw Lucifer's ass out of heaven. You might want to rethink your choice of sovereign there, buddy."

Moloch snarled and charged them. Katie patiently waited, yawning. The soldiers lowered their weapons and watched as he got closer and closer and she still did nothing. When he was only feet away, Katie shoved her shield in front of her and smashed it into his nose, stopping him cold. She leaped into the air and out of harm's way. Moloch tumbled forward, his nose bleeding and his forehead gashed. He slid through the dirt and came to a stop, then laid there motionless.

Katie dusted her hands and slung the shield on her back. "Well, that was easy."

Then Moloch put his hands down and angrily pushed his body up. He was not done with the fight. Not in the least.

Angie held tightly to Juntto, squeezing her eyes shut. For several moments she heard nothing but the sound of Juntto's beating heart in his cold chest. Slowly, she picked up her head and looked around, wondering if the battle was over. A loud crack sounded, and beams of light shot through the edges of the doorway.

The doctor looked up at the same time, unsure what was going on. Angie shook her head. "She must be summoning her angel powers. At least, I think that's how it works."

The doctor lifted his eyebrows. "Hopefully, she can hold him off a little longer. We're coming up with weapons."

A loud blast sounded and daggers of light streaked across the doorway from the outside. Angie whimpered and buried her head in Juntto's neck. Her hands were trembling, so she wrapped them around his blanket.

She needed him to come back and be the man—or alien —he had been before. "Juntto, please! You always made me feel so damn safe. You always stood tall, fearless in the face of danger. You may never have wrapped your arms around me or held me close, but that was what it felt like every time I saw you. I knew you watched out for me during fights. You protected me when you thought I wasn't looking. You're something like a thousand years old, but your life was just getting started. You'd turned into a Leviathan that anyone, well, almost anyone, could love and care for. We had such a hilarious time shopping, eating, and even doing your stupid laundry. You fell in love with fashion and gaming, a hard combination to find in a man."

Angie took a deep breath. She wasn't sure he could hear her, but she didn't care. A war was raging outside the building, and this might be her last chance to tell him how she felt. "I loved being able to kick your ass at those games.

You might have pretended it never happened, but I know you liked it too. In fact, sometimes it felt like you were trying to let me win, even though I am the master. God, just come back and let me make you steak and shrimp. Nothing spicy, because we know where that leads. Fuck, I'll even do your damned laundry."

Angie laughed through her tears, squeezing her arms tighter around him. "The truth is, when you first came, I wanted to hate you. You were the personification of everything I loathed in a man. You were angry, drunk, and violent, and had no respect for anyone. You may have been with us only a short time, but I could see you changing. I believed you were changing. I saw you save those people. I saw you protect me and Katie and Calvin. I saw you risk your life for perfect strangers, soldiers who would have never made it home if it weren't for you."

Another loud crash swayed the hangar on its frame. "I don't know anything about your people, but if we all come from the same place, the same stars, the same God, even, then I know that what I saw was possible. The truth is, I miss you, Juntto. I miss everything there is to miss about someone."

Angie couldn't believe she was pouring her heart out to this cold blue monster, but she didn't know what else to do. At that point, Doctor Ozu had one hand on the guns and the other on the failsafe. Neither of them knew if they would get out of there alive.

Angie sniffed loudly and sat up, looking around the hangar. Gunfire rang out in the distance and screams from the soldiers dying outside cut the air like a knife. It was only one demon, but it sounded like an all-out war. It was worse than the battles she'd helped with in the past. People were being killed, and she didn't even know where Katie was or if she was still fighting.

Something heavy hit the building, and it creaked and tilted crazily to the right. "Juntto, come on. You have to be in there. You have to fight through whatever this is. You have to come out of there and help us. There's a reason you are still alive."

A thud shook the ground outside, and the sound of a building collapsing struck fear into the pit of Angie's stomach. She held her chest as tears flooded down her cheeks. She turned back to Juntto and held his head. A tear trickled down her cheek and fell from her chin, splashing onto his blue cheek.

The ground shook again. Angie buried her head in his chest and moaned, "Juntto!"

Angie closed her eyes and held onto him. Slowly, the coldness began to dissipate from beneath her. A warmth she hadn't felt in a long time radiated from Juntto's chest. She turned her head, eagerly searching his face. She brought her hand to his cheek.

His eyes popped open, and he gulped air in huge gasps. Angie bolted up and looked at the doctor, who jumped from his chair and ran back into the main area.

The soldier was on his feet, shaking his head. "Everything just went wild."

Doctor Ozu approached Juntto. The frost giant was gaping at the ceiling, eyes wide, his chest moving heavily up and down.

Angie tilted her head to the side. "Juntto?"

He blinked once and groaned softly. "You guys keep it fucking cold in here."

Angie, tears still streaming down her cheeks, burst into laughter. She laid her body across his chest and hugged him tightly. His giant arm came up and over her back, giving her a light squeeze. He began to move and she jumped off the platform, helping him sit up. He swiveled his legs around and rubbed his face.

The doctor reached out to take his pulse, but Juntto shook his head. "I have taken my own readings, and everything's fine. Thank you, doctor."

Doctor Ozu looked slightly thrown off. "You're...you're welcome."

Angie looked into Juntto's eyes and shook her head. "How did you come back from this? I mean, we've been trying to figure out what the hell we had to do to get you back. Katie flew all the way to Rome."

Juntto lifted an eyebrow. "Wow. That's definitely impressive, although you didn't find an answer, did you?"

Angie shook her head. "Not in any scroll or book. One of the priests suggested the energy of emotion, but we had no idea what that meant."

Juntto nodded, impressed. "Smart, for a priest."

Angie looked at him strangely. "I don't understand."

"I'm not human." Juntto reached out and held her tiny hand in his large one. "You see, when emotions change in our bodies, we shut down. We aren't dead or sleeping. We're hibernating. Our body has to change to efficiently produce the chemicals that create those emotions. Basically, I was growing a heart while I laid there. My body has changed. It's been morphing to use *positive* emotions—

friendship, love, and compassion. Before, it was all anger, violence, hatred, and despair. Those were the first emotions I learned here on Earth."

Angie shook her head. "That's terrible. That was what we projected? Makes me think we have a lot to do to change this world beyond just killing demons."

Juntto gave her a kind smile. "You are part of, if not all of, the reason I am awake."

Angie narrowed her brow. "How? I didn't do anything."

Juntto chuckled. "Sure, you did. You holding me, crying, and caring for me? That was the energy I needed to restart. I was lost in this in-between place, but when you touched me, I started to come out of it. I could hear you, but you sounded like you were in a tunnel. When your tear hit my skin, it brought me back to the surface."

Angie was amazed. "So…love brought you back."

Juntto nodded. "I suppose it did. But more importantly, *you* brought me back. And Katie too. Her caring and desire to help me out of friendship brought me back. You all cared for me like I was your family."

Angie winced as the ground shook again. "How are you feeling?"

Juntto shrugged. "Like brand new, actually. I don't need to eat like you humans do, and my body manifests what I need when I'm unable to care for myself. Except for tequila —my body doesn't manifest that."

"And your body needs tequila, does it?"

The ghost of a smile touched Juntto's blue lips. "Okay, maybe *need* isn't the right word. Putting me in this icy area was a smart move, by the way. If you had kept me warm, I might have been out for centuries." Something crashed outside, and Juntto turned toward the door. "What's going on out there?"

Angie sighed and shook her head. "We came to see you, and then a portal opened. They say it's Moloch out there. I assume he came for Katie, but he's been killing soldiers right and left. She's out there fighting him by herself. None of the small arms are working."

Juntto furrowed his brow. "I need clothes."

Doctor Ozu pointed to a rack of military camouflage. "There are those. We, uh, we don't have anything for giants. And, uh, we're low on boots."

"I'll make do." Juntto grinned and shrunk to human size. He was a large, blue-scaled human, but he could now wear the clothes. "Thanks, buddy."

Angie turned as he got dressed, mostly to hide the bright red of her cheeks. Juntto just chuckled, knowing she had seen him naked. When he had finished dressing, he rolled his shoulders and stretched his back. His body flickered and changed from one form to the next, Van Damme and Morpheus appeared briefly, but ultimately he went back to his frost giant form. His beard was long and scraggly and his long hair was silvery-white, but there was something about it that Angie thought was hot.

As he worked out his stiff muscles, his eyes shifted to Angie. "And by the way. I *definitely* let you win those video games. I didn't want you to be upset. I know how feisty you get."

Angie put her hands on her hips. "Is that right? What about the tantrums you threw?"

Juntto waved her off. "All for show—and you're one to

talk. You threw a bag of gummy bears at the television. They were stuck there for days."

Angie shrugged. "All for show."

Juntto raised an eyebrow, a smile creeping onto his face. "Mmmhmm. Sure. Now, what kind of spears do we have around here?"

16

Katie rocketed toward Moloch and grunted as she slammed into his arm. She slid down to his wrist like she was on a fireman's pole. He shook his arm trying to fling her off, but she held on tightly. She wrapped her legs around his wrist, turned upside down, and grabbed his middle finger. *Okay Pandora, this is where I need you to work my ab muscles, please.*

She roared as she bent his finger backward, hearing a loud wet snap. He squealed and shook his hand, trying to get her off. "I just fucking got that arm back, and now you're going to fuck it up?"

Katie laughed and let go, latching onto the scales on his forearm. As he nursed his finger, she shinnied up over his elbow to his bicep. She easily ducked when he attempted to swipe her off. When his hand had passed, she hurried up and over the crest of his shoulder. Quickly, she crawled into the crevasse between his neck and collarbone. She leaned back to avoid his hand and then pulled out her pistol. She pressed it hard against his shoulder and pulled the trigger.

The bullet entered his body, traveled through flesh, and exploded out the tip of his finger.

He screamed.

Katie jumped, flipping sideways over his head and landing on the other shoulder. Moloch shook his arm, blood squirting from his fingertip. "You fucking bitch. I swear, when I get hold of you I will torture you to the brink of insanity, nurse you back to health, and do it all over again."

Katie smirked. "Uh-huh. And what arms are you going to do that with?"

"Huh?" Moloch grunted. He glanced around in time to see Katie pressing her gun to his other shoulder.

Katie smiled and let out a small giggle. Moloch tried to reach for her, but he was in serious pain from the special metal. "Don't you do it, whore."

Katie sighed. "Didn't say the magic word. You have no manners at all. It's a shame, really."

She pulled the trigger and Moloch's head flew back, an earth-shaking roar escaping his throat. The sound echoed across the base. The soldiers covered their ears until he was done, shaking their heads at one other.

Moloch moaned, his arms hanging limply at his sides. "I came out here to do a job that wasn't even mine to begin with, and *now* look at me. Two fucking useless arms and a slut on my shoulder like a goddamned parrot!"

Pandora chuckled, taking over Katie's voice. "Squawk. Moloch is an ass. Squawk. Moloch has no balls. Squawk. Moloch is a pussy."

Katie laughed and spread her wings, gliding to the ground. She hunkered down and hid behind a piece of metal, breathing heavily. *This is fun and everything, but I don't know how much longer I can do this on my own, Pandora.*

Pandora sighed. *I know. I'm giving you everything I've got.*

Katie peered over the metal at Moloch, who was mumbling to himself and pulling energy into his wounds. *How long will it take him to heal?*

Pandora thought about that for a moment. *Well, he heals slower on Earth, so...about three minutes.*

Katie rubbed her face. *Fucking perfect. I am out of ideas.*

The door to the hangar bay flew open. Katie looked over the hunk of metal, her jaw dropping. Ducking through the doorway, fully dressed in battle gear and fully bearded, was Juntto in all his glory. Katie immediately stood up and put her hands in the air. "Juntto, you magnificent bastard! Did you take a long enough fucking nap?"

Juntto grinned as he ran to Katie. "Never leave a friend behind."

"I think I remember that from somewhere." Katie smiled at him.

Juntto put his hand on Katie's armored shoulder. "I'm tagging you out."

"For once, I'm not going to argue with you."

Juntto stepped in front of Moloch, who was licking his wounds. Slowly, Moloch's eyes shifted upward, going from Juntto's bare feet up his pants, and over his strong, camo-covered chest. His lip snarled as he stared Juntto in the face. He couldn't believe the Leviathan was still alive. "I thought you were dead."

Juntto beat his fist on his chest. "It will take a lot more

than some puny pussy-ass fucking demons to get rid of Juntto."

Moloch was enraged. "You sick sonofabitch. You work for *me*! You came here for *me*! I woke you up on the side of that frostbitten mountain, and I decide what you fight for. How dare you come at me like you have something to prove?"

Juntto cracked his knuckles. "You're mistaken, Moloch. I work for myself. You're nothing. There have been far too many years of you and your sick fucking demented demons controlling the people of my planet. These humans have shown me it's far more heroic to stand for something instead of falling for your bullshit. I decide what I fight for, and I fight for them."

Moloch's arms started to twitch. "I'm going to ball your fucking Leviathan ass back up and send you back to your planet the long way. When you arrive, they won't even be able to recognize Juntto the Great. You'll be the laughing-stock of every frozen runt on your miserable planet. And while I'm at it, I'll make sure to send you parts of your friend Katie and your little girlfriend Angie. When you wake up, you'll have a reminder of what happens when you fuck with Moloch!"

Juntto gritted his teeth and yelled. He grew even larger, his new camo splitting around his muscles. He sprinted toward Moloch and rammed into him. Juntto grabbed Moloch by the shoulders and slammed him to the ground. Moloch bounded up, got his arms to work, and slashed his claws at Juntto, slicing him across the arm. Juntto growled and kicked him hard in the stomach, sending the huge demon flying across the runway to land in a pile of junk that had once been a plane.

Moloch jumped up and raced toward Juntto, but the frost giant ducked to the right at the last second. He waited until Moloch had passed him and grabbed the back of his neck, slamming him to the ground again. Juntto stomped on Moloch's forehead, whereupon Moloch growled and grabbed his ankle, flipping him over in the air and sending him face-first into the asphalt.

Soldiers ran from the battling giants, afraid of being stomped underfoot or battered by a giant flopping limb.

Juntto groaned as he pushed himself up, shaking gravel from his hair. Moloch was already on his feet, laughing at the Leviathan. "I thought you were supposed to be superior in strength. Maybe once. Now you seem like you're less than human."

Juntto grinned and spat a chunk of rock out. "That was just a warm-up, you mewling quim. Don't worry, your fate will find you."

Before Moloch could respond, Juntto rammed his shoulder into the demon's stomach, knocking him back a few feet and pushing the air from his lungs. Juntto didn't hesitate. He slammed his foot into Moloch's chest. The huge demon flew back, landing on the original side of the runway.

The door to the hangar bay opened and two Marines ran out carrying huge, handmade weapons. They handed them to Juntto with a grin. "We sure as hell are glad to see you back. The doc made these real fast. I hope they help."

Juntto saluted. "Thank you, guys. Let's see if we can't send this fucker back to his cave."

Juntto turned, holding a weapon in each hand. Although they would be huge for someone Katie-sized, Juntto couldn't even get his finger on the trigger. He put one weapon down on the ground and held the other between thumb and forefinger, carefully pulling the trigger with his nail. A grenade launched, flying through the air like a slug of potato from a potato gun. As it landed on the ground, it bounced twice and exploded right in front of Moloch.

Juntto looked at the weapon and sighed. "Why can't they build Juntto-sized weapons?"

Moloch hopped to his feet and roared at Juntto, then turned and ripped open a gate. Juntto started to chase him, but Katie put her arm on Juntto's leg. "Wait! Let him run back scared. I promise that Lucifer will not be happy with the fucker. Moloch's jumping out of the frying pan into hell. It needs to be over for today."

Juntto grumbled but didn't move. Moloch disappeared into the portal, and it snapped shut behind him. Juntto sighed. "Glad I came when I did."

Katie groaned and stretched her back. "Me too, big guy. I don't think I could have taken another bashing. My head was starting to hurt. Thanks for that."

Juntto shrank down to something like human size. "I told you. You have my back, and I have yours. You've had my back since you brought me onto the team. I will always have yours."

Katie lifted an eyebrow. "You seem different—almost gentler."

Juntto chuckled. "Maybe, or maybe I just handle my temper better. Don't tell anybody. I did have one hell of a rest, that's for sure. The only thing I remember was the smell of meat. When I woke up, though, there was no meat."

Katie laughed. "We had to build a freezer big enough to handle your ass. Until we could finish it, we stowed you in a meat locker at a local butcher shop."

Juntto looked surprised. "Just like the Italian mob. Nice."

"Yeah, except those were dead bodies, and yours was just, like, stuck or frozen. You were glitching hardcore. We had to figure out how to get you back. Which reminds me, what woke you up?"

Juntto shrugged. "Honestly? You and Angie. My body reprogrammed itself to work off caring, friendship, and honor. That was why it froze. I was…rebooting, I guess. I only ever knew anger and bitterness until I met you and Angie. Her tears brought me out of my sleep."

Pandora choked. *Oh, that's fucking rich. It's like a modern-day fucking fairy tale where Juntto plays Sleeping Beauty, and Angie is the prince. This story fucking sucks.*

Katie giggled. *I personally think it's sweet and romantic.*

Whatever. As long as you don't start making me watch chick flicks, I will let you have this dumb fairy tale.

Juntto and Katie looked over when Angie burst from the hangar. Juntto grinned wildly and started forward, meeting her in the middle of what had been a war zone minutes ago. She launched herself into the air, wrapping her legs around his waist. Quickly, she climbed up his body and rubbed her nose against his. They stared at each other in the eyes for several moments.

Katie looked the other way.

Pandora made a gagging noise. *Kajesus, get a fucking room.*

They had better. Juntto's clothes didn't survive that fight with Moloch.

The Ice King and his fire bride. Gross.

Katie smiled. *I think you're jealous.*

Me? No, thank you. I've been married to the literal worst being you can be married to. Let them have their artificial love. Everything will come crashing down when Angie gets knocked up by a Leviathan and gives birth to a seventy-two-pound blue Viking.

Angie ran her hands through his long beard and smiled. "I knew you would come back."

Juntto lifted an eyebrow. "Did you? I think I recall you asking…no, begging me to. And I'm pretty sure you said you'd do my laundry for the rest of time."

Angie grimaced. "You heard that? Well, how about a trade?"

Juntto narrowed his eyes. "For what?"

Angie leaned in and whispered something in his ear. Juntto's smile went from tight-lipped to a full-on grin in two seconds flat. Whatever she'd said was enough to get him to agree.

The doors of the base began to open and military members emerged, looking around at the damage. They formed a circle around Katie and Juntto. For several moments everyone was dead silent, then one person in the middle of the crowd began to clap. That one clap turned to two, then three, and before they knew it, the crowd erupted in cheers around the combatants.

The captain pushed through, clapping his hands. "Well

done, guys. Well done. I think this calls for a little party, don't you?"

Katie wasn't about to turn down a party, that was for sure. "Let's do it!"

Juntto cleared his throat. "Can I party like this or do I need pants?"

"Free-ball it!" a random soldier shouted.

"Pants," Angie blurted. She scowled at the soldier. "Don't encourage him."

Angie jumped off Juntto and took his big hand, leading him toward the hangar to get more clothes. Behind them, one soldier whispered to another, "I thought that guy was dead."

The other soldier shook his head. "Nah, man. He's an alien. He was frozen or something while he healed. But shit, when our people were under attack, he woke right the fuck up and he didn't hesitate to jump in. It was a good thing he did. We may be celebrating, but there are a bunch of bodies to clean up."

The two soldiers stopped and looked around at the carnage. The first soldier put his hand up. "Everybody, hold up. I know we want to celebrate this victory, but we have brothers and sisters here who deserve a hero's burial. I think we should all band together to take care of them first."

Katie made her way through the crowd and patted the guy on the shoulder. "Good thinking, and you're absolutely right. We can save the celebration for another time. We may have pushed Moloch back, but he took multiple lives. These men and women deserve mourning and respect. They were heroes. I'll be happy to help you."

Juntto stepped out of the hangar dressed in new camo. "As will I. These men and women are responsible for bringing me back to the land of the living. I owe it to them."

The entire base put aside their celebration and began the cleanup. Members of the medic team came out with body bags and stretchers. It was a hard job since many of the bodies were in pieces or horribly mangled from the damage they had received, but they were shown the utmost respect.

When all the bodies had been recovered, everyone stood around the flag in the center of the base. The military members saluted the flag as two soldiers slowly lowered and folded it and walked away in a ceremonial march. The reality of the evening came flooding over them. Many had died. They had sent the demon back to hell, yet Moloch was still out there.

He was still lurking in the shadows, waiting for them to make a mistake.

Brock sat crouched in an abandoned house, wondering where the original inhabitants had gone. Sean stood watch at one side of the window. His assault rifle was at the ready in case anything crept up on them. Eddie came down the stairs and gave Brock a nod, letting him know it was all clear.

Turner was sitting on the edge of the couch wiping the clotted blood off his pistols. "I swear the bastards have tar running through them. It's fucking awful to get this shit off."

Brock put his last two magazines in his guns and holstered them. "Just be glad it's *their* blood and not yours. Okay, team, let's count them up. How much ammo you got left? I've got nothing for my rifle, two magazines for the pistols, and my blade." His blade was a longsword of special metal, and it was leaning against the wall. "Turner?"

Turner shrugged. "No rifle ammo. I got one-and-a-half magazines. And the daggers."

Eddie shook his head, holding up his short sword. "Pig-sticker's what I got. No bullets."

By the window, Sean patted his assault rifle. "I got a magazine for this baby and about seven loose bullets in my pocket."

"How did you get loose bullets?" Eddie grinned and shook his head.

"I got a bullet for your mouth, you tattooed freak." He grabbed his crotch. "This bullet right here." Eddie laughed and shook his head, and Sean chuckled. "Other than that, I got a couple of daggers."

Brock grunted and sat down in a chair. "We're almost out of supplies, and HQ radioed in to say they won't be able to resupply for at least two hours."

Turner groaned, throwing his head back. "What the fuck are we supposed to do with nothing to fight with? Last time I checked, unless you're Katie, fists don't do much good—not that I wouldn't have a field day running around this place punching fucking demons."

Brock chuckled. "It's all fun and games until you get a claw in the eye."

Turner pointed at Brock. "Good point. No punching. I'm happy using my daggers, but there are a fucking shit-ton of demons out there. I don't think I have the stamina to keep up that amount of thrusting."

Eddie snickered. "That's what she said."

Turner threw a pillow at him. "That's not what your mother said."

"My mama did what she needed to do to survive. No shame." Eddie winked at Turner, who burst out laughing.

Brock rolled his eyes. "Now that we've progressed to the your-mama jokes part of the evening, I say we make a Plan B and go with it. We have to figure out a way to conserve ammo until HQ gets us more."

"I don't know, bro. We barely have enough rounds to hold down this living room, let alone clear the town." Eddie shook his head unhappily.

Turner shrugged. "Personally, I think we can only fight if we're equipped."

"Truth." Sean sighed from the window. "We're pretty much the only ones left, so preserving our lives until we can re-up on ammo is probably the smarter choice."

Brock shook his head. "I hate knowing there are innocents out there who could be killed while we sit on our asses and wait for supplies."

Turner leaned forward. "Bro, a lot more people will die if you're six feet under. If a demon rips you a new asshole, you won't be able to help anybody."

Brock sighed. "I know, I know. Okay, so we sit it out somewhere. Obviously, *here* won't do. One demon finds us and they're all going to flock, and we'll trap ourselves in here. Any idea where else we can go?"

"The church," a thickly-accented voice pronounced from the other room.

All the guys stood up and pointed their weapons in that direction. A woman walked from the back of the house. One side of her head was shaved, the other in long dreads. She was wearing a cutoff shirt, a short pair of ripped jeans shorts, and black lace-up boots. Her black eyeliner was thick, and her lips were pouty and ruby-red.

Turner's mouth dropped wide open.

She walked with her hands up, narrowing her eyes at Turner. "I don't think so."

Brock lowered his weapon. "Who are you?"

She put her hands down. "You can call me Sasha. This is my house. Well, my parents' house, but they jumped in the ride and took off as soon as the portals opened. I pulled up just as the shit was going down and hid out in the pantry. Who the hell are you?"

Turner chuckled, liking the attitude. "We're the US Anti-demon Task Force. Pretty badass motherfuckers."

She was not the least bit impressed. "And you're out of ammo."

Brock stepped forward. "You said the church?"

She pointed out the window at a tall steeple about two blocks away. "That's the only church in town, and it's safeguarded and very holy. You can hide out there and be safe from the demons. If you can get there, of course."

Brock walked to the window and looked out. "Yeah, we were in there once today already and that was how it worked. I think that might be our best bet. After we resupply, we'll take any survivors we find back to that church. We have enough to get there."

Sasha cleared her throat. "What about me?"

Brock pulled one of his guns. "You know how to shoot?"

Sasha took the gun and pointed it at Eddie. "Yes, point and pull the trigger. Aim for the head."

Eddie grimaced and moved out of her line of fire.

Brock pushed the gun down. "Right. Okay. We move out, then. Let's get there the quickest way possible. Beeline for the front doors."

The team readied themselves. Brock opened the front door and was about to bolt for it, but he stopped at the sound of an opening portal ripping open above them. They all looked up as several portals ripped through the sky, pushing a wave of heat down on them. All across the town demons and humans alike stopped to gaze up into the black abyss.

Suddenly, a glop fell and landed in the front yard, setting fire to the grass. Brock stepped back in alarm. "What the fuck?"

The whole team stared as molten red liquid began to pour from the portals and shower the town. Turner couldn't believe what he was seeing. "That's motherfucking *lava*. Those assholes are dropping *lava* on our asses."

Brock shook his head. Things just kept getting better. "Well, we can't stay here. We gotta make it to the church."

The team formed a line and made a break for it, keeping Sasha in the middle of the formation. All across the town, both humans and demons screamed. The flowing lava burned whoever it touched, no matter which side they were on.

The music from Baal's band was louder than normal. He ordered them to really take it up a notch to drown out the voices in his mind. His brain was running over everything and getting it all tangled. He no longer knew where his plan ended and Beelzebub's began. That demon was dangerous. He was a threat to Moloch's and Baal's lives.

But things had gotten worse.

A messenger brought Baal word that Moloch had attacked Katie and Lilith, and it hadn't gone well at all. He didn't know all the details, but the name Juntto had been mentioned, and that definitely wasn't a good thing. Still, if Moloch were that upset, Baal would be hearing from him very soon. Moloch wasn't the kind of demon to keep to himself when he was pissed, which was most of the time.

His glass of whiskey shook slightly from the throb of the stand-up bass. He reached over and picked it up, taking a sip and closing his eyes as he swallowed. "I'm glad I stopped and got this a couple of decades ago. It's perfect now."

He glanced at the Suntory Yamazaki 1960 Whiskey on the shelf. He still chuckled every time he thought about it. The bottle of whiskey sold on Earth for close to a hundred thousand dollars, but he had lifted it right out of the distillery. Waiting forty years in hell was nothing, but waiting forty years on Earth felt like an eternity. Nonetheless, it was one of the best whiskeys he'd ever had.

There was a light knock on his living room door, and a new demon scurried in carrying a tray of pickled ferrets. Baal had given in to the allure of luxury. He had his chef in the kitchen around the clock and had several demons to do his bidding inside the house. At first, he had felt guilty, but then he remembered he was a demon.

The demon servant set the tray on the table next to him. "Anything else, Your Grace?"

"No. That will be all. The rest of you can go home, or wherever it is you go when you leave here."

All of the demons quietly packed up and left Baal to his thoughts. The room was silent then, no music or scurrying servants. Baal opened the box and let out a deep breath as he removed the scroll. He began studying it closely.

Baal frowned and paused. He set the scroll in his lap and sniffed the air around him. His eyebrow went up, and he sat forward, smelling the pickled ferrets.

He burst into laughter and set the scroll aside, finished. "Found you!"

Katie sat in the hangar bay watching the medics tend wounds, mechanics try to fix broken machinery, and soldiers talk to each other about the events just past. They had enjoyed celebrating the night before, but only after respectfully tending to the dead. Juntto and Angie sat close to one another, lost in their own world as they whispered to each other.

Katie's phone vibrated in her pocket, and the general's name flashed on the screen. "General. I was wondering when you were going to call."

General Brushwood cleared his throat nervously. "Katie, so good to hear you're okay."

Before the general could go on, Katie gave him the rundown. "Yeah, it was crazy. We were here checking on Juntto when all of a sudden, a portal opened and out came Moloch. He was a tough sonofabitch. We fought for what felt like forever. Several soldiers here gave their lives, and many more were injured. I was almost beaten, General. I'll admit that to you. I don't know when I've felt so weak and helpless. Then the door to the freezer swung open, and Juntto emerged in all his Leviathan glory. He tagged me out and started beating on Moloch. A lot of the base was destroyed, including much of our hardware, but Dr. Ozu managed to rig up some weapons. When Juntto started haphazardly shooting them, Moloch opened a portal and got the fuck out of here."

The general chuckled. "No following him to hell this time?"

Katie snickered. "No. It was a good thing he left because we weren't prepared. I don't think we could have taken him down. Juntto arrived in the nick of time. We'll be better prepared next time, for sure. I need large-grade ammunition to fight that bastard. Personally, I would rather cut his head off and be done with it. We can place it next to T'Chezz's. But a huge-ass missile launcher would be okay, too. In any case, we have to destroy him. As long as we keep sending him back to hell, this war will continue to drag on."

"In due time. What's important is that you're all still standing and Juntto is back.

"Juntto has changed in some ways, but it's a good thing."

"That's fantastic news. It's nice to have good news today. How is Pandora?"

"I think she had more fun than she should have knocking Moloch's ass all over the base. Then again, she's waited a long time."

Pandora scoffed. *Damn straight, and I can't wait to do it again. I...*

Pandora's voice trailed off, sensing something wasn't right.

"I'm glad to hear it, but unfortunately, that isn't why I was calling." The general's voice went low, making Katie nervous. "The latest operation in Europe took a dark turn. As far as we know at this point, it was a complete loss."

Katie stood, immediately thinking of Brock. "What happened? I don't know if we've ever had a complete loss before. What do you mean by that? As in no demons were killed, or no survivors?"

The general let out a deep breath. "Well, the demons used a new tactic. They flooded the town with lava, using portals in the sky. They killed many of their own in addition to the humans. All hands not accounted for are MIA and presumed dead. I'm sorry to tell you, but that includes Brock's entire team. I wanted to tell you before you heard it from someone else. They were valiant and strong fighters for the cause. It's a great loss for the world, but I know they were friends of yours. I'm sorry, Katie."

Katie's eyes went blindingly red as she tried to wrap her head around what he had just said. "Don't worry about sending a counter, General. I'll respond to that personally."

Before the general could argue with her, she hung up the phone and slammed it onto the bench next to her. The loud noise grabbed Juntto and Angie's attention. Katie sat and put her head in her hands, her shoulders heaving as she sobbed. What the general had told her had been like a knife in her soul.

Angie moved her legs off Juntto's lap and started to go toward Katie, but Juntto grabbed her hand. He shook his head. "I think it's best if you give her a minute alone. You'll know when it's the right time to comfort her. I have a feeling whatever this is, comfort will be the last thing on her mind."

Angie looked at her and back at Juntto. "But she's my sister. Obviously, something terrible happened. She shouldn't have to go through it alone. Remember, we're a family, and that means we're there for each other when something bad happens. We don't leave each other to cry alone."

Juntto pressed Angie's hand to his lips. "You're right, but remember that she *isn't* alone. She has the best support system a girl could have right inside her."

Angie sat back down but kept her eyes on Katie. "Right...Pandora."

Juntto nodded. "Let her handle this her way, and when she's done, we'll armor up. When you were mourning what you thought was my loss, I bet she gave you space to breathe and handle things in your own way. Now we'll do that for her. Look. I can see it now, as I've seen it many times before."

Angie furrowed her brow. "See what?"

Together they watched Katie straighten. Her tears were tears of blood, and her eyes were no longer full of grief. They blazed red with fury.

Juntto whispered, "Our angel has become an angel of death."

17

Everything seemed to slow to a crawl in Katie's mind. Even Pandora didn't have any words for her. She could feel Katie's rage swirling wildly, pushing back the soft calm of the angel. The anger fueled a burning desire for revenge. Something was twisting deep in Katie's chest. She pictured her last moments with Brock before he left for the mission. The rose petals. The wine. The bed. She could almost hear his voice echoing in her head. It was an indelible sound, one that would stay with her for the rest of her life—especially if she weren't able to find Brock alive.

She had never felt that way before. She had been angry, hurt, and even destroyed by the death of a teammate, but this was personal. It touched her in a way she couldn't quite understand. She realized that she cared for Brock more than she had ever thought she could, but she didn't want to start thinking about that. If she did, she might stay frozen, standing forever in that hangar bay like Juntto in his frosty sleep. The world would tick by around her, but she would never be able to move forward.

Katie looked grimly from Juntto to Angie. Tears of blood ran down her cheeks, and her eyes burned red with anger. She walked to them, her tears leaving a trail of red behind her. Katie swallowed, mustering the strength to speak. "I need all the special metal you can pull together, and I need it *now*."

Angie stood up, shocked by her friend's fury. "What's going on, Katie?"

Katie closed her eyes. "Brock and his team were at an incursion in Europe. The demons somehow dumped lava over the entire town. The military is calling it a total loss, and anyone MIA is being presumed dead. Brock and his team never checked back in."

Angie put her hand to her mouth and thought about reaching forward, but comfort was clearly not what Katie wanted at that moment. Katie was rigid, her whole body tense. She wanted action, she wanted revenge, and she wanted to show those sonsofbitches that they couldn't do something that terrible and get away with it. Angie whispered, "I'm sorry, Katie."

Katie took another deep breath and spoke as if she had not heard Angie's words. "So yeah, all the special metal we can muster. Start with this base. I'm going to figure out what we have at the home base and what Joshua can give me as fast as possible." Her voice caught, but Katie snarled her final words, "I won't allow them to continue to kill us. *I will not let this go*."

Juntto nodded. "Neither will I."

Angie put her hand on Katie's. "Nor will I."

Katie looked at them, thankful. "I'm going to head to the home base. I need to get prepared for this, and I don't want to do it over the phone."

Juntto joined Angie next to Katie. Angie met her eyes. "Then we'll go with you. Every step of the way, right?"

Katie forced a smile. "Every step of the way. But Juntto? You might want to shrink a bit. Not sure the plane can handle you at that size."

Juntto looked down at himself. "Oh, shit, that's right. Hmm, let's see. What was the name of that actor you liked —the one in the movie where they danced like girls at strip clubs?"

Angie sang out, "Channing Tatum."

Juntto snapped his fingers. "That's it. Give me one second."

Angie and Katie stepped back. Juntto's blue frost giant form melted away, changing into a Channing Tatum look-a-like. His camo gear faded into Magic Mike tear-away pants, and his shirt disappeared altogether. Angie giggled, and even Katie cracked a smile. "Come on, you two."

They left the hangar and went to a waiting plane. Luckily, it had been refueling on the other side of the base when Moloch had rolled through, so it was not damaged. As Katie walked, the vision of Brock resurfaced in her mind. She felt instantaneous anger that she couldn't hold back. Demons. The lava. The bodies of her friends. The thoughts drove her mad.

They boarded the plane and Katie pulled out her phone to call Korbin. By that point, she was enraged again. That was good. If she was angry, she could use it. Korbin answered the phone, surprised. "Katie, good to hear from you. Not much has changed here."

Katie answered softly, "A lot has changed here."

Noting the tone of her voice, Korbin became serious. "What's going on? What do you need?"

"I need all the metal you can spare. I also need any RPG-type weapons you guys have. If it slows down production, I'll personally apologize to the company or the government." She held onto the arm of the chair tightly.

Korbin was writing it down. "Okay. What effect are you looking for?"

Katie breathed in through her nose and out her mouth. She shut the window shade. Right now she preferred the dark. "I need something that will explode."

"Is this for a portal or for a building?"

"A portal. More like *in* the portal."

Korbin paused, thinking about the strange structure of portals. "Maybe we can have something made that would create a lot of pressure."

Katie liked the idea. "Yes. I'll be there soon, and we can get on it. Just go ahead and talk to Joshua."

"I got you."

Korbin hung the phone up stared at it. He'd never heard that tone in Katie's voice before. He got up quickly and jogged out of the main building and across the courtyard to the armory. He winced at the noise and grabbed a pair of headphones off the wall to muffle it. They were attached to a microphone that allowed Joshua to communicate with everyone without constantly shouting.

Korbin clicked on the microphone and switched it to Joshua's channel. "Hey, man, where are you? I got a call from Katie, and I need us to do some brainstorming before she gets here."

Joshua waved from a workstation at the back of the building. "Over here, dude. In the left corner at the desk."

Korbin spotted him and walked over. "Sorry, not used to the new layout."

"Yeah, I have to admit it took me a minute, too. But having assembly upstairs and admin above that really keeps things on point. So, Katie's coming? What's she looking for?"

Korbin nodded toward the soundproof meeting room. "We should go in there for a bit more privacy."

Joshua lifted an eyebrow, not knowing exactly what that meant. "Okay."

They walked into the room and clicked off their headsets, hanging them on hooks on the walls. They both took a seat at the long table. Joshua folded his hands together in front of him. "What's going on?"

Korbin shook his head. "I'm not exactly sure, but from the sound of Katie's voice, she means business."

Joshua chuckled. "When does she not mean business?"

Korbin sighed. "True, but this time it's different, I can tell. Something's happened, and I feel like she's on the warpath. She wants as much metal as we can spare. Ammo as well as RPGs. She said if it messes up production, she'll personally apologize to the clients. She also wants something that'll *explode*, or so she explained. I suggested something that has a lot of pressure. I think she wants to vaporize something very big."

Joshua ventured, "Does this have anything to do with the lava drop in Europe?"

Korbin pursed his lips. "I assume it does. I know enough to guess where her mind is at the moment. They want to drop lava on us? Well, we're building a bomb that's going to obliterate a portion of hell. They might think we're the *real* demons after all this."

Joshua took a few notes and looked around the room. "Things sure have changed from the beginning. Just think, it wasn't long ago that we even made our first bullet. Now, I'm creating weapons of mass destruction."

Korbin stood up. "The demons are playing dirty. To me, that tears up all rules of engagement."

Katie was leaning her head against the window, looking out at fat gray clouds. On the other side of the aisle, Juntto admired his new face in his own window. He kind of liked that fellow. He had a good jawline. Angie was curled up against his arm in the seat next to him. Her eyes were shut and she was fast asleep, making him wonder how much sleep she'd gotten while he was away.

Juntto looked at Katie, alone and huddled against her window. He reached across the aisle and tugged her elbow. "Hey, you doing okay?"

Katie sighed and shrugged. "I'm stuck in an airplane when I have a thousand things to do. How are you feeling?"

Juntto half-smiled. "Good as new. Angie said you went

across the world looking for the right energy. How did you know energy was the key?"

"I got a little help from Gabriel," Katie admitted.

Juntto nodded his head. "I see. I'm surprised he helped you. He and I had a run-in several centuries ago. Or more? A long time ago, anyway. It was one of those moments when we weren't looking for each other and didn't have time to battle it out...well, not fully. He left me with a pretty good scar across my lower back, and I got him right in the side. I hear he's the only angel with a scar."

Katie was surprised to hear it. "Didn't think they got scars."

Juntto smiled. "God made them, but He didn't make any creature indestructible."

"No, I suppose not."

Juntto eyes shifted down. "I hope we can find the team."

Katie looked at the ceiling, the grief striking deep in her chest. "I'm trying not to be sad until I know for sure they're gone. Until that's beyond proven, I won't give up on my team. Like I did with you, you know? I didn't give up on you. You were brash and angry, but you were coming around. We'd brought you onto the team, and we weren't going to change our minds about that. There was hope from the moment they froze you, and I made sure everyone thought you were dead until I could find an answer. Even Angie was kept in the dark until after the funeral."

Juntto looked at Angie and whispered to Katie, "Poor girl. She looks like she's been through the wringer. I'm glad we didn't get together sooner. I was an asshole, and I would surely have hurt her."

Katie pointed a finger at him. "I'm still not above removing your balls. Just remember that if you try to slide right back into your old ways."

Juntto put up his hands, chuckling. "Not going back there. Even if I wanted to, I couldn't. My body is different now."

Katie leaned her cheek against the headrest. "I wish I could change the way I felt just by taking a long, cold nap. Might make this all easier to take."

Juntto's face went serious. "I only worked those couple of times with Brock and the others, but they were good guys. He was brave and didn't give two shits about being liked or sugarcoating anything. He said what was on his mind and stuck with it. I respected him for that. I respected all of them, but I know you were close with Brock."

Katie shook her head. "I *am* close with Brock, present tense. I've lost too many people in my life, so I'm not going to give up on them before I know it's true. Brock and the guys are seriously resourceful motherfuckers. They could easily have gotten themselves to a safe place. Maybe they can't check in because their equipment is damaged. I haven't given up yet."

Juntto smiled. "Is that why we're making the mad dash to the base and creating weapons?"

"Yes and no. Whether or not Brock and the others are alive, these demons need to know I'm not fucking around. They will not change the rules without us responding in kind. If they want to come here and drop lava on innocent people, I can make sure they have an even bigger problem in hell. They need to know we're not backing down."

Juntto chuckled. "You would think that by now they would know not to fuck with you or Pandora. They just don't seem to be learning their lesson. It's wild to me that Moloch showed up after he killed all those people. You would've thought he would wait for your response."

Katie wrinkled her nose, not having thought about that. "That's a good point. At the same time, though, he's been trying to catch me off-guard. He might have figured that was the perfect time to come rolling in. Strike again before I had a chance to reevaluate the situation. I don't know why he didn't throw it in my face, though. He seems like the kind of douchebag who likes to fucking brag."

"He definitely is that, but who knows?"

Katie picked up the mug of tea in front of her and took a sip. "Right now, I have to do my part for this war. Then, when that's taken care of, I'll go look for Brock. No matter how long that takes, I need to see it for myself. His absence is not proof. I need evidence, proof I can see with my own eyes that he's gone. As far as I'm concerned, he's out there somewhere waiting for me."

18

The plane touched down on the base, and Katie looked out the window. The base was crawling with soldiers working on what she assumed was damage from their recent fight. Everything looked decent enough, though, and the armory building was still in one piece. Juntto took a deep, nervous breath. Katie noticed he was looking out the window at the quickly-approaching Korbin. She patted him on the shoulder. "He's just a man."

Juntto chuckled. "Yeah, a man who's survived the demon war longer than any human alive today. And he was your teacher when you were first infected. Even Leviathans pay attention to the legendary warriors."

"You need to tell him that. He'll get a kick out of it."

Pandora woke from her nap. *Are we here? Where are my assholes? I've missed them.*

Katie grabbed her bag and climbed out of the plane, immediately giving Korbin a tight hug. He held her longer than usual, sensing something was wrong. When they pulled apart, Korbin lifted his eyes to Juntto, who still looked like Channing Tatum. Katie made the introductions. "Oh, sorry. Korbin, this is Juntto, the Leviathan."

"Frost giant. Leviathan is my title."

"Right. Juntto, this is Korbin."

Juntto bowed and stuck out his hand. "Nice to meet a fellow warrior."

Korbin looked at him strangely but shook the offered hand. "Good to see you aren't frozen anymore."

Juntto glanced toward Angie. "I've got some good friends."

Korbin's eyes twinkled. "Yeah, I think I know what you mean. Okay. Let's head on over to the armory. I know you want to get straight to the nitty-gritty. Joshua started working on your new bomb as soon as we got off the phone. If anyone can help you with this, it'll be him. You know how he is with this stuff."

Katie followed him to the armory. "That I don't doubt. I just want to make sure we are giving those bastards what they deserve."

When they were apart from the others, Korbin pulled Katie to the side. "I know there was an incident with lava, but I can tell there's more. What's going on?"

Katie looked down. "My team, Brock and his guys, were on that mission. They haven't reported back in. The military is considering them KIA."

Korbin tilted his head back. "Oh, man. Oh, *man*, that's fucking brutal. Katie, I'm so sorry. He's a good kid, and one hell of a fighter."

Katie smiled slightly. "One hell of a person, too. I'll let those demons know just how bad they've fucked up."

Walking in single file, their feet moved over the

threshold into the boisterous room. Juntto and Angie took headphones from the wall and sat in a couple of armchairs in a makeshift waiting room. Korbin led Katie to the glass soundproof room at the back of the armory. Inside, Joshua had all kinds of parts laid out and was working on them wearing goggles and long, thick gloves. When they entered, he was maneuvering a few parts with a clamp and forceps. He bit his bottom lip and pressed until a small metal piece clicked into place. He had made a small gun attached to some sort of lever.

Katie reached out to touch it, but Joshua quickly dropped his tool and firmly grasped her wrist. "I haven't made it merc-friendly yet. I wouldn't touch it."

Katie's hand flew to her chest. "Right. Sorry. How's it coming along?"

Joshua pulled his goggles down. "Well, I'm kind of rolling through ideas, creating as I go. I want to do something more intense than an explosion. You want it to be long-lasting. I think just an explosion or implosion will make little impact."

Katie agreed. "So how long until you're done?"

Joshua's eyes fell to the table. He prodded a few parts. "About two days."

Katie's mouth dropped open. "Two *days*? I thought this was something that could be done quickly. God, they could flood ten more cities with lava in those two days."

Korbin cleared his throat, taking over the conversation. Katie was pale-faced and ready to implode. She was clenching her fists so tightly that he could see her knuckles turn white. "Katie, Moloch could do that whether or not you bomb him."

She glared at him and crossed her arms on her chest. Korbin glanced at Joshua briefly, then eyed Katie. "You don't want to rush revenge. You know very well it's a dish best served ice-cold, with a lot of violence and more importantly, results. An explosion will be like fireworks for them. It's not going to be intimidating. Jumping off too quickly reduces results in the military."

Katie's face began to relax slightly. She wrinkled her forehead, putting up her finger.

Korbin slowly lowered her hand down, shaking his head. "Military planning is not an oxymoron, no matter how much you want to think it is."

Katie stuck her hands in her pockets and blew the air from her lungs. Heat flashed across her neck as she looked at Joshua, who was hastily moving through the parts. "I'm sorry, Joshua. I didn't mean to snap at you. Take whatever time you need to make sure we're doing it right."

Joshua's mouth curved up on one side and he tapped his head with his wrench. "I'll do the best I can."

Katie's eyes met Korbin's as she opened the door and headed to the front. She flipped her head toward the main door, and Juntto and Angie quickly followed her outside. Korbin was a few steps behind them, shutting the huge metal door and silencing cacophony of the armory.

Angie rubbed her hands together, feeling the calluses from the weapons she'd used recently. "What's the plan?"

Katie pulled out her phone. "I'm going to call and let the base know it will be a few days. Then I'm going to spend that time in Europe looking for Brock and the team."

Angie's eyes flashed toward Juntto. "We'll go with you."

Pandora cleared her throat. *She should stay behind. Three is a crowd. We don't know what we're walking into or what to expect. Besides, no need to take the plane. I'll take you through a shortcut.*

How?

We're going down.

Down?

Down, baby.

Katie squeezed Angie's small shoulder. "Sit this one out, okay? We're going to be going through hell to get there...literally."

A rush of scalding air cut through the dense forest as a portal cracked open. The Leviathan put one foot on the leaves, his breath fogging in the afternoon sun. He reached back and Katie took his hand, stepping out behind him. Pandora let out the breath she had been holding, and the portal slammed shut.

Katie gripped the piece of paper in her hands, furiously waving it in the air. The paper was red and smoking, a line of red flame moving quickly across the ink-blotted map. Pandora growled. *Don't shake it! Don't you know things burn faster in fucking air?*

Katie clamped her fingers around the edges of the paper, but it was too late—the last burnt bits turned to ash. The wind blew them from her fingertips in a cold breeze. *I'm not the genius who thought bringing a map through hell was a good idea. Now we have to figure out how close we are to the city.*

Pandora yawned. *I would estimate about three miles, give or take. I think. Probably.*

And how the hell do you know that?

Pandora snapped, *Because I'm a demon who travels from place to place all the time. And I haven't been here in...I don't know, three of your lifetimes? It's a ballpark guess. Besides, I know how little you remember after a good humping. Don't give me shit.*

Katie gritted her teeth. *You're fucking impossible. You think you know every damn thing, yet here we are lost in the fucking Carpathian Forest. And guess what, know-it-all? I know that because of all the trees around us.*

Pandora laughed. *Or the fact that I said it before we walked through hell.*

Katie crossed her arms. *Let's ask Juntto. Maybe he can help us.* "Juntto, would you please tell this mouthy bitch..."

Katie turned in a circle, peering at the woods surrounding her. Frost glistened over everything, and the trees were spaced so perfectly it looked like they had been planted that way. It was like a maze of trees. There was no sign of Juntto anywhere.

Katie threw her hands in the air. "Great, now we've lost the Leviathan."

Juntto jumped from the trees above her, landing with a thud in front of Katie. She gasped and stepped back, her feet tangling on a fallen tree limb. Juntto grabbed her arm, pulling her back upright. His cheeks dimpled as he chuckled, little pieces of bark falling to the ground. "We're ten miles away."

She shook her head at him. "Okay, then. That answers *that* question."

Juntto crossed one foot over the other and leaned against one of the trees, taking in the foliage. "I've never actually taken the time to look around the woods when I'm in them. They're quite calming."

Katie rubbed the bridge of her nose, frustrated. "Yeah, great, Jacques Cousteau. I'm definitely not going to walk ten miles. Stand back. I have a shortcut."

Juntto pressed himself against the tree. Katie rolled both shoulders and shut her eyes, letting a puff of air come from her lips. Her long feathered wings sprouted from her back, the m-shaped curve slowly unraveling. The feathers blew gently in the breeze as her wings spread.

Juntto's eyes grew wide, and he hastily stepped forward. "Please tell me you're going to give me a lift."

Katie pursed her lips. "If you shrink to…maybe Peter Dinklage size."

Juntto tilted his head to the side. "Do I know Peter?"

She rolled her eyes. "Tyrion. Tyrion Lannister."

Juntto laughed. "Oh. Why didn't you just say that?"

Juntto shrunk to a smaller size, yet he still looked like Channing Tatum. "That is the strangest thing I've ever seen. I'm pretty sure a miniature Channing Tatum dancing on a chair will forever be burned into my mind. Come on, no time to waste."

Katie stretched her arms out like a mother beckoning her child. Juntto came to her and she picked him up, settling him on her hip. "For a little person, you're mighty heavy."

Juntto nodded. "We tend to be dense."

Pandora snorted. *No shit.*

Katie tried to hide the smirk pulling at the corners of

her mouth. Her head tilted back, and her eyes fixed on the canopy as she ascended through a break in the trees. The branches of the trees rubbed against her wings as she broke into the open air and hovered over the forest.

She could see the city burning in the distance.

Billowing clouds of smoke floated ceaselessly toward the sky. Below, there was a faint shimmering where the fires still burned. Rivers of dark reds and purples flowed throughout the entire town. *Lava.* "Well, I guess we know we're in the right place."

The wind whipped through her hair as Katie soared toward the town. Juntto laughed as he took in the forest from the air, loving the whole idea of flying. Katie's lips twisted into a grin despite the serious nature of her task. The Leviathan was actually having a good time. She found it kind of endearing.

As they got closer, they scanned the area, finding a ramshackle forward operating base set up on a ridge over-looking the town. Katie descended and set Juntto carefully on his feet. Immediately, he grew to over six feet tall and beamed with excitement. "We should see what more we can do while we're searching for people."

Juntto stared hazily at the clouds. Katie snapped her fingers in front of his face. "Juntto. Earth to Juntto."

Juntto shook his hair back and looked at Katie. "Huh?"

Katie closed her eyes for a moment, calming herself, and started quickly toward the tents. When the soldiers saw her, they all stopped what they were doing, their mouths dropping open. The commander of the operation stood in the middle of the base, staring down at a stack of papers and barking orders. "Johnson, you're taking the left quadrant. Johnson? Johnson, goddammit. Am I talking—"

The commander's eyes met Katie's. He fumbled with his papers, passing them off to a soldier standing next to him, and his boots slapped the ground as he jogged to meet Katie. "Katie and…Channing Tatum?"

Katie sighed. "No, this is my friend. He's a shapeshifter."

The commander nodded, taking it all in stride. "Right. General Brushwood didn't tell me you were coming."

Katie looked over the town. "I'm here of my own accord. I have some people out here I'd like to search for. I figured if I can lend a hand while doing so, then hey, why not?"

The commander wasn't going to tell her no. "Right now, we're searching for survivors. There are still a few demons lurking around, so if you're interested in taking care of those, we'd appreciate it."

Katie forced a smile. "Anything I can do."

The commander waved his hand at the soldier holding his papers. "Get me a comm."

Katie shook her head, her face grim at the sight of the town below them. "I can't help staring. I've never seen anything like it—a whole town flooded by lava."

"We're still trying to make sense of it." The commander handed her the comm gear. "If there's anything you need, just let us know."

Katie clipped the relay on her belt and the microphone to her shirt. "Will do."

With that, she and Juntto headed down the hill toward the town. They immediately started to search and found more people than they had thought they would. The people were resourceful, banding together and hiding in all sorts of places out of the lava's reach. They spent all day searching, only occasionally being called to a specific area to take down rogue demons.

By the time the sun was low on the horizon and casting orange and red stripes across the sky, Katie had nearly given up. There was no sign of the guys. The commander walked up next to her and crossed his arms. "Sorry you haven't found your friends yet. Don't lose hope. We've been pulling survivors out all over the place. We set up a tent for you. Hopefully, you can get some rest."

"Thank you." Katie turned toward the base. "Oh, and my friend?"

The commander smiled. "Already sawing logs next to your tent."

Katie waved at him and headed toward the tents, hoping she could get at least an hour or two of sleep. That, however, did not seem likely.

19

The search the next day did not help Katie's mood. Her nerves caused a hollow feeling to spread through the pit of her stomach. In addition to the few survivors, they found bodies. They were completely encased in cooled lava. It gave them a terrifying statuesque appearance. Their faces were haunted and deformed and their mouths hung open, their eyes wide and empty. They almost looked like some sort of eerie art installation. The adults had been caught writhing through the lava rock until they could no longer move. The children had almost all been enveloped on the ground.

Plumes of chemical smoke floated from the ground, burning the inside of Katie's nose. Pandora worked dili-gently to clear the air she was taking into her lungs. Her wings flapped tiredly across the sky with a small Channing Tatum clutched tightly in her arms. He pointed his short arm at a steeple toppled to the side in the distance. "That might be a good place for survivors. It's holy ground."

Katie didn't say a word, just shifted her wings and

glided lower. Her feet hit the church roof. Juntto grew to his regular size and they walked across the singed surface, the sound of cracking shingles ringing in their ears. Katie's eyes combed the rooftop for a way to get inside. Juntto leaped onto the crest of the roof, teetering back and forth on the peak. "Over here. There's a hole in the roof."

They carefully situated themselves at the edges of the jagged hole and peered inside. Katie wrinkled her nose and sighed. "It doesn't look like there's anyone inside. The place did stay fairly clear of lava, though. I wonder if anyone got caught in it trying to escape."

She stepped over the hole and unfurled her wings, steadying herself in case the roof collapsed. She looked over the edge of the church into the yard below. It was covered in a layer of black tar with smoke slowly rising from it. Juntto moved next to her. He shrugged. "Let's go look for bodies."

He stepped off the edge and Katie gasped, sticking her arm out for him. "Don't."

Too late.

Juntto's bare feet hit the ground and he wiggled his toes experimentally, then grinned up at her. Katie jumped into the church, letting her wings carry her gracefully to the ground. "I don't understand. How in the hell are you able to walk on this so soon? It's only been a little over a day since the entire thing happened. I thought for sure this place would still be a smoldering pit."

Juntto cleared his throat, putting up his finger. "I was around when Vesuvius happened, and I learned a thing or two about lava. It only takes ten to fifteen minutes for lava to cool, and that creates an insulating layer sturdy enough to walk on."

Katie's eyes grew wide. She was impressed. "And to think I used to believe you were just a giant hunk of angry alien."

Juntto scowled. "Hey, believe it or not, this giant hunk of alien does have a brain. And may I point out, it's bigger than a human brain."

Katie shrugged. "Something's gotta fill in all the empty space up there."

Juntto glared. "That's not funny, bitch."

Katie pointed her finger at him, her eyes gleaming. "Aha! *There's* the Juntto I know and despise. I was wondering if you were going to walk around for the rest of your days like a wide-eyed church kid."

Juntto grabbed his junk and stuck out his tongue. "I may be caring and thoughtful now, but I didn't lose my sarcasm."

Katie patted him on the arm. "Good to know that not everything in this world is upside-down. Come on, let's look for bodies."

With every step, Katie's heart beat faster. She wondered what she was going to find around each and every corner. The lava's surface was flat, hard, and not as deep as one might think. If anyone had fallen victim to it, their remains would still be visible. The two of them searched the entire building. They went down the cellar stairwell as far as they could but found nothing. Katie walked back up to the main floor and joined Juntto. "I just don't get it. Not a single body here. Maybe no one was at church that time of day."

Juntto peered out at the street and scratched his forehead. "Or they all left when the lava hardened. But you'd think we would have found them, or at least the other soldiers would have. They can't just be wandering around town."

Katie rubbed her palms on her thighs as whispers of Brock's voice floated around in her head. She couldn't bring herself to believe he'd died. He was too strong and too smart for that. She had to believe he figured out a way around the lava, but if that were true, where was he? Katie had no idea what to think.

Moloch stood tall with his shoulders slightly forward, his arms out and his palms up. "You should have seen them, marching their Leviathan out there to save the fucking day. It was disgusting. He's a traitor, and I'd like to see him as dead as Katie. Too bad we don't get the Leviathan souls when they die. He would be a nice addition to my fireplace."

Beelzebub's large hand fiddled with a stack of papers. "The Leviathan should be the least of your concerns. He's just a dumb alien. If his friends die, he'll simply go back into hibernation and be on your side again a century from now, or whenever he's called upon."

Moloch's forehead wrinkled, and he dropped his hands to his sides. "Then we'll focus on that bitch and her demon. I know that joining forces to take out her main base will secure us a win. I need her and fast. Lucifer isn't going to wait forever."

Beelzebub wrapped his clawed hand around a glass and

threw back the contents. Black liquid seeped out of the edges of his mouth, and he wiped it away with his arm. "She can't be as big of a pain as you think. I personally believe it's mind over matter. If the Leviathan hadn't shown up, you would have tired her out and eventually beaten her. She's no walk in the park, I get it. But still, this should be an open-and-shut case."

Moloch crossed his arms and frowned. "You're underestimating her strength and power. She's an angel with Lilith inside of her. That's like a double-fucking-whammy."

The other demon snorted and cleared a wad of spit from his throat. "She's part-angel, which makes a huge difference. Besides, like I told you before, I have demons who can weaken her. In fact, I have the whole plan laid out. You're worrying for nothing at this point. Everything happens for a reason, and you coming to me is exactly what needed to happen. There's no shame in not accomplishing this all on your own."

Moloch chewed the edge of his tongue. He glared at Beelzebub. "The only one who could have done it alone would be Lucifer, and even he wouldn't be able to set foot on Earth without summoning the angel army."

Beelzebub shuffled across the dirt-covered cave floor. His expression never changed, and he responded with very little. Moloch got the feeling he was listening out of courtesy and nothing else. He'd always been a hard-headed sonofabitch. Beelzebub motioned for him to sit, but Moloch didn't move from his spot. There was no way he was sitting on one of those old dusty chairs.

Beelzebub cleared his throat, not noticing Moloch didn't sit. "We'll take care of her, but you'll need to get her here, to hell. At the same time, you'll need to get rid of that bitch Lilith. Weakening her human will allow you to do that. Once you've pulled her out, you can take her by the neck to Lucifer, and he'll forgive your few mistakes."

Beelzebub stood slowly from his chair and put his arm around Moloch's shoulder, ushering him from his cave. They stepped out into the cooler-but-still-blistering heat of the outer ring. Lightning flashed across the black sky. "This is not going to be hard. Lucifer will welcome you back with open arms. You worry too much. It's one of your worst traits."

Beelzebub's mouth curled into an evil smile, and Moloch's followed suit. Beelzebub took a step back and waved his hand, disappearing from sight. As soon as he was gone, Moloch's face fell to a deep frown, his smile no longer needed. "I don't know what I've gotten myself into. If this doesn't work, Lucifer will be wearing my nuts as a necklace."

Katie's feet tapped to the sound of the radio playing in one of the tents behind her. She was back at the HQ, taking a dinner break. She planned to go back out before the sun started to go down. She wanted to search as much of the town as she could. It wouldn't be long until the military was done and pulled out, but she couldn't let that happen without figuring out what had happened to Brock and his team.

When her phone rang, she leaned her head back and stuck her hand in her pocket to pull out her phone.

Korbin's name flashed onto the screen. "Hey, Korbin. Tell me something good."

Korbin chuckled. "Well, we finally have the right weapon. It's time for you to come back. We are ready for you as soon as you get here."

Katie's eyelids were low as she stared at the quiet town in front of her. "Right. Okay. I'll grab Juntto, and we'll head back as soon as we can."

Before she could hang up, Korbin added, "Katie, did you have any luck with Brock?"

Her heart fluttered in her chest, and she quietly shook her head. "We haven't found him yet. We've rescued some survivors and killed the rest of the demons, but there's no sign of the team."

Korbin knew that wasn't the worst news. "That could be good, though. That could mean they got out. Maybe they sought medical attention in another town or something. From the pictures on the news, it doesn't look like you'd be able to miss a body if it were there. The lava was brutal, obviously, but not deep."

Katie pulled herself to her feet. "Yeah, I suppose that's true. Anyway. I'll grab Juntto. See you in a bit. I want to get this shit going."

Pandora mustered her strength as they walked away from the HQ. *Don't worry, we'll come back and look for him. Right now, we have to maneuver our way back to the base.*

Katie stared at Juntto's back as she walked. *Right, and*

don't forget to bring us out a little bit away so we don't have any of those bastards following us back.

Pandora could feel the energy gathering over her. *Aye-aye, Captain. Now hold still, I'm ready.*

Katie tapped Juntto on the shoulder and gave him a nod. The two stopped on the outskirts of the woods and turned their bodies toward the setting sun. Pandora lifted Katie's arm and formed a claw. She slashed downward, ripping a portal in midair. Juntto stepped through first and Katie followed him, staring at the ground as she walked. As soon as she was through the portal, a heavy hand pushed her stomach. She stumbled to one side as a demon lunged at her with its fangs out.

Katie grabbed her sword off her back and slashed it in a wide arc, taking the demon's head off. *Wow. Drop us right in the middle of a demon fucking disco.*

Pandora growled. *It's not a perfect science, bitch.*

Katie felt the need to let off a little steam. *Well, while we're here, why not?*

Juntto was already in action, grabbing demons by the arms and ripping them in half. Katie smiled and jumped up and down, the adrenaline starting to pulse through her. She gripped her sword tightly as she slashed it through the air, slamming into a demon's forehead. The sound of the scales cracking and skin tearing was music to her ears. There was no holding back at that point. Katie whirled through the group, taking off limbs, heads, and anything else her sword touched.

The last demon faced her, his arms curved to grab her and his veins popping out of his black skin. He showed his pointy, jagged teeth and raced toward her. Katie screamed as he ran at her, holding the sword to one side like a baseball bat. She swung hard, but instead of decapitating the creature she lodged the blade in the demon's neck. She put her foot on his chest and yanked it out, dropping it to the ground. From her holsters, she pulled Tom and Harry and pointed them at his head. "Fuck you, motherfucker."

With that, her finger firmly pulled the trigger and sent bullet after bullet into the demon's skull. She walked forward, screaming, until she stood over him, emptying her guns into the demon's chest. She ran out of bullets but continued to pull the trigger, listening to the hollow clicking. Juntto put his hand on her shoulder. "We should go."

It was like he had broken a trance.

Katie looked down at the pile of ash beneath her feet and holstered her guns. "Fine."

She let Pandora rip open another portal. They stepped through into a field about two miles from the base. Katie didn't say a word; her face was frozen in disgust. She grabbed Juntto without asking him to change and spread her wings.

Juntto whooped loudly as they flew toward the base. He put out his arms and Katie grunted, her fingers digging into his stomach to keep him in the air. "Don't squirm or you'll be a pile of smashed Juntto."

Juntto laughed wildly, his eyes excited and his hair blowing in the wind. "I would more likely put a crater in the ground before I hurt myself, but thanks for looking out for me."

Katie wrinkled her face, grunting. "I'm looking out for myself, but yeah, you're welcome. Still, stop fucking fidgeting, or I'll carry you upside down by your ankles."

Given the way he wiggled in her hands, that didn't seem like a deterrent. Katie ignored him and kept her eyes on the base. She was impatient. She didn't want to waste any time getting back to Romania. Brock could still be out there, and she had to find him.

As they lurched over the fence, Katie put her feet toward the ground, sweat beading her forehead as she lowered Juntto. She landed behind him, breathing heavily.

Juntto clapped his hands. "That was awesome. Thank you."

Katie cracked her back. "Sure."

Both their heads snapped up as Angie opened the door to the barracks and waved at them. Katie replied with a short wave while Juntto put his fist in the air. Angie giggled and put her other hand in the air, holding up an Xbox controller. Juntto pumped his fist and took off toward her, looking back with a huge grin at Katie. She couldn't help but smile.

Pandora groaned. *God, love is so disgusting these days. You got Leviathans and humans and you—you who kill people with your vagina.*

Katie's face went blank. *First of all, if that were the case, he would have kicked it a long time ago. Secondly, don't shit on their happiness. They just want to chill and play whatever game it is they play together. It's been a while, remember? He was a giantsicle.*

Pandora blew a raspberry. *Oh, please. That's not what they're dying to do together. Did you see what Angie was wearing? Where did she get a pair of short silk shorts and a flowy tank top out here?*

Katie hadn't even noticed. *Probably from Stephanie or Timothy. It's not like we brought a ton of clothes with us.*

Pandora giggled. *Yeah, well, I bet he doesn't play three games before Angie is boinking his brains out. The tension between the two of them is thick enough to trip over. They are like two rhinos in heat. I wonder if he can change his dick when he changes characters?*

Katie frowned. *Just stop. Please, for the love of God, stop.*

20

A crowd was gathering outside the soundproof room in the armory. The girls had taken a break for lunch, but instead of dispersing like usual, they wanted to see what was going on. Joshua was focused completely on the large bomb he was assembling.

Two of the girls stood close, their hands clenched as they watched him. Keira breathed, "I call this his science mode."

The other girl flinched when he moved another wire. "I call this a dangerous thing to be doing in a building full of explosives."

Keira sighed and pursed her lips. "I think that thing right there is huge enough that if it went off a mile from us, we'd be fucked. It might be a quicker death if we're right next to it."

Her friend let go of Keira's hand and stared at her with a straight face. "You are the worst at comforting someone."

She rolled her eyes. "Oh, come on. We fight demons and make weapons. How soft can you possibly be?"

The girl clicked her tongue and nodded rapidly. "Okay, you're right. I was being a drama queen. Probably better if we're right up close."

Korbin pushed open the front door, looking down at his phone as he entered. He took several steps before realizing there was no noise from the machinery. He stopped. He raised his head slightly, the fear nipping at the back of his neck overtaken by curiosity. He spotted the group of women gathered around the soundproof booth, whispering to each other. He could make out the top of Joshua's head inside the room, but he couldn't see what he was doing.

Katie's hands ran over the edge of the chair she was sitting in to watch Joshua work. She had been doing that since she'd gotten there, and she hadn't wanted to disturb him. The door opening brought her attention to Korbin as he came into the room. His eyes landed on Katie as if he'd been looking for her. "How's everything going?"

Joshua lifted one finger to silence them. He was staring down at a small screen. He carefully set the screen inside the bomb and closed the metal door over it. His fingers pressed against the glass and a green light began to flash. "I think I got it."

Katie stood up so fast the room spun a bit, but she wasn't about to stop for that. "Okay, so what do we have here?"

Joshua rubbed his hands together proudly. "We have a specialty weapon that will only be harmful to those in an atmosphere like hell's or Damned standing nearby. You launch this sucker straight into hell and walk away. Preferably, you aim it and know where it's going, but firing blindly would probably work too. It would just be less dramatic."

Katie examined the thing. "And it does what?"

Joshua smiled evilly. "Well, the bomb has a liquid H_2O core with an emulsified powdery substance mixed in, none other than my special metal. When the bomb hits, the core will break, spilling its contents into the streams of lava. Special metal mixed with simple water will create a steam cloud."

Katie let her head fall slightly back, and her shoulders went slack. "We're going to kill demons with steam?"

Joshua laughed. "Not just any steam, my friend. This is going to be a steam cloud of death. The combination of chemicals in the lava will interact with the special metal particles, and the cloud will spread through hell. Anything that breathes it will ultimately suffer a terrible and very painful death. It's probably the most amazing thing this armory has ever created."

Korbin looked at it nervously. "And probably extremely fucking dangerous in the wrong hands."

Joshua nodded reluctantly. "Which is why I only made one. We'll make sure this baby goes off when it hits the lava. Once it's broken open and airborne, there's no way they'll be able to replicate it. The sheer heat of hell will evaporate the water almost immediately."

Katie smiled and slapped Joshua's back. "Well done, Einstein. Well done."

Korbin leaned across a dining table toward Katie,

Stephanie, and Calvin and waved his hands as he told a story from when Calvin was new to the team. "I swear, he looked like his whole body was going to explode right then and there. It was amazing."

Calvin's cheeks were red and hot, and he shook his head. "Hey, I was new to all of it. That fucking demon had three heads. Three not-so-attractive heads, I might add."

Katie laughed and patted Calvin on the shoulder. "It's okay. We've all had at least one piss-your-pants moment, like Juntto with the ice cream man demon."

Angie and Juntto were whispering in the corner, not realizing they were being discussed. Everyone stared at them until they looked over in confusion, and a roar of laughter filled the room. Katie looked at her friends, remembering what it was like to be together with a team so close that they were family. Except for Brock and his team, of course. As soon as the thought crossed her mind, she couldn't shake the sick feeling in her chest.

When the laughter died down, everyone went sullen, remembering reality. Stephanie took a deep breath and grabbed an empty tray that had once held a dozen donuts. "Well, we've still got an hour of light outside. We could all go out there and enjoy the fall breeze. I think I have a couple of bottles of wine in the fridge."

Korbin scoffed. "Try like ten, but okay. I need to build this woman a wine cellar."

Stephanie spun, almost losing the tray. It flipped in the air and she clapped her hands together, sandwiching it in between her palms. "Finally, you catch on."

The door to the dining hall flew open, and Timothy raced in with his tablet. "A portal. There's a portal."

Everyone stood up quickly, Calvin's chair falling over and hitting the floor. Korbin held up a hand. "Okay, calm down. Tell me where."

Timothy put one hand on his hip and breathed in and out repeatedly. He could barely get his lungs to take in air, much less speak. After a moment of everyone staring at him with confused looks on their faces, he pointed straight up. "The sky. Above us."

Korbin ran to the door, hitting a red button on the wall. Emergency lights started to flash, and sirens howled overhead. "Everyone, grab your weapons and gear up. We want to be on top of this one."

Timothy stepped quickly over to Korbin. He tapped him on the shoulder and held up his tablet. "Everyone obviously should be in place regardless, but why don't we try out our new anti-aircraft guns first? Let's see if we can send them back before they hit the ground."

Korbin bit the inside of his lip and stared at the screen. "They can be aimed where the portal is being detected?"

Timothy nodded. "Yep."

Korbin ran his eyes over the room and everyone paused, looking at him. "Okay. Gear up and meet me outside, but no one fires until I give the word. We spent a shit-ton of money and time on these guns, so let's see exactly what they can do."

The whole team hurried to grab their weapons from the training room, then ran out the side door. They swerved around the corner and came to a stop next to Korbin. Their defenses included six anti-aircraft guns, all remotely controlled from Timothy's tablet. Katie stood shoulder to shoulder with Calvin and Juntto, holding her pistols in her hands. A huge flash of light tore across the sky, and a portal appeared above them.

Timothy pressed his tongue between his lips as he adjusted the position of the guns. "Ready and in position. Tell me when to fire."

Korbin narrowed his eyes, watching the dark hot abyss swirling above the main building. As soon as the first demons began to drop, he pointed at Timothy. "Fire!"

Timothy said a prayer and pushed a button on his tablet, and the guns instantly started firing round after round. They rotated slightly, sprayed bullets from one end of the portal to the other. As the demons fell, they turned to dust, disintegrating before they could hit the roof of the building. The guns continued to fire for another three minutes.

Korbin waved his hand at Timothy. "Okay, hold off.

Timothy turned the guns off, and they watched the portal with bated breath. The flow of demons had stopped.

"Let's see what's next."

The portal wavered and flickered for a moment before slamming shut. Everyone jumped into the air, cheering loudly. The soldiers behind them cheered as well, holding their guns up over their heads. Korbin hugged Stephanie tightly and kissed her on the cheek. "Nice work, Timothy. Nice fucking work."

Pandora sniffed the air. *Don't start celebrating just yet.*

Katie's head snapped toward Timothy. "Check your radar."

Timothy's smile fell as he switched screens. His eyes went wide, and he spun around, looking across the field. "Another one. There's another one coming just on the other side of the base. These guns can rotate, but they can't do a one-eighty."

Korbin hefted his assault rifle and nodded at the others. "This one we blast from here. Men, when that portal opens, shoot it with everything you've got."

The soldiers got into formation. A line of men got down on one knee and steadied their rifles. Katie gripped the thick handles of her pistols. Her eyes found Juntto, who was already looking to Katie for orders. The same deafening crack echoed across the marsh, and a hot wind blew across the base. The portal split wide open and was met with a shower of gunfire from everyone on the base.

Juntto fired at the portal with a borrowed rifle, but he scooted closer to Katie. "We should be out there. We can take those bastards."

Katie fired one more bullet. "You read my fucking mind."

She holstered her guns and found Korbin. "Keep firing. Juntto and I are going to flank them. You guys hold the line in case any of the demons get past us."

Calvin ceased firing. "I'm coming too."

Katie squeezed his shoulder. "I wouldn't expect anything less."

The three of them took off to the right, going around the gunfire to avoid being shot. The last thing Katie wanted was to end up with a bullet in her back. She had way too much to do to worry about that. Juntto roared loudly as he raced forward, ready to take down demons.

The beasts poured out of the portal, angrier than Katie had ever seen them.

They were small but ferocious, jumping in groups and

piling on top of one another to get at the three of them. Katie fired with deadly accuracy, shooting as many as she could as Juntto ripped through the horde throwing heads all over the place. Calvin was a bit taken aback by their anger and danced in and out of the demons, slashing his short sword through their skulls.

Korbin put up his hands. "Hold your fire. Let Katie, Calvin, and Juntto do their thing for a minute. We don't want to accidentally hit any of them."

Angie wiped the sweat from her forehead. "Please. We've had enough of that lately."

Stephanie frowned and slid her hand into Korbin's. They stood watching the demons rage, slashing their claws violently. Whenever one would break the line and head toward the base, a soldier would light it up, blasting it into dust.

Stephanie's face was contorted in horror. Timothy stood there with his tablet pressed to his chest, his mouth slightly open. "I've never seen those baby demons move like that. It's like someone filled them with caffeine, shook em' up, and let em' loose. Damn."

"They're getting stronger and fiercer," Stephanie agreed. "I haven't seen a battle rage like this one in a very long time."

Korbin's breath caught as he took it in. "I know. Everything about these demons has been drastically evolving."

He relaxed his brow and squeezed Stephanie's hand tighter. His eyes shifted down to hers, and he brushed his other hand across her cheek. "We knew one day the war would really kick into high gear. I'm not worried, though. We have a good leader and everything we could need to fight them. Let's just hope those three can handle themselves out there. They've moved in front of the target, so unless we want to shoot them, we can't fire as a group."

Stephanie gulped and glanced at the long scar that went up her arm, a relic from her first fight after Katie had brought her back. She would never sacrifice her friends to fight off the demons, but she sure as hell wasn't looking forward to hand-to-hand combat.

Timothy scooted closer to Stephanie and took her other hand. She tried to give him a reassuring smile.

He stared at Katie, Juntto, and Calvin, who were fighting the wave of snarling beasts. Behind them, the sky was growing darker by the second. "Maybe we should go out there and help them. You know, give them backup?"

Stephanie tightened her grip on his hand. "Our leader gave us orders, and we're going to follow them. We'll be okay. They're just a bunch of ferocious little bastards this time around. But then again, when are they not?"

Timothy smacked his lips. "I think all they need is a week-long spa retreat and some really nice shoes. That will make anyone happier."

Stephanie's lips curled into a smile. "You're so good in these situations. You could make me laugh if I was holding a head in my hand."

Timothy shook his head, his eyes closed. "*No*, ma'am. You are not ruining that manicure."

A loud bang sounded, and everyone turned their attention to Katie. She was whaling on a medium-sized demon. They watched as the three bodies fought valiantly in the night, stomping out as many demons as they could. Timothy pulled his tablet back and started pressing buttons. "I should turn on the lights out there. That might help."

As soon as he pressed the button the great spotlights flashed on, blinding the soldiers for a split second. Stephanie's hand flew out and grabbed Timothy's arm. "What the fuck just happened? A moment ago we had three people fighting those demons out there. Then you flipped the lights on."

"So?"

"Look. Now there are only two."

21

Located in the southern part of Kangding in Sichuan China, Minya Konka towered above the clouds. Better known as Mount Gongga, the Chinese mountain was white from bottom to top, and the weather was always cold and rainy. The air was thin and quiet on the seven-thousand-meter peak of the mountain. Very few ventured to these parts, and only twenty-four humans had ever reached the top.

On that rainy October day, the clouds sat below the peaks, and the horizon was a zigzag arena of mountainous terrain. On the tallest peak of the range, a loud snap echoed, sending a heat wave down the ice-covered slope. A large demon stepped out onto the icy ground, the snow and slush immediately melting beneath him. Steam rolled off his shoulders and back as he looked out over the horizon.

The muscles in his back began to twitch as he turned, revealing Baal's furrowed brow and snarling lips. He shivered, patting both sides of his arms. "Fucking nonsense. It's cold as fuck up here."

His hands went to his hips as he scanned the top of the mountain. Slowly, he pulled a rolled-up map from the fanny pack around his waist, then zipped the pouch again and unrolled the map. He ran his finger down the parchment but glanced up from time to time, trying to figure out where the hell he was. A strong burst of wind swirled around the mountaintop, and he lost control of one side of the map. He grumbled as he caught it and turned his back to the wind.

He looked up again, seeing two slightly shorter peaks across from him. "All these damned mountaintops look alike. Why can't the assholes who make maps smarten them up a bit?"

Grumbling as his feet sloshed through the mud and stone beneath him, his eyes narrowed as he squinted into the distance. His eyes moved from one fixed point down to the map, back up to a mountaintop, then to the map one last time. He snorted loudly, the air rippling the map. He lifted the paper and turned it from side to side, finally nodding and flipping it over. "Ahh."

He pointed to one place on the map and glared to his right. Sighing, he shook his head and rubbed his nose on his arm. "Well, *that* might be the right one."

He rolled the map back up and shoved it into his fanny pack. Zipping it again, he shivered, all the scales on his body vibrating against his flesh. He swiped his hand down diagonally, and a gate opened with a loud crack where he stood. "Well, here's hoping."

Baal disappeared into the gate, and it slammed shut behind him.

Calvin was buried in a swarm of snarling demons. He slashed and cut, and still they came.

His short sword bit into a demon's skull, and it burst into dust. More demons pushed against him, and he leaned back as a demon's claw flew at his face. He snarled and narrowed his eyes. "You fucking ass, you almost cut this beautiful face."

The demon roared loudly, spattering spit all over Calvin's visage. He closed his eyes and wiped his hand across it. When he opened them, the demon was charging again. "Oh, that's the last straw, motherfucker."

He struck out hard with his right leg, planting his foot right under the demon's chin. Its whole body flew back and Calvin pounced, swirling his sword in a circle and slicing the demon's head off its shoulders. Katie was a few feet away and looked down as the head bounced to her and turned to dust. "Nice one."

Calvin took a bow, stabbing a demon behind him as he did. "Why, thank you. I'll be here all week."

Katie laughed as she grabbed a demon by the neck and flipped over him. She landed and pressed her forearm to his throat, then placed her palm flat on its forehead. With a quick snap, she broke the thing's neck. The demon crumpled to the ground, turning to dust. Calvin nodded. "Not a lot of flare but I like it. Simple and to the point."

They both looked at Juntto. He raged, ripping his shirt

open and then grabbing two demons. He slammed their heads together until they went limp in his hands and finally exploded into ash.

Calvin grimaced, but Katie giggled. Calvin hadn't seen him fight like that before. "Yo, your boy is scary as fuck. Just thought you should know."

Katie took off at a run toward Juntto, giving Calvin a thumbs-up. She soared through the air, slamming her foot into the neck of one of the demons sneaking up on Juntto. Juntto whirled but stopped in his tracks when he saw Katie. Pandora tilted her head. *Aw, you calm him like Betty Ross calmed the Hulk.*

Katie slammed her fist into another demon's face, breaking its nose. *Yeah, except she died at the hand of Hulk's arch-nemesis.*

Pandora cleared her throat as Katie shot the demon in the face. *True, but as we learned last week, she's been resurrected.*

Katie shook her head, backing up toward Juntto as more demons approached. *I don't want to be resurrected. If I die, leave me dead, please. At least then I can sleep.*

Katie pulled out Tom and Harry and fired into the oncoming horde. Pandora sighed. *You would think that, but the afterlife comes with a lot of jobs and responsibilities. If you're looking for rest and relaxation, look elsewhere.*

Great. More missed sleep. Wonderful.

A loud hum reverberated throughout the courtyard, and all of the demons began to turn. The portal was clos-ing, and they made a mad dash home before it did. The demons had started to learn that when they were left on

Earth, very few returned unscathed. In fact, most who returned were banished to the depths of hell for failing.

Juntto swung around as Calvin jogged up. "The portal is still open."

Calvin turned to watch. "It's doing something weird."

Katie pulled out her knives and moved her eyes from right to left. "What do you guys say we kick some of these demon's asses? Make it harder for them to come back here."

Calvin raised his short sword and nodded. "Hell, yeah. Been a while since I got to fight with my girl."

Pandora giggled. *My black hero. Swangin' dicks and breakin' legs.*

Katie tried not to make a face, but Calvin noticed. "I miss you, too, Pandora!"

Juntto chuckled at the two and raised his arms, stretching. "You know I'm always down for a bit of massacre and fear. I mean, hell, it's been quite a while."

Juntto clapped his hands and took off through the demons, coming to a sliding stop about seven feet from a medium-sized beast. It froze, its eyes wandering over Juntto's body. It could tell what Juntto was. It was just trying to decide what to do with him. Juntto yawned and snapped his fingers to wake the demon up. "Are we going to fight here, or are you going to ogle me like a fangirl?"

The demon snarled and ran at Juntto, who took a knee and flipped the demon over him. The frost giant swirled around and slammed his fist into the demon's head, crushing its skull. Juntto shook the blood off his fingers, wrinkling his nose. "Fucking gross."

The demon turned to ash beneath him. Juntto watched

as Katie and Calvin sliced and stabbed demons, one after the other. He looked at his bloodied fist, then at their blades. "I really need Juntto-sized weapons. Then I won't be stuck human-sized during fights."

Katie kicked a demon in the nuts and yelled, "Right, but how many times do you actually get bigger?"

Juntto shrugged his shoulders. "Not often."

Katie slid her knives into their sheaths and spun, kicking four demons in the chest as she whirled. When her foot came to a stop, she pulled her guns and fired until there was nothing left except a circle of ash. She let out a deep breath and put her guns down, looking across the courtyard. "We got them all, I think, or at least those that didn't flee back into the portal…which is still open."

Juntto and Calvin stood beside her and stared at the swirling portal. "Maybe they forgot. You know, like leaving the front door open or something."

Katie raised an eyebrow. "Or this is just the beginning."

As if caused by her words, the portal vibrated slightly and split open wider. A blast of heat and energy hit the three of them like a wall and threw them back. They slid across the ground and came to a stop, dirt and grass all around them. Katie shook her head, her ears ringing. Pandora sniffed. *Oh hell, not again.*

Juntto, Katie, and Calvin looked up as Moloch stepped through the portal, growling as he came. He was healed except for the slight limp. He put both clawed feet on the ground and clenched his fists, his body growing until it towered over them.

Moloch looked around and began to laugh. Muscles twitched violently in his arms and thighs as he came to a stop. "Pathetic humans. You can't even stop a small incursion. Look at this mess. And what did you think—pointing guns at my other gate was going to stop me from coming here? Pathetic!"

He bellowed louder, showing his sharp, pointed teeth. Saliva dripped from his fangs and splashed on the ground. He spotted Juntto and Calvin scrambling to their feet. Katie was already up, and this time she wasn't fucking around. She pulled in her energy and lifted her arms, and a bright flash of light stopped Moloch's laughter in its tracks.

Her golden armor snapped to her body. A heavenly sword appeared in one hand, a shield in the other. She took off across the lawn, screaming the pain and grief that had been consuming her. Before Moloch could move, she was in the air slicing her sword across his stomach. She flew past him and rolled forward, hitting the ground and tumbling a few feet before finding her legs.

Moloch put his hand on the cut and licked the blood off his fingers. An eerily calm smile spread across his lips. "Bitch, you don't scare me anymore. You aren't even fully an angel. You were only able to kill T'Chezz because he was weak!"

Juntto lumbered toward them, his gaze locked on Katie's. She nodded, and Juntto began to grow. Channing Tatum disappeared and in his place was the original blue badass frost giant, pumped and ready for a fight. He slammed a fist hard into Moloch, and the two faced off. They grappled like massive wrestlers as Juntto attempted to push him back through the portal. Calvin sprinted to Katie and looked at her shield. "That's a nice touch."

"You know me—go big or fucking go home. I'm tired of

this sonofabitch ruining my plans. Come on, let's give him a little leg action."

Katie wiggled her eyebrows and Calvin laughed, pulling out his sword. "I go right, you go left?"

Katie opened her mouth to agree when the portal flashed again. Another demon stepped through, this one larger and even stronger than Moloch. Katie stopped in her tracks, wrinkling her nose and staring at the crooked beast. *Who the fuck is that?*

Pandora snarled. *Fucking Beelzebub. I should have known. I bet he's the one behind this lava bullshit.*

As soon as Katie heard the word "lava" she saw red. The metal of her sword hilt warmed in her hand, and she gripped it tighter. Staring at the beast, she snarled, "Okay, Calvin. Plan's changed. Let's take both of them down."

Calvin whooped and ran toward Moloch, slicing his sword across the demon's large ankles.

Katie ran toward Beelzebub, her shield held high in front of her. She slammed into the demon, expecting the force to knock him back. Instead, she bounced off of his scales, falling backward onto her ass. Beelzebub looked down at Katie and began to laugh. "*This* is the human you were so terrified of? She's pathetic."

Pandora was fuming mad. *What the fuck is he doing here? He was exiled to the outer rings decades ago. Now he's fighting alongside Moloch. Oh, girl, I think something crazy is going on. We may have just entered a whole new level of the War of the Damned.*

Katie stood and shook the dirt from her hair, backing up. *What does that mean?*

Pandora sighed. *I don't fucking know. I need more information. What the piss is happening here?*

Katie couldn't just stand still. Calvin and Juntto were still fighting Moloch. Katie spun back around to face Beelzebub and found his face was level with hers, huge and crooked. Katie gasped and slammed her shield into his nose. He winced and backed up, rubbing his face.

Katie shouted, "What the fuck do *you* have to do with this fight? If you're looking for glory, you came to the wrong damn place. We own this planet, and neither you nor your lackeys are going to take it from us."

Beelzebub laughed loudly, putting his hand on his stomach. "You stupid bitch, I will take what I want whenever I want to take it. It so happens that today I'm here for you."

Pandora screamed, *Shit. Get out of there!*

Before Katie could react, Beelzebub's hands were swinging toward the ground. As they made thunderous contact, bolts of electricity shot in every direction. Katie put up her shield, and the electricity slammed against the metal, then dissipated. She slowly picked her head up and narrowed her eyes. Her teeth ground against each other, and she bolted forward, swinging her sword as hard as she could. The blade cut through Beelzebub's massive leg and he wailed, tumbling to the ground.

Katie's eyes grew wide as she watched him trip over his feet and smash into Moloch. Juntto backed up as they rolled across the marshland. Katie pumped her fists but slowly stopped. Lying on the ground where the demon had stood was Calvin, his head bleeding and his body twitching. "Calvin!"

She ran to his side and knelt beside him. He blinked his eyes until Katie came into focus. "What the hell happened?"

Katie wiped the blood away from his forehead. "I'm so sorry. I didn't think he would fall into Moloch like that. This is all my fault. You never should have been in harm's way."

Calvin reached up and batted at her long dark hair. "You know, this is probably the fourth time I've seen you with your hair down. Looks good."

Calvin was lying half-dead in the marsh, and he *still* couldn't help thinking about other people. Tears sprang to Katie's eyes. "Oh, God. Just hold on, okay? I'll get you out of this fight. You just have to hold on. Don't give in to whatever pain you feel."

Pandora yelled. *Drag him to the sidelines. I've got an idea. Just get him out of harm's way. Those two fools will kill him faster than they can say my name.*

Katie swallowed hard and carefully picked him up. She groaned as she tossed him over her shoulder and ran him to safety far from the snarling demons. His blood ran over her shoulder with every step she took.

When she reached the edge of the courtyard, she laid him gently on the ground. He coughed. Blood splattered through his teeth and down his chin. Katie didn't know what to do, and panic was taking over. *Pandora, you have to do something. What is this? He's fucking dying.*

Pandora hushed her. *Calm your fucking tits, woman. I'm working on it. I need it to be fucking quiet.*

Katie looked back over her shoulder. Juntto was taking on both of the huge demons at once. He was strong, but she wasn't sure how long he'd be able to keep that up. She was strong as hell, and fighting only one of them had exhausted her. The demons were powerful—more so than ever, it seemed. At that moment, she missed Brock and the team. If they had been there, things would have been different. They would have been fighting their asses off. But that wasn't the way that it had turned out.

Pandora took a ragged breath. *Okay, here's what we are going to do.*

Pandora whispered in Katie's head, letting her know every aspect of the plan. Katie wasn't sure it would work, but they couldn't sit around waiting for something to happen. *Okay. If you think it'll work, let's fucking do this.*

Katie scooted on her knees back to Calvin's side and took his hand in hers. "Do you trust me?"

Calvin chuckled. "With whatever is left of my life. Why?"

Katie shook her head. "I just need to know you're open to me."

Pandora barged in using Katie's voice. "Hey, big man. Pandora here."

Calvin smiled his bloody smile. "Well, look who the cat drug in. I was starting to wonder if you were real, but I remember seeing you across the table from me. I watched you fight those assholes for our freedom."

Pandora smiled. "You're keeping tabs on me, are you? I thought you had a girlfriend."

Calvin laughed, then winced as the muscles on the left side of his body cramped up. "Hey, Pandora, you got any magic up that sleeve that can help me heal? I don't think my demon can handle this level of injury."

Pandora leaned close to his ear and whispered the plan

to him. His eyes immediately darted to hers. "Are you sure?"

Pandora nodded, then gave their body back to Katie. Calvin saw the change in her eyes. "Katie? Are you sure?"

Katie gave him a grin. "Hell, yeah, I'm sure. Let's get this shit over with, shall we? Those sneaky motherfuckers aren't going to take one more thing from our lives. Not our friends, not our family, nothing."

Calvin reached up and grabbed Katie's hand, his arm shaking. "Fuck, yes!"

Katie nodded. *Okay, Pandora, you're on. I hope you know what you're doing. This guy's important to me.*

Pandora drew energy around her and turned Katie's body toward Calvin. He lay on the ground staring at her, then gasped. His body twitched and was still. For a moment Katie thought Calvin had died, but when his eyes began to glow, it was obvious Pandora was up to her old tricks.

Katie leaned forward and whispered into Calvin's ear, "Stay down there like you're injured. Wait until this plays out before giving them any inkling of what's going on. Understand?"

Calvin nodded slightly and relaxed to the ground. He faked several coughs as Katie clenched her fists and stood up, her back to the two demons. She mustered her angelic powers, her jaw clenched and her eyes blazing blue. The anger and angst of the loss of Brock and his team gave her the extra fuel she needed.

Moloch stepped aside as Beelzebub was fighting Juntto. He could see Katie standing over Calvin. "Hey, human meatsack. You just gonna stand there or you gonna join the fight? Or hell, are you sending in Juntto because you don't care if he lives?"

Katie spun, her eyes shimmering blue before dimming to a dull red. She clapped her hands, and her armor and weapons disappeared. She grabbed the front zipper of her shirt and slowly pulled it down to reveal her heaving cleavage. Because Pandora had created them, her massive breasts stood up on their own, violating the laws of gravity—and morality laws in several states.

Katie bit her lip and began walking toward Moloch. She used every bit of seduction she could conjure. Her hips swayed from side to side, and her ass jiggled in time with her steps. Her lips curled into a feral grin. Moloch stumbled over his words for a second as he watched her. Katie laughed loudly. "Oh, poor Moloch. Never seen a pair of these before? Doesn't surprise me, since you are a straight-up cocksucker."

Moloch snarled and then roared as Katie lunged toward him at full speed. She put her arm up and summoned her shield and sword again. The gold on the shield reflected the overhead light, blinding Moloch for a moment. He put his arm up to block the light as she barreled forward and she went low, jamming her sword into the top of his foot.

Moloch screamed and began jumping up and down holding his bloody foot, Katie's sword was still protruding from it. After a couple of seconds he slammed it down, the rage on his face growing more intense by the second. Katie put her hand out, flipping her wrist. The sword flew from his flesh and landed firmly back in her hand. "You want some more?"

Moloch swiped at Katie, but she dropped to the ground

and rolled to the right. His deadly claws grazed the top of her head. Behind Moloch, Beelzebub grabbed Juntto by the neck and threw him. The frost giant landed with a crash, sliding in the dirt beside Calvin and groaning as he came to a stop.

Beelzebub turned, watching Moloch fighting Katie. He smiled and slashed his hands through the air, creating a new gate. The heat rays quivered at the edges of the portal. Katie pushed herself back to her feet and looked at Korbin and the others. She really hoped this was going to work. Otherwise, she was going to be completely screwed.

Beelzebub called to Moloch, "*Now*! Don't waste time. Do it *now*!"

Moloch growled, swiping his hand and grabbing Katie. She didn't even attempt to fight him. They were playing along with her plan perfectly. Beelzebub stepped through the gate and went back to hell, with Moloch hot on his heels. Juntto jumped to his feet and started to run toward the gate, but before he could reach it the gate snapped shut.

Katie was gone.

22

The blinding heat hit Katie like a freight train, and she gasped for air as Moloch dropped her on the molten ground. He laughed, pacing around her. His body shrank to seven feet tall, but his chest was still twice the girth of a normal person. He flexed the muscles in his arms, on a high he hadn't felt before. "I didn't think he could pull it off, but fuck me running, he did! Not sure where that bastard got off to. I guess it doesn't matter, does it, Katie and Lilith?"

Katie looked at him with narrowed angry eyes. She struggled to her feet, pushing through the unbearable heat, ready to beat the hell out of the demon. She was sorry Beelzebub had already vanished. She gripped her sword tightly and lifted it as she charged him. He easily swatted her, knocking the sword from her grasp. She watched it bounce across the ground and slide to a stop on a ledge of volcanic rock.

She growled loudly and rammed her shield hard into his face. He fell back, grabbing a boulder to catch himself.

She staggered right and left, a look of determination on her face. Katie adjusted her grip on her shield as Moloch slowly stood back up, holding his bleeding nose. His eyes flashed bright red, and he chugged forward. She raised her shield, and he grabbed the edge before she could hit him again.

Moloch reared back and punched Katie hard in the stomach. "You fucking bitch. I'm so tired of this. That will be the last time you ever hurt me."

Katie gritted her teeth, her legs shaking. "No wonder Lucifer blamed this all on you. You're weak and pathetic."

Moloch yelled and punched Katie in the face. She flew back, losing her grip on her shield. She covered her face with her hands and groaned. Her face began swelling almost immediately. Moloch was pacing in circles around her writhing body, furious. "How dare you come to my home and think you can hurt me?"

He kicked her in the side. Katie could only lie there, stunned. She moaned and rolled over, grabbing her stomach. "Bitches like you deserve every bit of the torture you have coming. You and Lilith both. I wish I could be there when Lucifer breaks your precious demon."

He kicked her in the stomach, and his laughter was like thunder. Moloch was enjoying beating the hell out of Katie more than anyone he'd ever tortured. He walked to the edge of the cliff and looked over, trying to judge how much damage a fall would do to the human body. Katie winced and spat blood as she pushed herself to her feet. She took a deep breath, letting her angelic powers wash some of the pain away.

She pulled Tom from his holster and pointed it at

Moloch. "The problem with you is that you don't understand what real power means. You're a pawn in the game like everyone else."

Moloch whirled as she pulled the trigger. The bullet seemed to move in slow motion as it exited the gun and flew toward him. Moloch was much stronger in hell. He put up his hand before the bullet reached him and waved it to his side. The bullet whizzed past his hand and his head and shot into the open space behind him.

Katie shoved the gun back in the holster, and the two of them circled each other like prizefighters. Her face was bloody and swollen, and she held her stomach tightly with one arm. "You are so pathetic. You've never been able to hold up your end of the bargain. You mocked T'Chezz relentlessly, yet you haven't been able to do any better than he did. We're still on Earth, we're still running it, and your little incursions only bring us all closer together. You wanted chaos, but that will never happen. Humans are smarter than you think."

Moloch snorted. "Please. You're the people of a penniless world. You fight with each other over fake religions. You couldn't even get the bible right, and the damn thing was written just for you. You starve and kill each other. You commit sin after sin, yet you have the audacity to stand here and degrade me. I think not. You're all demons, you just don't have the scales yet."

Katie ran toward him, throwing her body into his. He easily knocked her aside. She stumbled over rocks and caught herself on the wall behind her. She could feel the heat of the lava, and in a moment her hand was bright red. "How can you be so proud? You couldn't even do *this* right.

I know you're being watched. I know you're being scolded. Why the hell else would they send another demon to do your job for you? Do you think I missed that? Other demons are fighting us now, which can only lead me to believe you got demoted."

Moloch's eyes flashed again, but he held steady. Her torture would come soon enough. "You have it all twisted, you fool. I'm the only one capable of doing something on this grand a scale. I'm the only one with the balls to get it done.

"You can't even come down yourself and fight me. You send your minions to try to distract us. But don't worry, when we killed them, we let them know you were responsible."

Moloch smacked the side of his head with one hand like he was trying to knock a thought loose. "Shut up! You don't know the slightest thing about me."

Katie scoffed. "Please. What is there to know?"

She backed up to the rock wall and slipped her hand behind her back. She grasped the handle of a hidden dagger in her belt and carefully drew it. Moloch had been so pissed that he hadn't seen her hide it.

He shook his head and put out his hand. He counted his accomplishments on his fingers. "You don't know anything. I was the reason all those cities across the ocean felt our wrath. I was the reason Incursion Day happened. Without me, your pathetic kind would still be hunting us down in the shadows. I got T'Chezz killed on purpose. I'm turning the world's eyes toward hell, and I will be the one who kills the almighty Katie. I will be the one who delivers Lilith to His Majesty on a platter."

"For most of those, we were there to head you off. You fled every single time. You left mass graveyards full of bodies and filled the world with hateful racist rhetoric. You haven't actually done one single thing to better this country."

Moloch laughed loudly. "You will never fully understand the paths I have taken. You will never know the sacrifices I have made. Though I do have to admit, I can't take credit for the lava flow. It was fantastic, it just wasn't my idea. Do you know whose idea it was? Beelzebub."

Katie's lip twitched. "So what? He'll die like you will."

Moloch shook his head. "No, see, that's what you don't get. You will never be able to kill him. He's been up against much worse than some little girl playing superhero. But hey, I'll take credit for the lava flow if it killed some of the people you loved. What was the name of that poor boy, the one who helped with fighting? Oh, yes. Brock."

Katie gritted her teeth. "Don't you say a word about him. Don't even let his name cross your lips."

Moloch's brow furrowed, then a smile played across his lips. "Oh, boy. Someone is pretty sensitive about that. What's wrong, little Katie? Did you fall in love with that boy? Did mean Mr. Beelzebub cover his pathetic corpse in lava?"

Katie stepped forward. "Shut up!"

Moloch leaned his head back, his laughter echoing through the canyons of hell. "Of course, I have no idea what happened to him. I knew he was there with his team. I remembered them all from their little expeditions into hell. If he's dead, don't worry. I'll find his soul in hell and plant it next to yours in my soul catcher. You two can spend an eternity writhing and screaming in my fireplace."

Moloch leaned against a boulder and nonchalantly crossed one foot over the other. He picked his teeth, laughing as Katie struggled to keep herself upright. "I bet if he *did* die, Brock cried like a baby the whole time."

Adrenaline mixed with anger flowed through Katie's entire body. It would only last a moment, but for that moment her legs worked again. She closed her fist around the hilt of the hidden dagger and ran forward. As she vaulted over a rock, she pulled her dagger from her back and slashed it at Moloch's head. His eyes went wide for a moment, and he ducked to one side. She hit the boulder he had been leaning against and grunted, knocking a huge chunk from it.

Katie breathed heavily, shoving the dagger in her back pocket. She leaned down and picked up the boulder. Moloch backed up, waving his hands to stop her, then tripped and landed on the ground. She lifted the rock and slammed it down on his scaly head. When it made contact, there was a cracking noise. The rock began to crumble in Katie's hands and she stepped back, looking for the next weapon to assault the demon with.

She figured if she couldn't trick him, she would just have to beat the ever-loving hell out of *him*. As she reached back to grab her dagger, Moloch began to laugh. "You idiot. You never just walk away."

Katie's eyes went big as she tried to yank the dagger from her pocket, but it was stuck. Moloch sprang to his feet, touching the blood on his forehead. He tsked loudly and shook his finger at Katie. "Didn't anyone ever teach you it's rude to come to another person's home and break their things?"

Katie sneered. "Fuck you, douchebag."

Moloch grimaced. "I think not. I can come up with at least a hundred other things I would rather fuck. Like, for instance, this boulder. Or maybe that hot lava stream down there. Maybe even one of those spiny demons we see running around."

Katie finally was able to yank the dagger from its sheath. She charged him again, but her strength was beginning to leave her once more. He put up his arm and grabbed her wrist, easily spinning her around and pinning her arm to her back. He whispered into her ear as he pushed his knuckles into her ribs. "What's wrong, Katie? Your demon not helping you stay strong down here like before? Are you realizing that without Lilith you're nothing? You're just the puny, self-absorbed, pathetic puppet of some man in the sky. Down here, I could make something of you. You could be a warrior on your own terms."

Katie breathed heavily, listening to him. "I would rather lick a dog's rancid asshole."

Moloch's face dropped and he pushed her across the ground, taking the dagger from her. He waved it in front of Katie with an evil grin. "Maybe it's time I taught you some fucking manners.

Calvin and Juntto walked back across the field to the armory. They had already geared up in the training room, but Calvin could tell it was going to take something extra-special to get Katie back. They began to load as many weapons onto their bodies as they could physically carry.

Calvin rubbed his finger across an old pistol he'd used twenty years before. He glanced at Juntto, who was even strapping holsters around his broad arms. "Sometimes I wonder how I am still alive after all these years. I can tell you right now, it's because of people like Katie. That's why I'm doing this."

Juntto nodded and picked up a compound bow, considered it, then put it back down. "I'm doing it for Katie as well. I'm doing it because she didn't leave me behind, and I won't do that to her. I'm doing it for Angie, too. Katie's the most important person in her world. A lot of people would be lost without her."

Korbin stormed into the room, Stephanie and Timothy trailing behind him. Korbin stared at Calvin, waiting for him to volunteer the information. When he didn't, Korbin snapped, "What's going on? Where's Katie?"

Calvin walked to Korbin. "Sorry to keep you in the dark, but we have to do this on our own. Katie gave up her freedom for us—for all of us. You just have to trust us. Keep your eye on the television. You might get a sneak peek at what we're up to."

Stephanie furrowed her brow. "And none of us can go with you?"

Juntto shook his head and strapped a short sword on top of another short sword at his waist. "No, this is something we have to do alone. There's a reason for it. You need to trust Katie. Know that she's doing the right thing."

Korbin and Stephanie looked at each other for a moment. "We trust Katie."

Angie walked into the room, holding her hands limply in front of her. "And I trust you, Juntto."

A smile crept across Juntto's face. He rushed to her, picking up her hands and looking at the blisters on them. She gave him a soft smile, her eyes twinkling. "I wasn't going to leave you guys out there on your own. I shot from a distance until they disappeared."

Juntto took Angie's face in his hands and leaned down, pressing his lips gently against hers. She wrapped her arms around his neck and stood on her tiptoes, kissing him back. Everyone went silent, covering the smiles on their faces.

Calvin's eyes flashed red, and he opened his mouth to talk. Instead of Calvin's voice coming out, it was another voice entirely. Pandora groaned. "We have shit to do. Get your shag on when we have my sister back."

Angie pulled away quickly, her eyes wide. She stared at Calvin. "Pandora?"

Calvin threw up his hands and spoke to the demon inside him. "Go on."

Pandora snarled, "Yes, it's me. Now, do you see why time is of the essence here?"

Angie nodded and pushed Juntto toward him. "Get my best friend and bring her back to us."

Juntto bowed and winked at her. "Of course."

Timothy's forehead wrinkled as he tried to figure out what the hell was happening. He put up his finger and opened his mouth to speak, but couldn't find the words. He sighed and shook his head.

Stephanie patted his arm, shaking her head. "It's okay, sweetie. We'll explain it to you when you're older."

Korbin just stared at Calvin, who returned the look. Calvin shrugged. "It's weird for me too."

Korbin shook his head. "I've seen a lot of shit in my lifetime. Hell, I've *been* through a lot of shit in my lifetime, but hearing Pandora come out of your mouth is not something I was up for."

Calvin's eyes flashed, and Pandora's voice echoed in laughter. "Hold on to your man-panties, 'cause you ain't seen nothing yet. I'm just getting started. They want to play dirty? They want to change the rules on us? Well, we're going to do the same."

Calvin's hand grew into Pandora's claw and sliced the air, and a portal tore open right there in the training room. Calvin bowed to Juntto, put out his hand, and said in his own voice, "After you, giant sir."

Juntto tipped an invisible hat. "Why, thank you, lady-man."

"You mean ladies' man."

"I meant what I said."

Juntto walked through the portal and Calvin followed. The portal slammed shut after them. Korbin and Stephanie slowly turned toward Angie and Timothy, blinking wildly. Timothy was still frowning, trying to piece together what just happened. "Was that Pandora in Calvin's body?"

Stephanie giggled. "A little slow on the uptake today, girl?"

Timothy eyed the empty space where the portal had just been. "If Pandora was in Calvin, then who's inside Katie? And what is that demon doing to protect her?"

Korbin let out a deep sigh. "That's a very good question. Unfortunately, that's something we won't be finding out anytime soon. Sometimes Katie and Pandora's ideas are so far out there that it's better not to ask questions."

Angie jumped. "Ooh! Let's turn on the television and see if anything comes on. Not sure what we're looking for, but if it's big, you know they'll broadcast it."

Timothy followed Angie out of the training room and down the hall. Stephanie wrapped her arms around Korbin's waist. "You okay? You look like you saw a ghost or something."

Korbin shook his head. "Yeah, sorry. I was hoping that whatever their crazy scheme is, they get to it before Moloch gets to Katie. Without Pandora, we don't know how long she'd be able to survive in hell. I'm not ready for another funeral, especially not one that will change the course of humanity's future."

Stephanie laid her head to his chest. "Me neither, Korbin. Me neither."

23

Katie stumbled to her knees and put her hand to her chest, wheezing. Moloch raced over and grabbed her by the neck, lifting her into the air. She clawed at his hands to try to get free, but her tank was empty when it came to energy. "What's the matter, your demon pet hiding for now?"

Katie blinked uncomfortably. Everything was getting blurry, even Moloch's face. She swung from side to side, trying to get free, but she feared all she was doing was making him grip her throat tighter. Moloch pulled her face close to his. She could smell the liquor and cheap cigars on his breath.

Moloch snarled. "Or did she get away when I wasn't looking? That's not like that ball-kicking sanctimonious bitch. I thought she was more dedicated to you than that. I figured she would come after you and protect you from anything. I guess this was a good excuse for her to tuck her tail and run. Then again, maybe I'm wrong. Maybe that bitch is still inside of you, and if I hurt you bad enough for long enough, she'll come out."

Moloch slowly pushed Katie back until he was pressing her against a stone wall. He pulled her forward and slammed her back again, knocking the wind out of her. "If she won't come out on her own, then I guess I'll have to lure her out. What better way to do that than to hurt her human body enough that she begs me to stop?"

Moloch ran the tip of his claw down Katie's arm and back up again. "It's a shame this has to be done, but I promise I'll make it hurt as much as I can."

Katie shook, her eyes darting around. Moloch steadied her and wrapped his hand around her arm. With a quick twist, he snapped the bone in her forearm. Katie's eyes went huge as the pain surged through her and she screamed, unable to control herself. The demon laughed as he prodded her broken arm. Darts of anguish shot into her chest. Katie had never broken anything like that before.

Moloch set her on the ground but kept his body pressed against her so she couldn't move. He rubbed her hair with his hand and chuckled. "Did that hurt? I hope it did. I hope Lilith is writhing inside you.

Katie turned her head from him, but he grabbed her cheek. "Speak, whore. Did it hurt?"

Katie sneered as she slowly met his eyes. She opened her mouth as if she were about to speak, but spat in his face instead. He breathed heavily, spittle hissing as it dripped down his nose and cheek. "I can see now that you're going to be a bit harder to break than the general run of human, but all it takes is for you to send that whore out here. I just want Lilith. You know you can command her to step out of your body here in hell, right?"

Katie tightened her lips and refused to answer his questions. Lilith was with Calvin, but the longer she withheld that information from him, the longer they had to execute their plan. She could take a few broken bones, right?

Moloch pressed his claw against the boulder above her head, laughing as if he'd lost his mind. "Oh, little girl, just wait until I start eating your fingers. They're like little crunchy snacks. C'mon out, Pandora. I can feel evil inside this little sack of charred shameless slattern."

Moloch sat there waiting for Pandora's legendary wrath to be unleashed. He wasn't quite sure that he could handle her, but he needed to separate them. He wanted to preserve Katie for his collection, so he was trying not to kill her. His selfishness was putting him at a disadvantage, but he didn't care. After a moment, he sighed. "Okay. You're right. I give up. No hard feelings?" He stuck out his hand as if to shake hers.

Instead of shaking it, he grabbed her other arm and laughed in her face. "Just kidding." He twisted the arm brutally, cracking the fragile bones. "*Come out, dammit!*" he bellowed.

Katie screamed and tilted her head back. Her eyes glowed bright red, and her body convulsed. Moloch licked his lips like a serpent. "Yes. That's right. Feel the pain and agony. *Feel it.* Come out of there, bitch."

He thrust his claw into Katie's chest, digging into her very core, and snagged the edge of a demon. "Gotcha, bitch!"

Moloch pulled hard, ignoring Katie's monstrous

screams—and ignoring the bright white light coming from her body. Her eyes changed from red to blue and back again. Finally, he pulled the entire demon out and threw it on the ground at his feet. Katie's screams instantly stopped, and her body collapsed to the ground. The pain was almost too much for her to bear. Everything was spinning wildly, and she couldn't pull air into her lungs.

Moloch tilted his head back and laughed loudly. "Look at that! Look at your precious Lilith. She's so weak, it's pathetic."

Moloch grabbed Katie by the face, staring at her eyes as they rolled in her head. She gurgled something, but Moloch couldn't hear what she was saying. He stepped closer and put her head to his ear. "What? Say it louder, bitch. Don't worry, your time is almost here."

Katie struggled to swallow and then righted her vision, staring directly at the side of Moloch's head. "I said, joke's on you, motherfucker."

Moloch looked at her strangely, not sure what she meant. "You're talking in riddles. Joke's on me? No, joke's on *you*, bitch. I have your writhing evil demon right here. She acted so big and bad. She talked so much shit. She acted like she gave a shit about you, but look at that lump of dry shit. She's as pathetic as she's always been. There's no glory or honor in this. Who knew that in the end, Lilith would cower in fear? All the years I wasted fearing her!"

Moloch was quite proud of himself. He'd not only gotten Katie, but he'd also gotten Lilith, too. Lilith was the real trophy, although he was excited to add a demi-angel to his collection of souls. "You are a one-of-a-kind prize for my collection. You will be the centerpiece of every conversation I have. You will be my prized soul. Don't worry, that only means you'll be tortured more often than others."

Katie's head bobbed, and she spat in Moloch's face. Moloch raged, grabbing her chin and pointed it at the demon on the ground. "Look, your protection is...your protection is... Wait."

He let go of Katie's chin and stepped back, bending down next to the demon. He picked up the demon's head by its long hair and stared at its face.

It wasn't Lilith. He'd gotten the wrong demon. He stood up quickly and faced Katie. "How can this be? You fucking *tricked* me!"

He grabbed Katie by the throat and slid her up the wall. "Tell me where she is. Tell me, or I will rip your heart out right here and now."

Katie's eyes shifted up his chest to his big, round head. When they met his, he knew he'd been had.

Katie sneered. "How about you tend to your balls first?"

Moloch's frowned. "My balls? Why my—"

Katie kicked him as hard as she could, slamming her foot into his nutsack. He froze and slowly looked down at her foot. "Balls?"

He released Katie's neck, dropping her to the ground. Katie couldn't get around him since her body was too weak to move. Besides, until Pandora arrived, she had no way out of hell. Moloch knelt on the floor in front of her, clutching his crotch and wheezing loudly. "Why is it always the balls?"

Katie shrugged, looking around. "You tried to take my most prized possession, I'll fucking take yours."

Moloch went silent, just sitting there clutching the

jewels of hell and breathing heavily. Katie struggled her way back to a standing position and looked past him for any sign that Pandora was coming. There wasn't anything in the air, not even the whisper of a gate. Her focus shifted back to Moloch as his shoulders shook, a deep laugh coming from his chest.

He put one hand on the floor and stood with a grunt. Still laughing, his eyes rose to meet hers. Tears were streaming down his face. "Oh, Lucifer's toes! I'm going to eat you slowly. I'll chop you up. I'm going to rip the skin from every small appendage and then play with your bones. I'm going cut open your brain like Doctor Lecter and feed you small pieces of it, deep-fried. I'm going to —URGGHHH!"

Katie whipped her head toward Moloch. She followed his bulging eyes to his chest, from which the tip of her angelic sword protruded. It shimmered and sparkled as his black, gooey blood ran into a puddle on the ground. Saliva dripped from his lip. He lifted his hand to touch the razor-sharp tip of the sword.

A smile moved across Katie's face. Moloch's eyes combed over Katie, trying to figure out how she could have possibly done that. She had been in his line of sight the entire time.

He put his lips together, trying to speak, his whole body beginning to shudder. Katie tilted her head to the side and leaned forward, whispering, "Tell me how much it hurts, whore?"

He growled, but the blade twisted in his chest. A voice came from behind him, and he closed his eyes. He could not believe he'd been fooled like that. "That was for Katie, you pompous piece of dog shit. You should have known not to hurt her."

Moloch put his arm down to try to push himself up. When he was almost there, his giant thigh shaking hard beneath him, a second sword burst from his chest. Moloch let out a deep whine as the other sword pushed hard, breaking through his chest and popping the scales off. He dropped back down to his knees, gasping for air. Katie lifted an eyebrow. "That looks like it hurts."

A loud whine came from his throat, but he wasn't able to say a word. Blood continued to pool at Katie's feet as a second voice told him, "That was for me."

A foot slammed between his legs from behind, kicking him in the nuts again. Moloch's eyes rolled back in his head, and drool ran down his chin. Pandora stuck her head around Moloch and smiled widely at Katie. "Actually, I can't take credit for that one. That was Juntto. He has bigger feet."

Katie chuckled, barely able to move her arms.

Pandora wrinkled her nose and sighed. "You poor thing, this fucking cock-monger really did a number on you. Sorry it took me so long. Had to push Calvin back through the portal when I jumped out of him. He was being stubborn, as usual."

Katie nodded her head, still trying to take a deep breath. She couldn't talk anymore, and she thought she might lose consciousness any minute. Pandora clapped her hands. "Okay, it's probably time we got this party started, right?"

Juntto chuckled. "I feel like this is the part of the evening when a party is usually starting to wind down. No one reacts well when you stab a guy a few times and crush his nuts. It usually breaks the party up and sends people running—and screaming—out the door."

Slowly, Pandora turned her head and raised an eyebrow. Juntto shrugged. "What? I've done it before. Yule party. I just wanted to test the waters. Some people even grabbed their gifts before leaving. Who knew you couldn't stab someone and still be friends? Humans are strange."

Pandora stared at Juntto. "I think perhaps the whole you-not-having-friends thing might have something to do with you being a psychopath. What exactly did this guy do to deserve the stab-and-jab treatment?"

Juntto thought about it for a second. "Oh, I remember. Yes, it was terrible. He took the last crispbread. I wanted it. It was my house, after all."

"What's crispbread?"

"Uh, crispy bread. Like a Viking Dorito."

Katie chuckled softly as she began to slide down the wall.

Pandora stared at him. "So you attempted to murder—"

"He died."

"Okay, regular murder. You committed regular murder and testicular injury because of a Dorito?"

Juntto nodded. "Yeah."

Pandora shrugged her shoulders. "I mean, that sounds legit to me. Those things are delicious. What do you think, Moloch? You want to weigh in on this one?"

Pandora wiggled the sword in his body and Moloch groaned, his head hanging. Pandora frowned. "I believe Moloch thinks that might be a bit over the top for one Dorito."

Juntto rubbed his chin. "Perhaps, but one man's Dorito is another man's salvation. It would be like him coming in and just snatching my lover from my bed. He gave no thought to what my needs and wants were. He didn't care whose hand was on the crispbread first. He just plowed through and devoured the last tasty morsel."

Pandora nodded her head. "Did you use that defense in court?"

"No, I just killed everyone who had a problem with it, fled the village, and started a new village—a village that made crispbread."

Pandora brightened. "Oh, this story has a happy ending! I wasn't expecting that."

Katie began to cough, blood splattering her lip. She wheezed, "I could really use your help right now. Any time would be great, but preferably in the next minute or so."

Pandora nodded. "Yeah, I think it's time to get this show on the road. Juntto, would you please do your magic?"

Moloch twisted, trying to move, but he couldn't. The two swords in his chest were crisscrossed, and Juntto stood behind him, holding them tightly. "You can squirm, but if you wiggle too much, I am literally going to cut you in half. I would suggest you just chill."

Pandora walked away from them and tossed Juntto a set of heavy chains they'd brought with them. Juntto moved quickly, winding the chains around Moloch, binding him tightly. He pulled up on the chains and lifted Moloch to his feet.

Pandora hurried to Katie, pausing to look down at the

demon on the ground. "Sorry about that. Your sacrifice did not go unnoticed."

She quickly slid back into Katie's body. Katie took a deep breath and gasped, her body instantly beginning to heal. Pandora went to work to ease the pain as much as she could. She couldn't heal her completely while they were still in hell, but she could make her well enough to move on to the next phase of the plan. *I'm going to numb your arms for a second and pop all those bones back in place. It's temporary, so don't go rock climbing or anything. It'll get you through the next part.*

Katie chuckled breathlessly. *Damn it, and to think I had plans to scale Mount Olympus today.*

Pandora rolled her eyes as she worked. *Zeus isn't real. Silly girl. Who believes nonsense like that?*

Katie blinked wildly, finally able to stand up without leaning against the wall. *I am a half-angel with a demon in me. I am, right now, standing in hell in front of a huge servant of Lucifer. There are literally volcanoes exploding everywhere and rivers of lava flowing below this cliff. I'm pretty sure that if someone said, oh yeah, Zeus is totally real, I would believe it at this point.*

Pandora made a tsking sound. *If you don't stand for something, you'll fall for anything.*

Katie raised an eyebrow. *Did you just quote George Bush to me?*

Pandora sighed. *No, no. That's a song. Bush was the one who screwed up "fool me once."*

Katie nodded. *That's right. I always get them mixed up.*

Pandora couldn't agree more. *I think it was Alexander*

Hamilton who said that, but not the musical rap version one. That one is just weird to me.

Katie sat humming one of the songs from the musical to herself as Pandora finished her temporary healing. When she was done, she moved Katie's fingers and arms for her. *How does that feel?*

Katie nodded. *It will do for now, thank you, now let's get the fuck out of hell. I probably already have tumors from all the shit I've inhaled here today. My ribs are practically in tiny bits at this point.*

Pandora winced. *Yeah. I'll get to work on that, and you get to work on him.*

24

It was just like any other day in New York. The fall decorations were out, the city streets were loud and boisterous, and people were milling about all over the place. Times Square was never dull; it was a tourist hub every day of the year. Traffic was jammed that time of day, with horns honking and people yelling at each other. All the wondrous sights of the Big Apple in one small space.

Harold, a taxi driver, rolled down his window and pumped his fist. "Come on, get the fuck outta the way. We're drivin' here."

He shook his head, looking in the rearview mirror at two girls who were excitedly taking pictures out the window. "Fuckin' mooks. This city can be such a hassle."

One of the girls in the back smiled. "I love it. There's always something crazy and wild going on here. It's like the city has its own pulse. Much different than Minnesota. Nothing ever happens there."

The other girl bounced up and down. "Oh, I wonder if

we'll get a view of Katie while we're here? She lives some-where in the city, and they say she flies around at night."

Suddenly, a loud cracking sound echoed from the center of Times Square. Harold slammed on his brakes, jolting the girls. Right in front of them, a large portal opened, heat peeling the paint from the front of his cab. "You might just get your wish, ladies."

The girls marveled at the portal shimmering in front of them. All around the portal people started to scream, grabbing their things and running away as fast as they could. No one knew what was going to come through that portal, and many still had terrible memories of the last major incursion.

Harold tried to back up, but he couldn't. "Oh, hell. This is going to be one for the books if we make it out alive."

One of the girls in the back pointed. "Look! Isn't that her? Who is that with her?"

Harold turned back around. Juntto, transformed into the guy from Far Cry 4, stepped through the portal. Katie walked through behind him. Juntto had chains wrapped around his arms, and he dragged a beaten and bloody Moloch through the portal and into the city streets. The frost giant lifted the chains and brought Moloch to his feet. Moloch groaned as the people around them screamed and gasped. The swords were still firmly planted in his chest, blood dripping down their blades. The demon wondered, not for the first time, where that second sword had come from.

The girls squealed in excitement, not really realizing there was a massive demon standing in front of them. "It's her! It's her!"

One of the girls opened the door and got out, taking a picture of the three of them. She tilted her head to the side, looking at Juntto. "Who's that guy?"

Harold lifted an eyebrow. "Apparently, the Leviathan *is* alive. The rumors were true after all, not that I listen to rumors."

The other girl giggled. "He looks like the guy from Far Cry. Either that or he's hitting up New York Comic-Con this weekend."

Harold glanced at her. "You know about Comic-Con?"

The girl gestured to her outfit. "Uh, *hello*, I'm wearing the Shimakaze costume from the Kantai collection. I don't just run around with these giant bow ear-things all the time."

Harold shrugged. "I see some crazy shit in this town, lady. Look where we are. Sitting in Times Square in front of an angel, a frost giant, and a demon. This is the real world, honey."

Pandora sniffed the air. *Ah, it's good to be home. Smog, smog, and more smog.*

Katie was glad to get some cleaner air into her lungs. "Any minute now the news and the cops should be rolling up. Juntto, you remember the plan?"

Juntto gave her a thumbs-up. "I sure do."

Sirens blared as the cops made their way through the traffic jam. News vehicles screeched up onto the sidewalks, and cameramen began surrounding the whole area. One reporter edged closer, eyeing Moloch. "Katie, Jane Arrows from Channel 8. Can you tell us what you're doing here in the middle of Times Square?"

The portal snapped shut behind them, scaring the

reporter for a moment. Katie put up her hand to quiet the gathering crowd. "I will make a statement in just a minute. Please be patient."

Moloch growled, bringing a gasp from the crowd. Juntto snarled and yanked the chains, jostling the swords in Moloch's chest. Moloch groaned and went to grab the handle of one of the swords to steady it, but his elbows were pinned at his sides.

Where *had* that second sword come from?

He glared at the humans. He didn't think he was going to get out of this easily.

Juntto stepped closer to Moloch. "Don't make me have to put you down in front of all these people. Be a good little demon and stand there quietly."

Moloch snorted. "At this point, anything is better than what Lucifer is going to do to me when he hears about this. I won't get out of torture for centuries."

Katie grumbled under breath. "I don't think that's something you're going to have to worry about for too much longer, buddy."

Pandora growled. *I'm so hungry. All I smell is food. They should be delivering us donuts while we wait for everyone to get here.*

Katie chuckled. *Patience, Pandora. We're just about ready to begin. The people of this country and this world deserve to have closure. They deserve to see the face of the demon who ordered the killing of so many of their brothers, sisters, mothers, fathers, and children. They deserve to see the beast who has haunted their dreams since Incursion Day. His death may not be the end of the problem, but this is definitely the beginning of the solution.*

Pandora settled down. *Amen, sister.*

When the last of the news vans had arrived, Katie took a deep breath and stepped forward. She put her arms out and tilted her head to the sky, pulling on her angel abilities. Golden armor flew from the light shimmering above them and molded to her body. Her shield slammed into her hand, and her angelic sword vibrated in Moloch's chest. The people oohed and ahhed as Katie unfolded her wings carefully and spread them wide across the street.

She addressed the people. "Citizens of New York, of the United States, and the world, I come to you with good tidings. For those of you who don't know me, my name is Katie, and I am a mercenary. I have been fighting in this war with other brave men and women for years now. As you can see, I'm part-angel. First and foremost, I am one of you."

Several people in the crowd cheered, and Katie nodded. "Mercenaries work behind the scenes with the brave women and men of the armed forces. We go where no one else will go. We do what no one else will do. I want to read you the Creed of the Damned. It is our way of life, and it is our dedication to you."

Katie cleared her throat, no longer needing a crumpled piece of paper to get it right.

"We are the ones who did not make it home.

We are the chosen.

The infected,

battling our demons night and day.

Protecting the uninformed from reality.

We fight where the stupid meet the clueless to perform

the asinine for our teammates every day.

We are cops, military, special forces, and SWAT,
medical techs, priests, and clergy.
We are the dimensional derelicts,
the legion, the host, the forgotten.
The feared.
The sheep can sleep at night because we don't.
We fight for humanity—yours—and for our own.
We are the Damned, and death is our enemy,
our escape,
and our tribute."

The entire crowd sat absolutely silent, completely absorbed in the words Katie had spoken. Goosebumps crawled up her spine as she stared at Moloch. "This is Moloch, a council member serving Lucifer. He was the main demon behind the attacks perpetrated against our planet and our people. Moloch has caused mass destruction from coast to coast, and beyond. Most recently, he and his cohorts were responsible for raining lava down on a Romanian town. There, people fled but were burned alive in the streets. Children were entombed in ash and soot, clinging to their mother's arms. And friends of mine were there, fighting for you and for all humanity. We still have not heard from them."

The crowd let out a low boo and people began throwing things at Moloch. Katie took a deep breath and put up her hands. "We aren't saying this will end the war, but you can go to sleep tonight knowing that this particular hellspawn won't be bothering you again."

Katie turned toward Juntto and nodded. Juntto put his hand on Moloch's shoulder and pushed down, forcing him to his knees. Everyone went silent again, shocked to watch what was happening right in front of them. The majority of the people wanted to kill Moloch themselves. They wanted a reprieve from the fear and chaos. They wanted to kiss their babies goodnight and know they would be there in the morning. What Katie was doing was very public, but she felt it was necessary. The country and the world had to unite, and the world had to know that Katie was looking out for them, too.

Moloch snickered, his body heaving as he began coughing, blood splattering on the ground. The crowd hissed and backed up a bit. Moloch forced his lips into a bloody grin. "You can't kill me, little humans. I'll be back. You know as well as I do that when we die here on Earth, we go straight back to hell. It won't take me long to climb from the depths and regain my power. When I do, I will rain terror on this planet like you have never imagined. I'll start right here in New York City."

The people muttered, creating a fearful low roar over the crowd. Katie put her hands up and smiled at the people in the streets. She turned back to Moloch and bent over, a smirk lurking on her lips. "Oh yeah? I think you might be mistaken."

Moloch narrowed his eyes and followed the shadow of Katie's demon sliding from her body. The crowd gasped as Katie stepped to one side and grabbed a light post. Her strength left with Pandora's exit. Pandora had prepared her body for it, healing everything she could, but Katie was still weak.

Pandora stood tall, her hair floating around her in the wind. Instead of her birthday suit, Pandora was sporting much heavier garb. Angelic robes whirled and hovered around her, shimmering in the autumn sun. She looked quiet and calm, a small, tight-lipped smile on her face. Instead of striking Moloch, she simply reached out and gently pressed her fingertips to Moloch's forehead. Smoke came from his skin and he tilted his head back, screaming at the top of his lungs.

Pandora slowly withdrew her hand. Moloch breathed heavily, growling deep in his throat as he watched her. She paused for just a moment before snapping her fingers. Moloch's eyes went wide as one of the angelic swords disappeared from his chest and reappeared in her hand. The blood was completely gone from the blade and it reflected the sunlight, creating a disco-ball effect on the crowd.

That was where the second sword had come from.

Moloch shook his head. "No, this cannot be! What's going on here?"

Pandora waved her hand, sealing Moloch's mouth shut. She held her sword high in the air and looked to the heavens. "By the rights and responsibilities I once rejected but which have been returned to me, you, Moloch, are sentenced to death. You will never walk the burning bowels of hell or the lush green grasses of Earth again. You will never harm another soul, living or dead. Let your fate be a warning to all those below who wish to test our holy vows. I will hunt you. I will find you, and when I do, your head will be mounted high for all to see, forever cemented in history. This war will end—mark my words."

Pandora gave Moloch a sly wink and whispered, "Nighty-night, cockstain" as she swung her sword hard and fast. The blade hit his scales but didn't stop, slicing through them like a warm knife through butter. It sliced through scale and flesh and unholy bone and reappeared in the open air. Moloch's great head slapped the ground meatily, then rolled forward. Katie put out her foot to stop it. When it settled, Moloch's eyes, once shimmering and shining red, flickered several times before completely extinguishing. Dead black orbs were left in their place.

His body didn't turn to ash or disappear like the others. Instead, it teetered back and forth on its knees, headless, spilling black blood all over the sidewalk. Juntto put his foot on the beast's headless corpse and pushed. The body fell over, hitting the ground with a thud.

The watching crowd stood there silently. On instinct, they began reaching for each other's hands. Not everyone knew one another, not everyone liked one another, but at that moment they were joined together in one common goal.

The television news cameras kept filming the scene, even though none of the reporters knew what to say at that moment. There were more demons out there like Moloch. The danger wouldn't end just because he was dead, but no one could deny that Moloch's death symbolized more than just the end of another fruitless battle. It showed that humans could stand together, even in the face of one of the gravest enemies they'd ever battled. They could rely on someone bigger and stronger to take the reins and protect them whenever she could.

The news cameras panned to Juntto, who dropped the heavy chains he was holding. Jane Arrows whispered to her camera, "This person, this Leviathan, is another symbol of our solidarity. Not only are we united across the country and the world, but across the whole universe. He's a symbol of the dedication and caring we all need to have toward each other. It doesn't matter what race, religion, nationality, or sexual orientation you are. It doesn't even matter what species you are. We're all holding hands. We must have courage."

Katie and Juntto made eye contact, and Katie winked at him.

The wind swept across Times Square as the crowd began to clap. Harold stepped out of his cab and put his hands in the air, cheering wildly. After a few seconds, the entire block was cheering so loud it echoed all across the city. The camera focused on Jane Arrows, who put her mic to her lips. "You are witnessing history here today, folks. In a Channel 8 exclusive of massive proportions, we can now say that not only is Katie herself part-angel, but her demon is as well. In a harrowing act of justice, Moloch, the demon who killed hundreds of thousands of people all over the world, was executed by Pandora, the demon with an angelic golden crown. The people in the streets are going wild. They're celebrating together, going hand in hand for the first time since the attack on New York City. If you are watching this from anywhere else, know that we have your hearts with us here today."

Katie watched Pandora as she stared at Moloch's head, huge and malevolent. She was so proud of her demon, who'd surprised them all. The crowd began to chant Katie's and Pandora's names. Pandora looked at all the faces she had refused to see for so many centuries. She had fallen from grace once before and lurched between hell and Earth searching for some cause to give her life meaning.

The warmth flowing through her was a better high than any she'd ever experienced. She felt alive. She was wrapped in grace's warm embrace. She would lead the humans back to salvation and safety. Something caught her eye on top of a building. Sitting on the ledge with his feet dangling off the roof, clapping his hands, was Gabriel.

Pandora snorted, whispering under her breath, "Asshole." Was she angelic? Sure. At the same time, she was still Lilith, the queen of the Damned.

Pandora raised her arms high and the crowd quieted, waiting for her to speak. Jane Arrows waved excitedly at the camera. "It seems that our heroine, Pandora, is about to say something. The crowd is completely enthralled. Let's watch it unfold."

The camera panned back to Pandora as she took a deep breath. Her eyes flickered from red to blue and back again, just like Katie's did. The sword in her grasp disappeared, and a bright white light shone down from between the clouds, spotlighting her. She closed her eyes and released her wings. They unfolded from her back and spread wide, the tips almost touching the buildings on either side of the street. They were gray with silver and golden wisps.

She cleared her throat and began, "It is time for the War of the Angels."

25

Baal took a sip of his wine and shoved several gerbils into his mouth, chewing loudly. Fur and blood splattered down the front of his scales. His servants had been steadily growing in number, but now they stood huddled in the corner, too afraid to approach him. He was growing more intolerant every day. He had thrown a demon down the steps to the dungeon and beat him to death the night before because his whiskey was one degree less than the perfect temperature. That was very difficult to achieve in hell, but Baal was demanding.

Baal grunted at the show on the television and grabbed the remote. "When does *Dancing with the Stars* come on? I love that show. One day I will perform, just you wait and see."

None of his servants said a word, and he didn't even notice they were there. Before he could press the button, an emergency broadcast came on. The sound hurt Baal's ears and he sneered, covering his ears until it was over. The news station popped up, and the newscaster looked disheveled yet hopeful. That was something Baal really hated about humans—their incessant need to be hopeful.

"A miraculous event has happened in the streets of New York City, and it was all caught on tape by our JLA affiliate. We take you to Times Square, where just moments ago Katie and her demon beheaded one of the major culprits behind the War of the Demons." The newscaster turned, and the television went full screen with the footage.

Baal sat forward, laughing at the image of Moloch in chains with two swords sticking out of him. Pandora, standing with her back to the camera, suddenly raised a sword high. "Oh, boy. Moloch is going to be pissed when he gets back. Not only will he have sword wounds, but that shit on his neck is going to take forever to heal."

Baal grimaced as the sword cut through his old friend's flesh. He paused, waiting for the body to turn to dust, but it didn't happen. Baal's face fell.

Moloch was dead. He'd truly been killed. Baal grabbed the remote and rewound it, playing the clip back in slow motion. "Wait a damned minute. That's not how it's supposed to work."

He watched Pandora, draped in a white gown with a small golden crown on her head, turn toward the camera. He pressed the pause button and moved closer to the television. "Holy shit."

Large on his screen loomed Pandora's face, her lips twisted into a grin. Her eyes gleamed bright blue on the screen. Her crown was a circlet of golden thorns, each sharp tip sparkling in the sun. Baal fell on his ass and scooted across the floor until his back met the chair. "She's...she's...an *angel*. By the hairs of Lucifer's rotting taint, Moloch isn't coming back."

Beelzebub slammed his hand on the wall and roared. He ran an arm along his desk, sweeping everything to the floor. A great plume of dust billowed into the air. Baal frowned and waved his hand in front of his face while he coughed. Beelzebub was livid, pacing back and forth in his study with his fists gripped tightly in front of him. "Those bastards. First, they publicly behead a member of Lucifer's council, then, they celebrate his death and mount his head in the center of New York City. On top of that, Lilith turned out to be some sort of recovered demon with angelic abilities. This is fucking insane. To top it off, those lazy, good-for-nothing humans dropped a bomb of death into the third ring."

Baal shook his head, his eyelids low as he leaned against the wall. "Really? Did you expect them to just behead Moloch and leave it at that? Did you think they were going to be satisfied with getting one of us? Please. These humans may be emotional, but they aren't stupid. I don't know what you expected when you dropped lava onto one of their cities."

Beelzebub screeched loudly, straining the veins in his neck. "I expected fear. I expected blinding, all-consuming fear. I expected them to begin to play nice. After all, no country wants liquid hell dropping on their people. I feel like they never learn lessons. They never process. They just point out what we're doing, call it evil, and retaliate."

Baal groaned. "They aren't the only creatures in the universe who don't crumble to fear, Beelzebub. We are one such species. If anything, you should admire their tenacity and ingenuity. They could have simply done what they did before, come down here and knock some demons around before getting their asses kicked. Instead, they came up with a scientifically viable weapon that not only fucked with us but sent a huge number of our demons either into the abyss or plummeting into the very depths of hell they had just climbed out of."

Beelzebub shook his head, stomping his feet on the stone floors. "These humans all deserve to die, and they have Pandora to thank for it. That bitch knew all along she was an angel. She knew it, and she kept it a secret from everyone. Can you imagine what would have happened if she'd tapped into those energies while married to Lucifer? She could have ended hell as we know it."

Baal yawned. "I really think you're being melodramatic. She wouldn't have beaten Lucifer. She's only one angel. Armies of angels have fought the dark lord and lost. I think Lucifer would have been happy to have an angel in his bed. It would be like a badge of honor of sorts."

Beelzebub winced. "That is sick and disgusting, Baal. Those creatures could not stand up to our grace and valor. They are not as strong as we are. They would have chased us from existence long ago if they could have."

Baal shrugged. "From Lilith's speech, I would say they now have every intention of doing so. It's a whole new game. Demons are no longer volunteering to go to Earth.

Before, they knew that if they died, they'd come back home. Now they know that if they face a legion of angels, they'll just die. Done. They'll no longer exist. I believe we need to rethink our strategies."

Beelzebub sat down at the table and put his claw to his lips. "I knew I should have stayed and helped Moloch. Better yet, I should have just done it on my own."

Baal snorted. "I know you think you're all high and mighty, but you wouldn't have survived either. She would have beheaded both of you with that golden sword of death and never given it a second thought. Your headless corpse would have been tied to a tractor-trailer and dumped next to Moloch's."

Beelzebub narrowed his eyes. "And you would be right here in hell, the only one left to tell the tale."

Baal turned his head. "Wait a minute, don't you dare imply that I wished this upon Moloch, or even worse, had anything to do with it. You know I like the behind-the-scenes stuff. I'm not the public face of any operation. I needed Moloch, but I don't want to be the next headless corpse because I made one too many careless choices."

Beelzebub stood up, knocking his chair over. "Careless choices? I set him up for complete success. That's more than you have ever done in this war. How dare you come in here and insinuate that I don't know how to perform my duties in the correct manner?"

Baal was getting frustrated. "I wasn't involved in the fighting because I chose not to be. I wasn't giving orders because it wasn't my fight. Unlike some demons I know, I don't let my ambitions get the best of me in these serious times."

Beelzebub marched toward Baal, shaking his fist. "You turd. You bleeding anus. You talking pool of vomit."

There was a loud pounding on the door to the cave. Beelzebub sneered at Baal and grabbed the door handle. He threw it open gruffly, yelling, "What?"

He blinked at the demon standing there. He was standing ramrod straight and wearing Lucifer's livery. Beelzebub cleared his throat and stood up taller. "My apologies. I don't get visitors from the king very often these days."

The demon kept a blank face and handed him an envelope. "Lucifer is demanding you show yourself to him immediately. You can follow me back to the castle."

Beelzebub swallowed hard, looking back at Baal. "Of course, I'll come. Catch you later, Baal. Lock the door on your way out."

Baal huffed, keeping his back turned. Beelzebub followed the king's demon. His palms began to sweat, and his bowels turned to liquid. He was, in short, terrified.

Beelzebub marched to his audience with Lucifer, plotting and scheming. He was looking for a way to save himself if things went poorly with the king of hell. If that happened, Baal would no longer be able to play in the shadows. Beelzebub would make sure of that.

High above the bustle of the city, Katie perched on the edge of a building. Her wings were folded behind her. She leaned back on her hands and stared at the stars shimmering high above. It was one of the few places she could see the night sky in the city, because the lights kept the stars at bay. Her base in Nevada was another story. There, she could see the entire universe, or so it felt.

A cool breeze blew over Katie and she shook her hair out, letting it cascade down her back. Pandora sniffed and sighed. *I like it right here; right where we are now. This is the perfect spot in the perfect city after one hell of an awesome day.*

Katie chuckled. *I would say that's an understatement. Not only did you come out of my body on national television, but you also came out with divine angelic powers stronger than mine. You really decided to leave your mark on the world this time around, didn't you?*

Pandora smiled. *I want to be in the history books. I want to be taught in school. Maybe even revered for my scientific mind, not* just *my tits and ass—though they could teach a course or two about my ass.*

Katie almost couldn't believe what she was hearing. *Look who grew into her wings over fucking night. You know, this whole time I thought you were capable of living outside my body. You just had to put your mind to it. Now you can go wherever you want whenever you want to.*

Pandora let out a sigh. *I know I can come out, but...*

Katie sat up. *Just say it, Pandora. You aren't going to hurt my feelings.*

Pandora was silent as she thought about her next words. Katie turned her arm over and stared down at her watch. She groaned and looked over the side of the building, appreciating the view. *We need to get back to the condo in ten minutes. I promised Angie some alone time with Juntto. Besides, I'm ready to get my stuff and head back to Europe. I've been gone far too long, and it could be bad for the guys and any other survivors who might be down there.*

Pandora didn't say a word, which rang just as loud to Katie as if she were screaming from the rooftops. It annoyed her that she knew what everyone was saying, but no one would just come out and say it to her face. Even her own demon wouldn't say how she felt, which was pretty much a miracle when it came to Pandora. *I know you have something to say about it. Hell, everyone has something to say about it. The only person who has even hinted at what they wanted to say was Angie. Even she wouldn't dive into it, though. Here's your chance, Pandora. Say whatever's on your mind. I'm tired of being tiptoed around.*

Pandora growled, frustrated that she had to say the words. *Look, Katie. I know you have all these high hopes. I know that on the inside, you can't even begin to fathom losing another intimate partner in such a horrific manner.*

Katie chimed in, *It's not just about that. He and his team are my friends, too. They are family like you or like Angie or like Juntto, Calvin, Korbin, and the rest of them. Would we be debating whether to search for Korbin if he went missing in the situation? No. Fuck no, we wouldn't.*

Pandora knew she was right, but still, there had to be emotion behind it. *He could be dead, buried in lava for no one to discover for hundreds of years.*

Katie looked out at the horizon. *Or he could be buried under rubble somewhere. Hell, he could be at a hospital. He could be in a military hospital, unconscious and without any identification. He could be tending to survivors. He could be buried underground, looking for a way out. There are a million possibilities of where he could be. Death is only one of those.*

Pandora sighed. *I get it. You're right. There are a million different things that could have happened to him. I just don't want to see you get hurt, that's all. I know what death did to you in the past when one of the team members died. For Brock, it's different. I'm terrified you'll crumble beneath the weight of it.*

Katie shrugged and stood up, tilting her hands back and forth. *And that, my dear, is why you have my back. If the worst is confirmed I'll cry on your shoulder, but I won't give in to that thought until I have personally and thoroughly done my own investigation.*

Pandora snickered. *I just want to point out something about crying on my shoulder. Like hell, you will. That makes my hair soggy, and then the humidity hits. Before you know it, I'm walking around with a huge bouffant. No one wants to see a flashback of Pandora in the time of bouffants.*

Katie put up her hand. *Uh, excuse me. I want to see that. It would be completely humorous, and it would be great to get a before and after shot, especially with you in your new robes. We could send out a postcard with you on the front, looking all angelic. You could be pointing at the camera with some sort of funny quip.*

Pandora laughed. *Once a poor beggar, now swimming with the angels. Do you have Jesus?*

Katie screamed in laughter, shaking her head. *You would look like that Buddy Jesus statue. That would be fucking amazing. You know, I am glad you're staying with me. I would be bored as hell without you.*

And saggy.

And saggy, yes. Come on, it's time to go back.

Before Katie could leap off the edge of the building,

sirens squealed by below. Katie leaned over and stared down at them. *Actually...*

Pandora got excited. *Yes, yes. Say it.*

Katie giggled. *I guess we have a few minutes to help stop those assholes.*

Yes!

Katie stepped up onto the ledge and spread her wings, then dove off the building and followed the cop cars. She flew high enough so they wouldn't see her. Pandora hollered as they flew between the buildings, "Slut Girl to the rescue! Solving crime and getting honeys."

Katie shook Pandora's voice out of her throat. "I don't get honeys, remember? And I would say we're more police than crime-solvers. I am definitely not Sherlock Holmes."

Pandora laughed loudly. *That would make me who?*

Dr. Watson. I do declare, Watson, we have a mystery on our hands.

Pandora giggled. *It would be more like Sherlock Prude and Doctor—*

Ho bag. We would make quite the team. I would constantly pull you away from strip clubs to solve crimes, and you would be on Tinder setting up dates.

Pandora was really into that idea. *And I would always end up hooking up with the murderer. That's how we would solve crimes. My vagina would sniff out the culprit.*

Katie swerved to the right, chasing the cops. She put her hand on her stomach, laughing loudly over the New York City streets. *Holy hell, a crime-fighting vagina. Would that technically be a third entity on our crime-fighting team?*

Pandora choked on her own laughter. *Hell, yeah, she would be. We would call her Detective Squeeze. She would taunt the confession right out of the villains in the throes of passion. One squeeze and they spill their entire life history.*

Tears flowed down Katie's face, and she had to admit it felt good to laugh. *Oh, oh, God. I'm really starting to think that if we see the end of this war, we should write adult fantasy fiction. We could have a fan base that was stupid-huge.*

Pandora clicked her tongue. *And there could be t-shirts. Me, you, and a walking hoo-ha. We could give her curly hair and glasses. Detective Squeeze. She could be the most sophisticated of us.*

Katie bellowed louder, blinking away the tears. The cops all stopped outside of the Macy's department store, and Katie slowed down and landed on the roof. The cops below talked loudly about the perp inside. "He's about mid-forties, red eyes, and snarling. That's the description we got. Apparently, he's holding some people hostage in Home Goods. They were out of the comforter he wanted, and he just lost it."

Pandora scoffed. *Oh boy, we got the male Martha Stewart in there ripping throats out because they don't have the down comforter he wants.*

Katie shrugged and walked to the roof entrance. She yanked the door open.

Her eyes flashed red. *Let's do a little redecorating then.*

A lawyer opened his office door, flung his coat over his arm, and headed home for the night. He paused at the corner. A ways down the street a dozen cop cars were parked in front of Macy's. He pursed his lips and took a deep breath, then leisurely walked down the steps and turned in the opposite direction.

The sound of huge wings flapping overhead made him look up. Katie flew overhead, slowing down as she approached the cop cars and the Macy's.

He watched her and smiled, his eyes flashing a deep ruby-red.

AUTHOR NOTES - MICHAEL ANDERLE

NOVEMBER 1, 2018

THANK YOU for not only reading this story but these *Author Notes* as well .

RANDOM (*sometimes*) THOUGHTS?

HOLY C@#$@# did the Juntto ending (in the last book) cause a SHITAKE ton of angst on the FB Group! Apparently, you really loved Juntto and had absolutely no desire to see him go.

This is the most response about a character I have received for all of 2018. While other characters are fan favorites, Juntto's apparent death was something that concerned readers to such a degree that they were signing online petitions and giving them to me in the PBTD Facebook group.

Message heard.

HOW TO MARKET FOR BOOKS YOU LOVE

We are able to support our efforts by you reading our books, and we appreciate you doing this!

If you enjoyed this or ANY book by any author, especially Indie published, we always appreciate if you make the time to review a book, since it gives other readers who might be on the fence a reason to take a chance on it as well.

AROUND THE WORLD IN 80 DAYS (rather, where am I writing these and what is going on?)

One of the interesting (at least for me) aspects of my life is the ability to work from anywhere and at any time. In the future, I hope to re-read my own author notes and remember my life as a diary entry.

For these *Author Notes*, I am sitting in the London Hotel in West Hollywood, California, which is one block (barely) away from the Whisky A Go Go club.

I spoke about the Stryper concert (from which just got back thirty minutes ago) in the *Barnabas* series *Author Notes*, so I'll skip it here. I will say I ate at the Panini Italian restaurant on Sunset Dr. (of Sunset Strip fame) and give it a very lukewarm rating.

The fried mozzarella was pretty good, but the pepperoni pizza was meh (bland). I added a lot of parmesan cheese and a good number of red pepper flakes just to give it enough zest to be worth eating. For me, pizza should have enough spices that adding those two elements is just a minor tweak to the taste.

Not a major procedure.

I won't be going back there any time soon (whether I find myself in the area for food or not.)

Life is too short for meh if I have a choice.

FAN PRICING

If you would like to find out what LMBPN is doing what the books we are publishing, just sign up at http://lmbpn.com/email/. When you sign up, we notify you of books coming out for the week, any new posts of interest in the books and pop culture arena, and the fan pricing on Saturday.

Ad Aeternitatem,

Michael Anderle

CONNECT WITH MICHAEL TODD

Want more?

Find us On Facebook

https://www.facebook.com/Protected-by-the-Damned-193345908061855/

BOOKS BY MICHAEL TODD

PROTECTED BY THE DAMNED

Torn Asunder (1)

Killing Is My Business (2)

And Business Is Good (3)

Sit Down, Shut Up, And Pull The Trigger (4)

Welcome To The Jungle (5)

Metal Up Your Ass (6)

Dirty Deeds Done Dirt Cheap (7)

For Whom The Bell Tolls (8)

WAR OF THE DAMNED

Resurrection Of The Damned (1)

No Quarter (2)

Dark Is The Night (3)

Dim Glows The Horizon (4)

Waking The Leviathan (5)

Subversive Giants (6)

Juntto (7)

Redemption (8)

BOOKS WRITTEN AS MICHAEL ANDERLE

For a complete list of books by Michael Anderle, please visit:

www.lmbpn.com/ma-books/

All LMBPN Audiobooks are Available at Audible.com and iTunes

To see all LMBPN audiobooks, including those written by Michael Anderle please visit:

www.lmbpn.com/audible

www.ingramcontent.com/pod-product-compliance
Lightning Source LLC
Chambersburg PA
CBHW031624100726
47898CB00006B/1945